Framed

Also by Tracie Peterson
in Large Print:

Controlling Interests

This Large Print Book carries the
Seal of Approval of N.A.V.H.

Framed

Tracie Peterson

Thorndike Press • Thorndike, Maine

Published in 2000 by arrangement with Bethany House Publishers.

Thorndike Press Large Print Christian Mystery Series.

The tree indicium is a trademark of Thorndike Press.

The text of this Large Print edition is unabridged.
Other aspects of the book may vary from the original edition.

Set in 16 pt. Plantin by Elena Picard.

Printed in the United States on permanent paper.

Library of Congress Cataloging-in-Publication Data

Peterson, Tracie.
    Framed / Tracie Peterson.
       p. cm.
    ISBN 0-7862-2696-X (lg. print : hc : alk. paper)
    1. Americans — Great Britian — Fiction. 2. Women
jounalists — Fiction. 3. Photographers — Fiction.
4. Great Britain — Fiction. 5. Large type books. I. Title.
PS3566.E7717 F73 2000
    813′.54—dc21   00-032533

Dedicated to my daughter Jennifer:

*God gave you to bless me, to teach me,
to keep my sense of humor sharp
and my perspective expanded.
But most of all,
God knew that as my firstborn,
you could show me
a special kind of love.*

I'll love you forever.

One

"I can't just drop everything to follow you to Europe, Janice," Gabrielle Fleming told her sister. Stretching out on the wicker lounge, she reached for an awaiting glass of iced tea and enjoyed the early summer warmth of her mother's solarium.

"But don't you see, Gabby," Janice protested, "this will fit *perfectly* with your job as a travel writer. You can be my traveling companion *and* see England and Scotland. It'll be great for you!" Her younger sister's enthusiasm was not lost on Gabby.

"But I have deadlines. Articles don't just write themselves. I have a stack of information on Kansas City that has to be compiled into a feature by the end of this month."

"But that's *ages* away." Janice whipped out a travel brochure and held it aloft. "Just listen to what's on the itinerary and you'll see the potential for yourself. Why, after this, you could write a whole *book* on England." She didn't wait for Gabby's reaction or comment before plunging headlong into the travel jargon so familiar to her older sister.

" 'Day One. Professional tour guides will whisk you away to the charm and wonder of nineteenth-century London. Explore the city, walk the hallowed halls of Westminster, view the Houses of Parliament, and see the changing of the guard at Buckingham Palace.' "

"Travel babble for 'wear yourself out on the first day and be grateful to ride the bus for the rest of the trip,' " Gabby commented absentmindedly.

Janice ignored her cynicism. " 'Day Two. Henry VIII's Hampton Court Palace and Stonehenge Monument are only two of the sights you'll take in on this portion of the trip.' "

Gabby held up her hand. "Janice, it sounds like fun, but honestly . . ."

Janice plopped down on the cushioned ottoman in front of her sister. "I really don't want to make this trip alone, and there's no one I'd rather travel with. You could write the whole thing off as a business expense and create a ton of stories and articles that would bring you more than enough money to compensate for your time and troubles."

Janice's pleading expression caused Gabby to seriously consider the idea for the first time. It wasn't like Janice to beg. Narrowing her eyes suspiciously, Gabby asked, "Why are you making this trip?"

Janice shrugged. "I'm majoring in English Literature. I thought it might be a smart thing to do, and I'm getting a real sweet deal on the trip because it's being set up for students."

"In case you've forgotten, I'm not a student."

"Students may travel with one family member and receive the same discount. The hitch is that I have to book the trip 'double.' Which means if I don't get someone to go along with me, I can't go."

"I hardly believe that they'll kick you off the bus because you're traveling solo." She still wasn't convinced of Janice's reasoning.

Janice's blond hair danced around her shoulders as she adamantly shook her head. "No, of course they won't kick me off. It's just that I'll have to pay out a whole lot more money if I travel as a single."

"So I'll spot you the extra."

"No!" Janice declared adamantly. "I want you to go with me. It would mean so much to me, Gabby. Please!"

"So what's the bottom line on this trip?

How much money? How many days?"

Janice smiled and Gabby felt as though she'd just been lured with exact precision into a trap. "The trip lasts fifteen days and it only costs fifteen hundred dollars. We get the special discount because it's through the college. Well, kind of through the college. The guy who owns the travel agency is good friends with the president of the college, so he sets up special student prices for some of his tours."

"That is an incredible price," Gabby had to agree. She'd priced trips to Europe and knew a person was lucky to get anything under two grand. "And it runs for fifteen days?" Mentally she calculated her upcoming schedule.

"Right. You fly overnight on the first day. Day two is when you actually arrive in London, and you spend that day as you like. I thought maybe we could take in a show. I know how you love musicals, and *Phantom* and *Les Miserables* are always running in London."

"Now you're fighting dirty," Gabby said with a sly smile and lost her suspicions.

"I have to. You never cut me any slack."

Just then their mother entered the solarium. Sarah Fleming was juggling her purse, car keys, and a well-worn canvas bag that she generally used when shopping. "What slack are you needing, Janice?" she asked with a hint of amusement.

"I'm trying to talk Gabby into going with me to England. I *know* she'd love it, and it would fit right in with her work. I was just explaining the possibilities —"

"More like dangling a carrot in front of my nose," Gabby interrupted. Getting to her feet, she offered her mother the lounge.

"I can't stay," Sarah replied. "I'm only here to tell you both that I'm headed to the market. Do we need anything special for the weekend?"

"Nothing I can think of," Gabby answered.

"No, nothing," Janice agreed.

Sarah smiled. "Well, you know Southampton will be packed with tourists before the end of the month. We should lay in a good supply of everything and avoid having to deal with the crowds." She paused and looked at each of them. "I can't begin to tell you how nice it is having you both here at home. I know a lot of parents might think it a drudge, but you girls are my pride and joy, and you're very self-sufficient. Frankly, you're doing me a favor by staying on."

Gabby shook her head. "No, you're doing *us* a favor. What with all the traveling I do it

11

would be a nightmare to keep a separate apartment."

"If you could find an apartment in the city," Janice chimed in. "I considered moving in with some friends next year. You know, finish my senior year in 'The Big Apple' and be the partying kind of kid? But who could afford the rent?"

Sarah and Gabby couldn't help but smile at Janice's words. It seemed Janice was always jumping into one experiment or another. She was the original partying kind of kid. Yet at twenty, she wasn't much of a kid at all, Gabby thought, and that only served to depress her. Janice was six years her junior, and sometimes her youthful excitement toward life made Gabby feel very old. That, coupled with the fact that all of Gabby's friends were either married, divorced, or working on second and third marriages. Considering all their problems, maybe single life wasn't so bad after all.

Sarah seemed not to notice her daughter's contemplation. "It's just as well. I can't imagine anyone wanting to live in New York City when they could enjoy a nice Victorian home on Long Island. We haven't got the noise or traffic here that you'd have to battle there, and your commute isn't so very bad, is it?"

Gabby noted her mother's tone of concern and instantly put her fears aside. "It's a great place to live, and I, for one, plan to stay on for a long time. On my salary, I could never hope to own a home like this, so I'll just enjoy it a little longer, thank you." She saw a look of relief pass through her mother's eyes. Ever since the death of their father three years earlier, Gabby had watched her mother fret and fear for her children as though they might be the next to go.

"Well, I hope you'll leave it long enough to come with me to Great Britain," Janice said, hurrying to her mother's side. "You *have* to help me convince Gabby to go on the trip."

"I think it would be nice if you two went together," Sarah said with little difficulty. "I know how frightening it can be on your own."

"But that would leave you here alone."

Sarah smiled. "I could go visit my sister in California, just like I keep promising her I'll do."

"That's it!" Janice took up the idea with great enthusiasm. "Aunt Jean would *love* it, and Gabby and I wouldn't have to worry that you were too lonely."

Their mother frowned at this. "I don't

want you girls to worry about things like that. If that's why you don't want to go, Gabby . . ."

Gabby patted her mother's arm. "Nonsense, Mom. Janice and I will talk it over."

Sarah offered a smile, looking from Janice to Gabby and then to her hands. "You're sure there's nothing you need from the market?"

"Positive," the sisters chimed in unison.

"All right, then. Janice, would you help me get the car out of the garage?" Sarah asked.

Gabby smiled as her sister went to help back out the Lincoln from the garage. In all the time since their mother had been on her own, she'd never once felt competent enough to get the massive automobile out by herself. *One day,* Gabby thought to herself, *Mama will feel capable of handling the car and our moving away.*

Leaving the warmth of the solarium, Gabby drifted aimlessly through the downstairs rooms and waited for Janice's return. She thought of her sister's request and felt a twinge of guilt mingled with suppressed desire. It *would* be fun to go to England and Scotland. It would make a great series of articles and possibly even give her ideas for that "Great American Novel" she one day

14

hoped to write. But there were also her deadlines. Deadlines for features she hadn't even begun to write. And why not? Why did the paper sit idly in the printer drawer? Why did the computer remain in the "off" mode? Gabby couldn't answer those questions.

Kansas City had been a whirlwind of colors, sights, and sounds. Her assignment had been to cover the top ten restaurants of Kansas City, Missouri. She'd eaten at ten restaurants in three days, never experiencing a complete meal at any one place — lest she be too full to review another restaurant before bedtime. Now she had six days before the end of the month, and still her zest for the article was missing and she was hard pressed to even begin.

I'm bored, she thought. *I'm bored with myself and the articles, and I'm tired of deadlines and issues that seem to never go away. Nothing holds any excitement for me anymore. Nothing and no one.*

She reached out to take hold of a most-loved photograph. This particular photo had graced the mantel of the family fireplace for many years. It was her parents' wedding picture. Her mother stood in yards of wispy lace and white satin, petite and waiflike and leaning heavily on the arm of her new husband. Patrick Fleming looked dashing in his long-tailed tuxedo and high, starched collar. On his face was an unreadable expression. Was it panic for the weight of the vows he'd just made, or was he simply aching to get out the dressy clothes?

Gabby traced the silver frame, a gift from Janice and herself on their parents' twenty-fifth wedding anniversary. It seemed ages ago and yet it had truly only been ten years earlier. Janice had just been a scrap of a kid. Ten years old and awkwardly beginning to find interest in the opposite sex, Janice had scarcely considered her parents' long years of marriage. Gabby had been a mere sixteen, but she remembered feeling very important in working hard to put aside enough money to buy the silver frame. Janice's contribution had been days of rummaging through the attic for just the right photograph. Gabby had readily agreed with her little sister's choice, as had their parents. It was a celebration to live through the passages of time and complications of life. Gabby sighed. Theirs had been a true romance, she remembered wistfully.

What must it be like to love and be married to one man for over twenty-five years? It baffled the imagination. Gabby had only been in love once, and even that was a questionable consideration between love and lust. His name was Dustin and he seemed to move the very universe with a mere glance. They had shared a college computer class and couldn't seem to keep from bumping into each other on a daily basis. She'd been driven by physical attraction to him, and when Dustin finally took a second look at her, Gabby was certain it was true love. It took a steady progression of dates and intimate moments to send her closer and closer to the edge of giving in to her feelings and forgetting her upbringing. Then Dustin finally popped the question — "Will you live with me?" Marriage was simply out of the question, Gabby learned, and the two drifted apart.

Twenty-five years. She looked at the hope and excitement in the faces of her youthful parents. They were blind to the future, just as she was now, but they would face it together. Together they would start a small shipping business. Together they would raise two daughters. Together they would bury an infant son. But always they would face the joys and sorrows as a team. Two, not one. Would there ever be someone to share her life that way?

She replaced the picture and wondered what was keeping Janice. Maybe she'd given up hope of talking Gabby into going on the trip. But Gabby knew better. Janice never gave up on anything when she was determined enough. Walking to the window, Gabby stood and watched as her sister shared some final comment with their mother. With the flick of her wrist, Janice was waving goodbye and hurrying back for the kill.

"I think Mother is getting more paranoid about leaving the house," Janice announced, bursting through the front door with the glorious fragrance of Japanese honeysuckle following her into the foyer. "She's actually considering using the delivery service for her groceries."

"If it makes less work for her, why not?" Gabby countered. "I think Mom's doing just fine. Remember, she just mentioned flying all the way out to see Aunt Jean in California. I think she's just trying to determine her comfort zone."

"What shrink gave you *that* idea?" Janice planted herself on the blue print sofa and settled in for a debate.

Gabby shrugged and came away from the window. "I think I read about it somewhere. People who lose loved ones go through many stages. Sometimes they just inch along, and other times they plow right ahead. Mother is an inchworm conquering little bits of territory at a time."

"But it's been three years."

Gabby sank into a well-worn winged-back chair and sighed. "I know, but compare that to over thirty years of marriage. If you think about it, Janice, Mother spent more time in life being a wife and mother than being a single woman. It's all she's known for so long that it's bound to be difficult to just switch gears. She'll make it through. After all," Gabby paused with a wary glance at her sister, "she has her faith."

Janice rolled her eyes as Gabby had expected. "Faith didn't save Daddy when his catamaran overturned in that storm, so please don't tell me how wonderful faith is."

Gabby shrugged. "I guess your alternative is so much better."

"Look, I don't want to fight, I want to talk about England." Janice had always been masterful at switching the conversation when the topic became too uncomfortable. "I really want you to go with me."

Gabby looked away from her sister's pleading expression. "I know, Jan, but I have to consider —"

"You'll have a blast and you know it," Janice remarked before Gabby could continue. "I just know it will be the *best* thing that ever happened to us. Please, Gabby? Please say you'll do this for me?"

"What's this really all about, Janice?" Gabby couldn't hide her skepticism. "You've never in your life cared whether you traveled alone or in a pack. You certainly have never worried about whether I came along."

Janice looked hurt. "I thought we were close."

"We are," Gabby agreed with the hint of a grin, "but I know you. You're driving this trip deal awfully hard. Why do you really want me to go?"

Janice shrugged. "I guess I thought it would be a good excuse for us both to do something different and get away from the normal routine. I know you travel for the magazine, but you've never been abroad and neither have I. I know you want to go, and the price is right, so why not just give in and do it? Be impetuous for once."

Gabby thought of a million reasons why she should say no, but instead her reply came in a more hopeful manner. "I'll talk to my editor. The concentration of the magazine has been on U.S. destinations, but if Sandy wants to do a layout on England and Scotland, I'll go. If not, you'll just have to be satisfied with going solo. I'll even spot you the additional money."

"I don't want the additional money. I want *you*."

Janice's adamant stand on the matter surprised Gabby. While they'd grown up as close as two sisters could be, Gabby had never known Janice to be so driven on the point of Gabby's participation in something.

"When will you call Sandy?"

"Let me put something constructive down on paper. I'll feel better knowing exactly what the trip entails, as well as the dates and such. I'll sketch out my ideas for a few of the possible articles and then I'll call her."

"I just know she'll say yes!" Janice was clearly elated and got up from the sofa with a bounce. "Get to it, and I'll call and save you a place on the tour."

"She hasn't said yes," Gabby argued.

"Never mind that" — her sister waved her upstairs — "she will!"

Gabby was still not convinced of Janice's reasons for insisting she go to England. She had barely reached the top step when she heard Janice pick up the telephone receiver. For some reason Gabby lingered to hear what Janice might have to say.

"Yes, this is Janice Fleming. I need to make a change in my travel plans. Of course I'll wait."

Gabby frowned in disappointment. Maybe

she was just calling to see if there was still an available slot for Gabby to go along. But then Janice was speaking again, and suddenly it all became very clear that Gabby's suspicions were merited.

"Yeah, it's Janice. Look, I talked her into it. She's upstairs right now plotting out her strategy for getting her editor to go for the idea." Pause. "No, I don't see it as a problem. You can count on her coming and if you can manage the rest, Gabby will make the perfect cover."

Gabby leaned back against the wall with an odd sense of trepidation. *The perfect cover for what?*

Two

"I suppose you have both read the morning newspaper?" a gray-haired man with a well-trimmed beard and mustache asked. Without waiting for an answer, he slapped down a copy of *The New York Times*. "IRA Bomb Explodes, Killing Four, Injuring Forty." The man looked up to meet the gaze of his two comrades. "Yesterday it was an explosion in London, killing six and wiping out half a block of stores. Two days before that, officials found a bomb at Heathrow, and now airport security has been boosted on all international flights out of England."

The men nodded affirmation, while the older man took a long drink of tepid coffee. "Things are heating up again between the Brits and the Irish Republican Army."

"Things will always heat up where those two parties are involved," replied another man. His youthful innocence and expression caused the older man to consider him a moment before continuing.

"We've had a fairly quiet time of it for the past few months, but as you know, our sources tell us that this situation is going to grow quite ugly in the immediate future. As you also know —" he paused to make certain he had their undivided attention — "there is widespread active support for the IRA here in America. The entire matter has been made into a 'Holy War' as far as those supporters are concerned, and they will stop at nothing to aid and abet the enemy."

"But exactly who *is* the enemy, if you don't mind my asking?" This came from a broad-shouldered man with piercing green eyes and a three-day growth of beard.

"Our job isn't to figure out the sides, it's to keep from taking sides. We're to uphold the Constitution, remember? It really doesn't matter whether I think the IRA is justified in their cause or not. It matters that their terrorist actions are killing innocent people and that they are gaining strong support here in the U.S.

"And as you know, there are two main groups we've been observing here at home. One seems to constantly be involved in some form of money solicitation. The other tends toward recruitment and arms dealings."

"I have the files on both," the younger man said, seeming quite proud that he'd thought to have these things available for the meeting. He held the folders aloft as though waving coveted prizes and smiled with thin, freckled lips.

"And what do your files tell us that we don't already know from the regular news media?" the older man asked dryly.

"Well, I have copies of receipts that show over one million dollars was raised for direct donation to the IRA. This was, of course, done in a covert manner, but these people seem quite bent on keeping precise records. Our agents had little trouble copying down the records."

"And was the money handed over?" asked the gray-haired man.

"Uh, it looks like . . . well, that is to say . . ." The young man looked extremely embarrassed and flushed. "We don't know for sure, but we think so."

"You *think* so? I need facts, man. I need absolutes. This new surge of activity could be the proof of that money in action. On the other hand, plenty of U.S. cash has gone the way of the IRA with little, if any, real repercussions."

"You mean, that we can see," the green-eyed man noted sarcastically. "Most of it probably went for pints of Guinness."

"That's neither here nor there," the older man replied. "Our second order of business this morning may well tie in with this funding. There has been a robbery of weapons from a South Carolina National Guard Armory. We have to presume it's possible those guns will be earmarked for IRA support."

"How many weapons and what makes?" asked the younger man. He searched for his mechanical pencil and set out to keep notes.

"The last count had it at one hundred thirty. The exact figures haven't come in from the guard unit."

"What are they doing in South Carolina, playing hide-and-seek? Surely they know exactly how many guns were on the premises." His youth and inexperience showed clearly in his impatience.

The third man interjected, "The robbery is scarcely twelve hours old, and the weapons in question were part of a transfer from another unit. I'm certain by morning they'll know the exact count and you'll have all of your figures in neat order." His green eyes flashed. "Maybe you can even make a new folder."

The young counterpart cast him a heated look. The older man ignored their flaring tempers and sat back with a nod. "I suppose we'll just have to wait — wait and wonder who the recipients will be."

The green eyes grew thoughtful. "The Irish are a strong possibility. We've been hearing rumors of a large weapons shipment for months now. My best educated guess would be that those army guns are headed for the bonny, bonny banks of Loch Lomond."

"That's in Scotland, you imbecile!" the youngest of the three exclaimed.

The man turned an angry scowl on his counterpart. "And well I know it. You don't expect them to just load up the boats and float them right into Belfast, do you?"

The younger man blanched but held his ground. "I thought Loch Lomond was land-locked."

The room echoed with the irritated man's fists against the table. "I only meant it figuratively. They'll run the guns into Scotland or transfer them off shore. From there, it's a short hop into Northern Ireland. Look at the map if you don't believe me. There's no more than fourteen miles in some places between Scotland and Ireland and a great many hiding places along the coastline."

The bearded man nodded and stared with indifferent eyes at the other. "But you can't be sure those guns are meant to benefit the Irish, can you?"

"No." The word was flat and unemotional.

"What about Bosnia? The Croats would kill to get their hands on the shipment. Even as few as a couple hundred assorted weapons would be a valued prize." This came weakly from the younger man.

"A possibility," the bearded man replied. "A possibility. But," he said, eyeing the two men in his office, "I need more than possibilities. I need those guns!"

The green-eyed man got to his feet and paced out a well-worn path on the ancient carpet. His summer-weight suit was far from cool, and in the outdated office of his superior it was a battle to keep from succumbing to the heat. Overhead, an archaic ceiling fan chattered in faulty circles but offered little relief.

The younger man, feeling the tension between his companions, suggested they also consider the possibility that the guns would go to Mexico or farther south into Central America. "I understand a DEA bust uncovered a large supply of Mexican heroin that was packaged and waiting for shipment. This would make an amicable trade for weapons, and we can't overlook it."

This stopped the pacing man in his tracks. "Of course we can't. We can't overlook any reasonable possibility."

The bearded man nodded. "From what I've been able to learn, the whole operation reeked of amateurs. They broke into the wrong building and made their way off with less than two hundred weapons when only fifty yards away was a building packed with a variety of explosives and other weapons that could have brought them three times as much money. The weapons, mostly M-16s as far as we can pin down, weren't even supposed to be in that building. They were shipped to the guard unit by mistake, and no one had arranged to send them on to their proper destination.

"Added to that, they crashed the gate with their truck, leaving streaks of bright yellow paint all over the broken fencing, and they killed three soldiers by —"

"We get the picture," the youngest interjected, seeming to have a distaste for the details. "The fact of the matter is that the deed is done, and now we have to find out who has the weapons and what plans they've made for their disposal."

"Well, as soon as this is finished," the green-eyed man said, finally retaking his seat, "so am I. I'm weary of these gruesome little affairs, and I want nothing more to do with any of it."

"Are you serious?" the other two men said in unison.

"Quite. I'll see this through, no matter how long it takes, but after that I'm done. I'm not even sure whose side I'm on anymore." His voice registered an air of disagreeable challenge, but neither man questioned him further. It was easy to understand his dismay.

"I suppose we each know our breaking point. I'm grateful to know that you'll see this through. I have the files you'll need." The bearded man reached into a desk drawer and pulled out a stack of manila folders.

"Is this a complete listing?" The green-eyed man reached out for the materials. "I want dossiers on all of the key players and suspects."

"It's complete, as far as we know."

Opening the folder on top, the two older men exchanged a look. "Janice Fleming?" the green-eyed man questioned.

"Yes," was the only answer forthcoming.

Three

Sandy Madison put down Gabby's latest feature on Kansas City and smiled. "Another winner! I don't know how you manage to keep cranking them out, but you've made this magazine what it is today."

Gabby smiled and waited for Sandy to continue. She didn't have to wait long.

"I am very excited about your proposed articles on Great Britain. I thought if you had time, maybe you could elaborate on the format you have in mind."

Gabby reached into her briefcase and pulled out the itinerary Janice had given her. "This guided tour will be very fast-paced, but I thought it would be helpful to our readers who might be planning just such a trip if I covered a similar itinerary rather than travel around the place with plenty of time and money."

"Yes, I think that's a good angle. Maybe we could get the tour company to advertise in our magazine." Sandy made notes to herself. "Better yet, most of these companies are so similar in what they offer, we could contact each of them, and those willing to advertise with us could have the additional reward of having their company mentioned at the end of the article."

"That would work for me. I think my sister mentioned that this particular group is rather small and privately managed. Something connected to the college, I believe." What she didn't add was that Janice had practically forced her into the trip, and the real reasons were still eluding her.

"Yes, I've already learned that." Sandy picked up a half-empty glass of diet cola. "What else?"

"Well, I see this as an opportunity to appeal to all the general issues of our magazine while focusing in on the details. We take the reader through each day of the tour. We highlight the areas to be seen, the tourist attractions and such, and if I'm lucky, the non-tourist attractions. You know, those out-of-the-way places people always want to know about."

"How will you have time to get that information?" Sandy asked, putting down the empty glass.

"I'll ask questions of the hotel staff and go

after hours if necessary. I'm not afraid to 'scoot about on my own,' as my grandmother used to say. I'll interview as many people as possible and pull together whatever bits of information make for an interesting side point. From experience, I've found better restaurants, bookstores, antique shops, and so forth this way than through any expert."

Gabby shuffled her papers and continued. "I'd like to contrast the price range, as well. While this will be a fixed-price tour, I'd like to show the readers that the total budget for their trip will vary greatly according to how they spend their free time. For instance, Janice and I have agreed we'd like to take in a West End show in London. Perhaps *Phantom* or *Les Mis*. An evening like this is going to be considerably more expensive than, say, a boat tour on the Thames. It will also determine what kind of clothes we take with us, as well as accessories and such."

"I like that idea. Readers will be able to determine for themselves what type of personalizing they'd be able to afford or even find interest in."

"Exactly. Also there are many tour days when you're given a free afternoon and evening. I would like to give information here that would provide a variety of choices. Janice has even agreed to do things separately so that I can interview her as to the degree of fun and expense she's entailed on her adventure versus my own."

"This will make a fabulous series. How do you see it shaping up as far as issues?" Sandy asked quite seriously.

"Depending on the space you want to give it, I'd say we could break it down as far as you want or compact it to maybe just include an issue on England and one on Scotland. Of course, there'll be plenty you can hang on to for later issues."

"I wouldn't want to drag it out so far that readers can't get the information they need within a short span of time. I think devoting one issue to England and one to Scotland would be the best. We can have other articles included and just make a complete run of it. I could hire a couple of historical writers to give us some royalty history. You know what an appeal that has here in the U.S."

Gabby laughed. "No kidding. Our neighbor's little girl knows that Prince Charles has a son named William who will be king someday, but she hasn't a clue as to the name of our president or his wife."

"Anglophiles!" Sandy said enthusiastically. "I don't know why I've waited to cash in on this for so long. People all across America are absolutely goofy for information on the royals and England. This could be very profitable."

Gabby grinned. "So I take it you don't have a problem advancing me the money I requested?"

"Not one bit. In fact, I have a surprise for you that I think will make this your best set of features ever!" The heavyset Sandy pushed back the copy and picked up her telephone. "Reba, you can tell Mr. Walls to join us when it's convenient for him."

Gabby lost her smile and raised a questioning brow as Sandy replaced the receiver. "Mr. Walls? Who's that?"

"You'll see. He should be joining us any time. In fact, go ahead and open the door."

Gabby got to her feet and opened the door about eight inches. "Sandy, what's going on?"

Behind the desk, Gabby saw Sandy shift rather uncomfortably under her scrutiny. This definitely wasn't like Sandy. "What kind of surprise?"

"I'm just sending a photographer with you." The words seemed to hang in the silence of the room.

"A photographer?" Gabby weighed these

words for a moment. "But I always take my own photos. Are you unhappy with the quality of pictures I've been taking?" She sank back into the leather chair opposite Sandy's desk.

"No. It's just that this is a big trip with a lot going on. I want you freed up to get a real feel for the story itself. I want you able to mingle with the people and hear their stories, talk with shopkeepers and tour directors, that sort of thing. You can't be writing down notes and snapping pictures and putting people at ease all at the same time. A photographer will free you up from part of the responsibility and assure us a professional layout for the magazine."

"You *don't* like my pictures." Gabby's voice sounded more and more dejected.

"Jarod Walls is one of the best free-lance photographers available to us. He's done quality book photography. You know, the coffee-table-type books. He's agreed to accompany you, and even though he's new to travel magazine work, I assured him you would be able to show him the ropes."

"Oh great. I get to baby-sit a photographer," Gabby protested.

"I assure you," a masculine voice sounded from behind her, "I'm hardly in need of a baby-sitter."

Gabby felt her cheeks instantly flush with embarrassment. Against her better judgment she got to her feet and turned to face the music. Well muscled and broad shouldered, he wore a casual black pullover tucked into jeans and an expression that suggested the utmost seriousness. When Gabby allowed her gaze to settle on his face, she was stunned by the intensity of his green eyes. *Irish eyes,* she thought, not really knowing why. Maybe it was the idea of shamrocks and rolling green hills. Maybe it was too many travel brochures and tour books.

"Jarod Walls, may I introduce you to Gabrielle Fleming. She's just plain Gabby to most of us, although the occasional insolent mail boy has been relegated to calling her Ms. Fleming."

At this, a smile broke across his face. "Some of your baby-sitting charges, I presume?"

Gabby wanted to crawl under the nearest piece of furniture and hide, but this man commanded her attention in such a way that she couldn't even look away. She wanted to say something that would identify her as independently strong yet witty. But while Jarod Walls' eyes surveyed her as though she might become his next photographic subject, Gabby felt completely tongue-tied.

"I . . . it's just," she struggled to begin. "Well, I'm used to working alone." There, she'd broken the ice and asserted herself as independent. Surely it hadn't sounded as weak in his ears as it had in her own.

Jarod nodded. "As am I. When Sandy suggested accompanying you to England, I can tell you I wasn't that enthusiastic about it. I find writers to be rather pretentious and insecure." Gabby's mouth dropped open as he continued. "I'm not used to having to pamper and spoil young women in the line of duty. I'm a photographer, not a nurse-maid or panty hose gofer."

"I beg your pardon?" Gabby finally found her voice. "Panty hose what?"

"Gofer," Jarod said casually. "The last time I teamed up with a woman, she was con-stantly putting runs through her pantyhose and sending me off to find her a new pair so that no one else would see her in that condi-tion. I'd gofer panty hose. I'd gofer aspirins. I'd gofer whatever else she thought to send me off in search of. I'm not doing that this time."

"Well, no one asked you to," Gabby said, putting hands on hips. Her eyes narrowed as her anger mounted. "I've been a feature writer for this magazine long enough to know better than to worry about panty hose. I dress appropriately for whatever story I'm covering, and I've never yet sent an assistant off looking for aspirin."

"Ding!" Sandy exclaimed from her position behind the desk. "That ends round one. Fighters, take your corners."

Gabby stared at her for a moment before calming enough to drop her stance. Jarod shrugged and walked casually to the empty couch that lined the south wall of Sandy's office. He sat down without invitation and stretched long legs in front of him. The set of his square but clean-shaven jaw left Gabby little doubt that round two was about to begin.

Turning a pleading expression on Sandy, Gabby decided to start. "I'm already accompanying my sister on this trip. I'd wanted to enjoy her company, not be caught up making notes and conversation with a photographer. I swear, I'll earn my keep and get you good pictures without the need for Mr. Walls to accompany me."

"Gabby, this isn't anything against you. I'm trying to make matters easier. Now, this is the way the magazine wants it. Orders from the top brass, in fact. I know we can work through your misgivings."

"Maybe I could sit at the back of the bus," Jarod suggested with a hint of amusement in his expression.

"Maybe you could sit on top of the bus," Gabby muttered and crossed her sweater-clad arms.

Jarod grinned at this and Sandy seemed encouraged. "See there, I knew you two would hit it off. Look, Gabby, I had no choice. The publisher wants it this way. I'm sure you and Jarod can work out your differences. I want a nice, tight article with eye-popping photos and record sales. I can get this if you two work together, I just know it!"

Gabby bit her lower lip and silently wished she'd left her long blond hair down so that she could nervously twist a piece of it as she considered her situation. But the tight French braid refused to give up a single strand, so she turned her attention to her immaculate linen slacks. Pretending to pick pieces of lint from her leg, Gabby tried to rationalize the situation. *It isn't fair,* she thought. *I've worked hard to earn the reputation I have, and now this complete stranger has the chance to ruin my efforts.*

She could feel his eyes on her, but still Gabby refused to look up. She wondered who he was and tried to imagine the arrangements and how she would communicate exactly what she'd expect from him. Certainly not panty hose!

"Don't you agree, Gabby?"

"What?" Her head snapped up and she met Jarod's amused gaze. It was almost as if he could read her mind. Gabby shook her head to shake free of the spell. "I was trying to remember whether Janice said the tour was filled or not. Besides, the tour is for students with the exception that they may take a family member along as a traveling companion."

"I've already arranged for Jarod," Sandy replied. "I took the information you gave me and contacted the tour company, a Mr. —" she shuffled through a stack of papers on her desk — "Mr. Bremel or Beamer." She finally found the paper. "No, Breman Butler. The tour director is Breman Butler. Anyway, he assured me there was space to squeeze in a photographer. It appears the tour is very small, and they were happy to have an additional person. They thought the publicity would be good for the company."

"Great," Gabby said without enthusiasm.

Sandy smiled weakly and got to her feet. "Why don't you and Jarod discuss strategies while I get your checks from Reba. I might be a few minutes so just, well, try to . . ."

"We won't kill each other while you're gone, if that's what you're afraid of," Gabby said in a rather dejected manner.

Sandy looked at Gabby as if contemplating the validity of this statement, then nodded her head and closed the door behind her.

"So we're to be traveling companions for fifteen days?"

It was more a statement than a question, but Gabby refused to leave Jarod's words unanswered. "Yes, and it will be a nonstop whirlwind. I hope you're up for it."

Jarod chuckled. "I'm quite fit, I assure you."

Yes, I can see that, Gabby thought to herself. There wasn't an ounce of fat on the man, and he looked as though he could probably jog alongside the tour bus and not even get winded.

"I meant professionally, of course," Gabby said, trying hard to think through each of her words before putting them into speech.

"Of course," he replied sarcastically.

Piercing green eyes refused to leave her, and Gabby noticed her ire rising. Why did he have to be so smug about it all? Couldn't he at least be graciously embarrassed that he'd been thrust upon her like a sack of unwanted laundry?

When she remained silent, Jarod gave her a quick once-over. "Surely that's not it? You aren't letting me off that easy, are you?"

"What else do you expect me to do?" Gabby got up and moved to the windows of Sandy's twenty-fifth-floor office. The view of downtown New York was rather limited by the building directly opposite them, but Gabby pretended to be quite interested in the world outside. "I don't like the position I've been put in," she finally admitted honestly, "but even I know when I'm beat."

"You make it sound like a real war is going on between us. I don't even know you, and you certainly don't know me. Shouldn't we at least have a better understanding of each other before we get too overwhelmed by it all?" Jarod seemed completely at ease with the conversation.

"I almost believe you're enjoying this." Gabby turned to face him.

He grinned. "I think I am, a bit."

"Well, stop it." Her statement came out so blunt that for a moment Jarod looked stunned. Moments later he was laughing out loud.

Gabby felt an overwhelming sensation of vulnerability. Her only defense was to put up a wall of anger. Without warning she picked up her briefcase, stuffed papers inside it, and made her way to leave. To her surprise, Jarod beat her to the door. His massive frame made escape impossible.

"What do you want from me?" she asked, turning her face slightly upward to meet his gaze.

Jarod's stern expression softened ever so slightly. "I want you to give me a chance and knock off with the hostilities until you have a reason to feel hostile toward me."

Gabby thought about her Christian upbringing and how her mother had always instructed her to be kind to strangers just in case, like the Bible said, a person might be entertaining angels. This made her smile. Jarod Walls was one big angel if that was the case. She guessed he must weigh at least two hundred pounds.

"I do prefer that look to all the others."

"What?" Gabby stepped back to get a better look at his face.

"I prefer your smiling to the anger, although I'm not sure why you're smiling just now. Either you see my merits and have decided I can be a productive benefit to you on this trip, or . . ." He let his words trail off for just a moment.

"Or?" she asked, instantly sobering.

"Or you're plotting my demise, and you've already imagined a particularly nasty way of eliminating me."

Gabby couldn't help but smile again.

"Ah-ha," Jarod said, crossing his arms and leaning back against the door, "you *are* planning my demise."

"No. I'm simply going to work hard to accept the fact that my plans have been altered," Gabby answered softly. "I'm sure you're very good at what you do and that in the long run I'll be happy to be relieved of the photography duties." She eyed him straight on and refused to look away. "Truce enough for you?"

Jarod held out his hand. "More than enough. Shake on it?"

Gabby allowed his large tan hand to close over hers. The action caused her to get goose bumps up one arm and down the other before she managed to pull her hand away. Jarod Walls was certainly more than she'd anticipated having to deal with.

Four

"A photographer?" Janice questioned while packing the last few articles of clothing she planned to take on their trip. "Why do you need a photographer?"

"Oh, I don't know." Gabby watched Janice with preoccupied disinterest. Her mind was focused on too many things at once. Things like why Janice needed her to be a cover for something, and why Jarod Walls couldn't suddenly develop some desperate illness for the next two weeks and cancel his participation in the trip. Not that she really wished him ill, but dealing with his smug attitude for fifteen days was not going to be easy.

"Don't you usually take your own pictures?"

"Huh?"

Janice paused in her packing and looked at her sister. "You haven't heard much of *anything* I've said, have you?"

Gabby tried to pull herself together. "Sorry. I guess my mind is on overload right now. I keep thinking that I'll forget to pack something or do something."

"Relax. You have your checklist, right?"

"Sure."

"So what's the problem? Pick out flattering clothes that are easy to pack and care for. Then relax. We leave in less than twenty-four hours. Who knows, maybe you and this guy will have some sort of summer fling. You know, a whirlwind romance inspired by the historic beauty of England." She made melodramatic gestures, clasping her hands to her heart, then lifting the back of her hand to her forehead. "I simply love love," she drawled.

Gabby rolled her eyes and got to her feet. "Look, I'm going to fix myself a snack. Do you want anything?"

"No, go ahead. I'm going to finish up here and give one last call to the travel coordinator. I want to make sure where we're all suppose to meet."

Gabby left the room but suddenly thought of Janice's mention of the call. She waited for a moment outside the door. She wondered silently if Janice had gotten herself into some kind of trouble at college. It would be just like her sister to hook up with the wrong kind of people. Janice was notorious for getting herself caught up in one cause or another.

After waiting several minutes and hearing nothing, Gabby wandered downstairs, still contemplating Janice. Maybe it was because Janice was her little sister and Gabby would always feel responsible for her that she couldn't stop worrying about her now. Sometimes Janice seemed so lost. She clearly had no interest in church or spiritual matters, and for the most part, her activities ranged in areas that Gabby couldn't understand or approve.

She couldn't begin to count the times she'd tried to talk to Janice about her lack of faith. *"God is for old people about to die,"* Janice had told her one day at the beach. That statement had started a running argument for three straight days and ended in an agreement to respect each other's differences.

With a heavy sigh, Gabby knew there was little to be done but wait Janice out. If she approached her with a direct question, Janice would just tell her it was a misunderstanding. Or she'd tell her it was none of her business, just like she always did where spiritual matters were concerned.

Then Janice faded from her mind, and

Gabby thought of her encounter with Jarod Walls. The man seemed willing enough to work hard, and his attitude, though smug, had certainly seemed independent and competent. But something about him — his cool manner and eyes that missed nothing — just set her on edge. For the first time, Gabby wondered what he might expect of her. He had a reputation to uphold, as well. Maybe he'd think Gabby's approach too feminine and one-sided. Maybe that was the real reason Sandy wanted a photographer to accompany her to Great Britain. This thought gave Gabby reason to reevaluate her style of writing.

She took up a jar of peanut butter, studied the fat-gram content for a moment, and opted for a bowl of cereal instead. Slicing a lone banana onto the awaiting flakes came as an afterthought, but it seemed to be just the right touch. Taking her bowl, Gabby moved into the solarium and stretched out on the wicker lounge.

Someone had opened the windows to allow the summer breeze to pass through freely, and with it came the sweet smells of meadow grasses, flowering trees, and the sea. Gabby sighed and took a bite of cereal. It was hard to imagine that in a few short hours she'd actually be across the Atlantic in England. It was even harder to imagine that she'd be sharing most of the trip with a total stranger. She thought of Janice's words about summer romances and laughed. There was such a secure guard up around her heart that such a matter didn't concern her at all. It was laughable. It was unrealistic. It could never happen.

For some reason the thought seemed to free her mind. Maybe it was Jarod's ruggedly handsome looks that affected her judgment in the matter. *There are certain people,* she thought, *who naturally command attention.* Jarod Walls was definitely one of those people, but it didn't need to concern her. She wasn't the kind of person to lose her head over a wink and a smile. And even if Jarod *did* have rather nice eyes, Gabby knew she'd be more concerned with what those eyes found to photograph than anything else. She began to relax even more and could finally see her way clear to enjoying the idea of traveling with Jarod in tow. The prestige of having her own photographer even began to make her feel important. She was still the magazine's representative. Jarod was just a free-lancer, and therefore he would come under her authority.

Smiling now, Gabby finished her cereal and deposited the bowl in the dishwasher.

Things were shaping up, and she finally felt like she'd regained her composure. *That's all that was wrong with me,* she mused and nearly danced up the stairs to her room. *Jarod Walls took away my control, and now I have a clear mind and understanding of the situation. I'll simply assert myself and take charge.*

~

From the moment they arrived at the airport and met up with the others in their group, Gabby realized that the only person she was going to be fooling was herself. Jarod lounged casually against a support pillar near the back of the group. He was clad in black jeans and a burgundy, black, and green sports shirt. The patches of green in the shirt seemed to darken his eyes and enhance their intensity. He met her gaze as if trying to decide if she was going to be civil or not, then looked away as if bored with the whole ordeal.

"Are we all here, then?" a voice sounded from behind Gabby. "I'm Breman Butler, and I'll be your tour guide for the next fifteen days."

Gabby turned around and found yet another pair of sparkling green eyes staring at her. What was with all these green-eyed men? Janice seemed instantly taken with

51

Breman and made somewhat of a spectacle of herself.

"I'm Janice Fleming," she said, thrusting her hand into his.

"It's a pleasure to meet you, Ms. Fleming. I believe we've talked several times on the telephone."

Janice smiled coyly, causing Gabby to openly stare at her in surprise. "Why, yes, Mr. Butler, I believe we have." Her drawl was thick and sugary. "I have so many questions about the trip — I wondered if you could possibly find it in your heart to sit with me on the plane?"

Gabby frowned. Now what was Janice up to?

Butler seemed instantly enchanted by Janice's put-on charm. "I think something can be arranged. I believe I was to share seats with a Mr. Walls, but if he doesn't mind changing with you, then —"

"He won't mind," Janice interrupted. "He's working with my sister anyway, and since I was to be her seating companion, it should work out perfectly."

Great, Gabby thought, sizing up the situation instantly. She had known Janice to get a little crazy over guys before, but never had she made such a public spectacle of herself.

Breman paused a moment to take a head

count, then reached into a small cardboard box. "I have a folder of information for each of you. When I call your name, please come forward and take out your packet. Many of your questions will be answered as you study the information. I believe the flight over will allow you ample time to acquaint yourself with everything. Should you have questions afterward, see me, and we'll talk about it."

He rattled off several names, and Gabby took special interest in seeing who else accompanied them on the trip. A giddy young woman named Ronny Davis took the first packet and instantly spilled the contents on the airport floor. Without thought, she tossed a thick brown braid behind her and bent to retrieve the materials. "I'm always clumsy," she declared. "Guess I should warn you all here and now."

Everybody laughed and encouraged her not to worry about it, while Breman hurried to hand out the remaining packets. Jim and Jason Evans were brothers who were majoring in theater and had an intense love of Shakespeare. Eager to see the homeland of the famous bard, they had signed up for the tour early on. Fred and Ginger Applegate were an older couple. Fred, a professor at the college, was the official faculty sponsor, but Ginger told everyone this was to be their second honeymoon. Everyone teased them about being the real Fred and Ginger dance team of movie fame, but Ginger assured them they couldn't dance a step.

As Breman continued, Janice excused herself for a moment and headed to the nearest rest room. When Breman called Janice's name, Gabby reached out to take the folder and was surprised when he refused to give it to her.

"Each member of the tour has their own folder. You are . . ." He waited for her name.

"Gabrielle Fleming. I'm Janice's sister. Janice slipped off to the rest room."

"Oh yes," he said, flipping through the folders. "Here's yours."

"I can hold Janice's for her until she gets back."

"No, that won't be necessary," Breman stated flatly, his green eyes seeming to bore holes through Gabby.

She found his reaction uncalled for, but since Janice had chosen that moment to reappear, Gabby decided to say nothing more. Taking her own packet, she simply focused on the outside logo and decided to forget about Mr. Butler.

Jarod stood last to receive his folder. Gabby had paid little attention to the faces in between, but when Breman called Jarod's name, her attention was instantly on the exchange between the two men.

"Mr. Walls, it's nice to have you on the tour with us. I hope you'll enjoy Great Britain."

Jarod nodded. "I'm sure I will."

"And do you mind the change in seating?"

Jarod flashed a smile at Gabby, causing her to realize that she was awaiting his answer with nearly the same interest as Breman. "I assure you, Mr. Butler, I don't mind in the least."

"Good. Now," Breman turned to the semicircle of travelers, "we'll all have to go through the check-in and security procedures. Have your tickets ready, passports and driver's licenses for photo ID, and follow me. Oh, and call me Breman."

Janice was instantly at Breman's side, leaving Gabby to stare after her in stunned silence.

"That's your sister, I take it? They make an unusual couple, don't you think?"

Jarod's words caught her off guard. "I can't believe she took to him just like that. Janice has been known to race into a relationship, but this is speedy even by her standards." Gabby watched the couple for a moment longer. She judged Breman to be somewhere around her own age. He was a head taller than Janice's petite five feet three, and his jet black hair was a harsh contrast to Janice's pale blond. "They do look a bit odd together." Gabby tried to put her mind at ease. If Janice was in too much trouble, surely something would have come of it by now.

Jarod laughed and hoisted his camera bag over one shoulder and his garment bag over the other. "Do you need help with your luggage?"

Gabby shook her head, still wondering about Janice. "No, I only have the two and I followed the travel brochure's advice and packed half the clothes and took twice the money that I'd originally planned to take."

"Smart girl." Jarod's words sounded sincere and almost complimentary.

"I try." She picked up her things and followed the entourage to the check-in counter. "After all, I wouldn't want to be accused of expecting you to be a gofer."

～

Two hours later, Jarod and Gabby sat side by side on the plane. The pilot advised the attendants to prepare for takeoff as he positioned the plane on the runway.

"You don't get nervous when you fly, do

you?" Jarod questioned Gabby.

"Nope. It's become second nature."

"What about all the terrorist attacks and accidents?"

Gabby smiled and thrilled to the feel of the wheels lifting off the tarmac. "I figure when my time is up and God's ready for me to go, I'll go. Whether it's in a plane or a car, from cancer or something else."

"That's a rather complacent attitude." He turned as he spoke the words, and their faces were suddenly only inches apart.

Gabby pulled back just a space and shook her head. "There's no complacence to it." She put up a wall of protective distance. Maybe Jarod would give her a hard time for her Christian faith, or maybe he'd make fun of her belief in eternal life. Silently, she waited for some assault, but when Jarod said nothing, Gabby couldn't help looking over at him. He was reading the in-flight movie list and seemed totally unconcerned with her response.

Easing back in the chair, Gabby breathed deeply and tried to relax. There was no need to feel like she was paired up with the enemy. For all she knew, maybe Jarod had his own faith in God. Either way, she'd never get through the trip if she didn't buckle down and concentrate on the job at hand.

"So are you and your sister close?" Jarod suddenly asked.

Gabby couldn't contain her surprise. "What makes you ask?"

He shrugged. "I don't know. You come on a trip to spend time with her, yet she clearly doesn't seem to have the same need."

This made Gabby smile. "Well, Janice has always been a bit unpredictable. But the fact is, we've always been close. We're six years apart, but we had more fun together growing up than most of our friends."

"Playing house and dressing up baby dolls?" he asked in a teasing tone.

"Perish the thought! Janice and I played super-spy. We had special names for each other and even made up our own secret code. It was a lot more fun than playing dress-up, although we did have to interrogate our dolls on occasion. I was still playing those games when I graduated from high school."

Jarod laughed. "I would have never guessed."

"I think Daddy got us started on it. He wanted boys, but when he found out he could play spy games with his girls, I don't think it mattered as much. He used to design maps for us and stories of intrigue. He'd send us in search of some missing article or give us a riddle that would turn into an all-day game. As we got older, the projects became more intricate and quite challenging."

"Sounds like he's a great guy."

"He was. He died three years ago in a boating accident in the Atlantic." Gabby tried not to dwell on the subject. "So what's our choice of movies?"

"Garbage mostly."

Gabby nodded. "Guess I'll try to get some sleep."

"What's wrong with a little more conversation?" Jarod asked seriously.

Gabby looked over to find his questioning expression. His reddish brown hair with its unruly waves seemed to beckon her to run a hand through, but she kept herself in check. "I'm a very private person, and to be quite frank, I'm not used to sharing the details of my personal life with a total stranger."

"But I'm not a total stranger."

"Maybe not, but you aren't exactly my closest friend, either." Gabby silently wished the flight attendant would hurry up and offer her a drink. Anything would be preferable to having to face those eyes again. Why couldn't he see how uncomfortable she was?

As if reading her mind, he spoke. "Look, I

sense that I'm making you uneasy, but I'm not sure why."

Please just shut up, Gabby thought to herself. *I can't bear for this conversation to continue.* She contemplated ignoring him but chose instead to disarm the issue. "I'm just trying to focus on the job ahead. My mind is going in about ten different directions. My discomfort is a matter of my profession. I'm always concerned about the details."

"Well, maybe we should discuss it since I'm going to be working with you."

Gabby wanted to scream. What had seemed like the perfect excuse only managed to dig her in deeper.

"You're still mad about me coming along, aren't you? You're one of those women who doesn't like having her plans changed for her."

This sounded like a challenge to Gabby, and just as she was about to bite, an attractive woman in a navy blue airline uniform was taking her drink order.

"Something hot would be nice. Do you have decaf?" Gabby questioned.

"Of course, both coffee and tea."

"Coffee would be great."

"And for you, sir?" The attendant looked over Gabby to Jarod.

"That sounds good for me, too."

The attendant served the drinks and moved back to the next row of travelers. Up ahead several rows, Gabby could hear Janice's animated laughter. What in the world was going on between them?

"Sounds like your sister is getting right into the spirit of things."

Gabby refused to look at him and instead nursed her cup of coffee. "Janice has always been a free spirit. She grabs life by the horns and doesn't let go until the ride is over."

"Maybe you could learn a thing or two from her."

"Maybe you could learn to mind your own business," Gabby snapped, not understanding why she suddenly felt so irritable. She downed her coffee and reclined her seat back. "I'm going to rest now." She leaned back and closed her eyes, hoping that Jarod would just leave her alone.

"Well, if you need a shoulder for a pillow, you know where I'll be."

"If I need a pillow, I'll ask a flight attendant."

"It won't be nearly as much fun," he whispered against her ear.

Gabby could feel her face grow hot. "No, but it'll be a whole lot safer," she muttered. It was going to be a long, long flight.

Five

Breman Butler listened to Janice Fleming's nonstop chatter. He would have liked to have had more privacy with her, but the fact was they couldn't have been seated in a worse place. Not only were they placed on the three-seat side of the plane, putting Breman next to a harried businessman with a British accent, but they were very near one of the rest rooms, and the constant traffic was irritating.

"When my father died," Janice was saying, "my mother was extremely lonely. Gabby and I agreed to live at home for a while longer. You know, offer her creature comforts."

"What is your mother doing while you're away?" Breman asked, not really caring.

Janice smiled attractively and her blue eyes fairly glowed. "She's in California visiting her sister. So you see, we're all very well taken care of."

Breman tried to figure out the mind behind the chatter. He'd been informed that Janice Fleming was very intelligent. She was, in fact, perhaps too intelligent. One thing was certain, she was a consummate actress.

"So what do you do for a living, Janice?"

"I'm still in college. I'll graduate next spring with a bachelors in English."

"Ah, a teacher, eh?"

Janice laughed a bit too loud. "Good grief, no. I'll probably go into law or business. There's no money to be made in teaching, and I haven't got a philanthropical bone in my body."

Breman smiled. A woman after his own heart. "Money is important to you, I take it?"

Janice sobered and the infatuated, girlish chatter left with her smile. "Money is very important to me."

The British businessman began snoring at this point, and Breman noticed the flight attendant was turning down lights in the cabin. "I suppose," he said, putting his unread book away, "that a bit of rest is in order. This is an all-night flight, you know."

"Yes, I know." Janice followed suit by putting her magazine in the seat pocket. She gave a brief stretch. Very brief considering the space, or rather the lack of it. "To sleep, perchance to dream . . ." Her words ended in a yawn.

Breman nodded and felt a strange excitement course through him. This affair might turn into more fun than he'd at first imagined. Only time would tell. He leaned over and whispered in her ear, "I'm sure you'll find some interesting facts about London in your folder. In particular, you might want to note the meeting I've arranged in my room before the get-acquainted drinks at the hotel."

Janice closed her eyes and smiled. "You're ever so accommodating, Mr. Butler."

As Janice nodded off, Breman mentally considered the dossiers in his briefcase. There was little doubt that things would move very fast once they arrived in London and met up with the rest of their group. He was relieved to know that his assistant in England, Roper Davenport, would be on the job and ready when the plane touched down at Heathrow. Roper would drive the tour bus, and because he was native to Great Britain and had already done this tour on three previous occasions, he would be familiar with the various travel routes. Breman couldn't believe his good fortune in securing Roper. It wasn't just the fact that the man could drive a bus and knew his way around, either. Roper seemed very amiable to the other ventures Breman had suggested. At first he'd started small in order to feel the man out. He had to see exactly where Roper stood when it came to the law and moral issues. He had to know his employee's politics down to the most intimate detail, just in case there should be any problem. Breman was no fool. He'd been in this too long to let things fall apart at the last minute.

This would be his final job. After this he would comfortably retire and pick up a new life, maybe writing or teaching. Teaching made him think of the delicate blonde who now dozed at his right. Janice Fleming had wasted little time in attaching herself to him. But he'd expected this. Perhaps she thought she'd win his favor in their upcoming transactions. No doubt she hoped to tip the scales in her favor. Breman smiled. Maybe she would at that, he mused. She was attractive and seemed very willing to share his company. Maybe the scales already had tipped.

Seven rows back, Gabby dozed fitfully beside Jarod. He'd watched her for a time before deciding to catch some sleep for himself. Turning out the reading light, Jarod motioned a passing attendant.

"I'd like a blanket and pillow, please."

"Certainly." The woman smiled graciously and produced the requested items. "If you need anything else . . ." Her voice trailed off in the hint of an invitation.

"I'm sure I'll be just fine for now, but if I do need something, I'll call."

Her dark eyes flashed as her brows raised ever so slightly. "I'll be here," she said with only a cursory glance at Gabby.

After she walked away, Jarod struggled to get the pillow into an acceptable position and to spread out the cover. He thought he'd finally managed to accomplish the feat without waking Gabby when she opened her eyes.

"Are you finished jumping up and down in that seat?"

Jarod grinned. "Sorry, I tried to keep from waking you up."

"I wasn't asleep," she replied softly. "I was afraid the flight attendant might drool on me."

He looked into her teal blue eyes with a questioning expression. "What are you talking about?"

" 'If you need anything else . . .' " Gabby said with the same sensual simper. "Who could sleep through that? If you're a diabetic, I'd take a shot of insulin to counteract all that sugar."

Jarod laughed in spite of himself. "Eavesdropper!" he declared in a whisper. He leaned closer to her and smelled the inviting scent of her perfume. It brought to mind childhood memories of his mother's flower gardens.

Gabby shook her head, not noticing his intense interest in her perfume. "How much longer until we're in London?"

"About five hours, maybe a little less."

"Five hours of sheer torture," Gabby moaned and shifted in the reclined seat to find a comfortable spot.

"It's all in how you look at it." Jarod stared at her closed eyes. Long lashes fell against her cheeks, sooty from a generous but not overdone dose of mascara. Jarod found himself wanting to reach out and touch her. She just didn't seem real.

From the first moment they'd met, Jarod had been completely captivated by her fiery spirit and independent nature. She was different from her sister, but not as different as she thought. It was true enough that Janice seemed to grab life by the horns, but Gabby didn't seem the kind of woman to let life pass her by. No, Gabby might not grab the bull by the horns, but she'd no doubt tame him just the same.

"Are you going to watch me all night?" she asked suddenly without so much as opening her eyes.

Amused at being caught red-handed, he answered her honestly. "I might."

"Let me know if I snore. I've always wondered."

Grinning, Jarod closed his eyes. "I'm betting you do."

She said nothing else, and with very little effort Jarod allowed himself to drift off to sleep. His last conscious thoughts were of a leggy blond-headed writer and her hard-as-nails facade.

six

Gabby awoke to the clatter and rattle of the flight attendant serving breakfast. Much to her horror, she was not only using Jarod Walls' shoulder for a pillow, but sometime during the night she'd draped her arm casually across his chest.

Easing away, praying that he was fast asleep and oblivious to her breach of travel etiquette, Gabby wanted to die when his voice called out, "I lost the bet. You don't snore at all."

She fell back into her own seat, unable to look at him. Embarrassed to the very core of her existence, Gabby opened her eyes and looked straight ahead. "Not one word, Jarod. I mean it. Not one word."

He started laughing, which only made it worse, and the hotter she felt her face grow, the more he laughed.

"Stop it!" she exclaimed between clenched teeth. "You'll have everybody looking."

"So what? I think you've already discouraged that sweet little flight attendant. What with the bear hold you had on me, she probably figured she didn't stand a chance. Bet she wishes she'd thought of throwing herself at me the same way you did."

"I did not throw myself at you!" Gabby jabbed her elbow into his ribs, but he was too quick for her and twisted away just in time. Turning to face him, Gabby stopped short of slapping him. His red-brown hair was tousled and hanging over his forehead into his eyes. There was a slight growth of stubble on his face that seemed a little heavier around his upturned lips. Gabby knew she had to say something.

"I can't work with you," she finally blurted out. This had just the right sobering effect.

"I beg your pardon?"

"You heard me. I can't work with you. Not if you won't respect me and cut me some slack."

"But I do respect you. And if you really knew me, you'd know that I've cut you a great deal of slack. I'm not offended that you shared my shoulder for a few hours of well-supervised sleep. I am beginning to feel offended, however, by your hot and cold attitude and this impenetrable wall you seem

70

intent on placing between us. I thought perhaps if I maintained a light attitude — you know, joked and such — that you'd relax and realize I'm not such a bad guy to spend time with."

Gabby was completely taken aback by this comeuppance. "I . . . I didn't . . ." Oh, what could she say? He was right on every count. There was no honest defense.

Jarod threw off the cover rather angrily. "If you'll excuse me for a moment, please." He motioned toward the lavatory, and Gabby quickly got to her feet and stepped into the aisle for him to pass.

He didn't say another word, and when he was well down the aisle, Gabby flopped rather dejectedly into her seat. She'd never met anyone like him before. He wasn't even attempting to play games with her or pretend to be something other than he was. He was there to take pictures for her articles. He was handsome and considerate and had a dry wit that was particularly attractive to Gabby. Her father had always had such a sense of humor. *But now,* she thought, *Jarod's mad at me, and I've brought it all on myself.*

Taking up her purse, Gabby pulled out her compact and hairbrush and worked to make herself presentable. She'd chosen to leave her long hair down and the tangles were almost impossible, while smudges of mascara gave her eyes a ringed appearance. She looked like a throwback to the sixties when women were given to wearing their hair long and straight and their eye makeup thick.

Making quick work of it, Gabby pulled hand lotion from her purse and a tissue. This was an old trick she'd learned while on the road. She smeared a tiny bit of lotion onto the tissue, then wiped around her eyes one at a time. This complete, she ran the brush through her hair, applied a touch of powder and lipstick, and finally felt ready to face the day.

Jarod appeared just as she slid her purse back under the seat. She noted that he'd managed to adjust his own appearance during his time away. Determined to keep her temper under control and Jarod's questions at bay, Gabby ignored him and read a book. The flight attendant arrived soon with breakfast trays, and to Gabby's grateful pleasure, a cup of hot coffee. This time, there'd be no decaf.

"So are you going to ignore me the rest of the trip just because you slept on my shoulder?" Jarod suddenly asked when the flight attendant had moved on.

Gabby had just taken a sip of strong coffee and at these words began to choke. Coughing and sputtering, she tried to pretend she hadn't heard him. "That's strong coffee." She turned her attention to a blueberry muffin and silently opened a pat of butter.

"Well?"

He wasn't touching his food and it was very apparent to Gabby that he expected to settle this thing once and for all. Meticulously, she slathered butter on the muffin, giving it far more attention than it deserved. "This breakfast looks really good."

"You aren't answering me."

Gabby stiffened and swallowed. There was no way he'd ever let this drop. Putting her fork down, she took a deep breath. "I've worked hard to be where I'm at. I don't want you or anyone else to mistake me for some simpering society writer who does this only because she can't work in the real world. There are a lot of people out there who think what I do is sheer fluff, and I won't stand for it from you. You waltz into my editor's office, and just by being who you are, you command attention and respect. I have to fight for every inch of recognition and consideration I get. Partially because I'm a woman and partially because I'm generally very mild mannered."

Jarod stared hard at her for several moments before his mouth curved into a grin. "So this is one of those men/women issues? You're intimidated by me and afraid that no one will take you seriously? Maybe people will even mistake us for being closer than co-workers? Is that what you're worried about?"

Gabby said nothing, but her cheeks were warmed by the thought. "No, that honestly hadn't crossed my mind. I knew you wouldn't understand, so please just eat your breakfast and leave me alone."

"Admit it and then I'll leave you alone and eat."

Gabby pushed the food around on her plate and sighed. "Admit what? That I'm overwhelmed by you and your position in my travel article?" She took a long, purposeful drink of coffee.

"*Our* travel article," he stated flatly. "Get used to the idea because I'm not going anywhere, no matter how indifferent you might appear. Be as angry or cool as you choose, but sooner or later you'll have to deal with me."

∼

Customs was a cinch compared to coexisting with Jarod Walls. Gabby cruised through the green channel with nothing to declare and had little to concern herself with until Jarod arrived at her side.

"Today's a free day. What do you suggest we do, maybe talk a little more?"

"I have a list of things I believe we should consider for the article. Talking isn't one of them."

"How will I know what you want pictures of?" Jarod questioned with a grin.

"I'll write it on paper or give you hand signals. Better yet, why don't you just take pictures of everything and I'll go off on my own. Janice!" Gabby called out, finally catching sight of her sister.

Jarod trailed after her and exchanged handshakes with Janice. "I don't believe we've formally met. I'm Jarod Walls."

"Janice Fleming. I'm Gabby's sister."

"My condolences."

"I see my sister has won you over with her natural beauty and sparkling personality." Gabby rolled her eyes while Janice continued. "Just don't judge her too harshly. Long hours of cattle-car flight can make anybody a little less personable."

Gabby held up her hand to put an end to the sarcastic comment she presumed was about to come from Jarod's mouth. "Look, I'm tired and I want a nap before —"

"But you slept rather soundly on the

plane," Jarod interrupted with a look that challenged Gabby to deny it.

Ignoring him, Gabby continued. "As I was saying, after I rest, I have a great many places to go in a short amount of time. What did Breman say about hotel transportation?"

"See that minibus over there?" Janice directed. "That is our home on the road. Breman's just now getting the driver's attention. We'll load up the luggage and go. Breman says there are four other people on this tour and they're already waiting at the hotel."

"Must be nice," Gabby muttered. She headed in the direction of the bus, hearing Janice whisper something and Jarod laugh.

~

Gabby watched the passing scenery with a writer's eye, albeit a very tired eye, and found herself slightly disappointed with London. So far it struck her as being no different than any other large city. There was the monstrous din of traffic, the confusion of pedestrians and bicycles, and as if it wasn't enough for London to be the largest European city, they did everything in the opposite direction from the U.S.

"I want to formally welcome all of you to England. I believe you'll find the Grosvenor to be a very accommodating hotel. We have used it on two other occasions and found it quite satisfactory," Breman announced over the motor coach's PA system. Roper maneuvered through traffic with the ease of a sea captain on a gentle ocean. "Now, before we arrive at the hotel and turn you loose on London, I have a list of announcements that are imperative to your well-being. It would be wise to jot down some notes."

~

Roper pulled the bus up alongside the hotel and stopped. Breman smiled broadly. "Well, here we are. I would like for everyone to bring their carry-on items and meet in the lobby. Roper will see to having your bags delivered to your rooms, so please don't stand about on the pavement waiting for the luggage compartment to magically open." There were several chuckles at this, but all Gabby really wanted was for Breman to excuse them. She was beginning to imagine the possibilities of her room and prayed the bed would be soft and accommodating.

"Oh, one last thing. All of your breakfast meals have been included in this package. You will have a Continental breakfast here in London, but most everywhere else will offer you a hot cooked meal."

"What do the English consider continental?" Ginger Applegate asked.

"The same thing Americans do. Rolls, fruit, coffee and tea, that sort of thing. Now, are we all ready?"

Gabby was more than ready. She was tired of having to be polite and personable and was overwhelmed by the man she would be spending the next two weeks with. She couldn't imagine what her little sister was up to that required Gabby to play the role of "cover." It was hard to think of the trip getting any more complicated.

To her relief and surprise, check-in was well organized and handled in a matter of minutes. She was grateful to finally open the door to her room and find not only the tour company's welcoming complimentary drink card but a charming double bed with canopied headpiece and lush floral spread. They were there only moments before the luggage was delivered, as well.

"This looks nice enough," Janice stated. "I see we'll be sharing a bed. I thought they were going to make it two double beds."

"I don't care how many people I have to share it with, just as long as I can have a nap. All I need is an hour!" Gabby declared.

"You heard what Breman said about jet lag. Besides, with your schedule, an hour is about all you have time to spare," Janice replied. Already she was kicking off her shoes and peeling out of her traveling clothes. "I just want a shower."

"Does it have a shower?" Gabby asked with a yawn.

"I never thought to ask. It has a private bath, so even if it's just a tub, I'm set." Janice threw open her suitcase and pillaged for her things while Gabby slipped off her shoes and pulled down the covers.

"I'll be right here if you need anything. Better wake me up in an hour."

"Will do," Janice replied. "Oh, by the way, what's with you and Mr. Walls?"

"Why do you ask?" Gabby hadn't thought anything could get a rise out of her, but this certainly fell into the category of things she couldn't ignore.

Janice laughed. "I saw you sleeping with your head on his shoulder. Are you planning a summer fling after all?"

Gabby groaned. "I fell asleep, and, well, when I woke up, I had my head on his shoulder and my arm across his chest. It was all perfectly innocent. Honestly, that man has tried my patience to the end. I can't work with someone who's so . . ."

"Attractive?" Janice offered, slipping through the bathroom door. She paused only long enough to see her sister's stunned reaction. "I guess your expression answers that."

"Oh, why do I bother?" Gabby plopped down on the bed as Janice laughed heartily and closed the door.

Gabby stared at nothing for several minutes, then with another heavy sigh removed most of her clothes and slipped into bed. *He is attractive,* she thought, then chided herself and snuggled down against the pillow. *Even so, it doesn't need to make a difference on this trip. After a nap, I'll feel much better and the whole world will look different.*

~

"Gabby. Gabby, wake up!"

Janice's voice came from a cloud of impenetrable darkness. Gabby struggled to open her eyes, but they were so heavy. "I told you to give me an hour."

"It has been an hour, and Jarod is on the phone asking for you."

"I'm so tired," Gabby moaned, easing herself into a sitting position. "What does he want?"

"I'd imagine it has something to do with your magazine article. Look, I'm going out with Breman. He promised to take me somewhere special."

"You already have a date with the tour director?" Gabby ran a hand through her hair and yawned.

Janice smiled and finished hooking an attractive gold belt around her slim waist. "Yes, isn't it exciting? I can date Breman and see the world!" She glanced at her watch. "Gotta go. I'll see you later." She hurried from the room so quickly that Gabby didn't even have time to ask where the phone was.

A quick assessment soon resolved the problem for her. "Hello?" she said, trying to stifle another yawn.

"Are you ready to go?" Jarod's warm, masculine voice questioned from the other end of the line.

"Go where?"

"I thought we'd do the Tower of London, unless you have a better suggestion."

Gabby sat down hard on the bed as Jarod hurried on to explain. "Look, it's a beautiful day outside. The sun is just right for some great pictures, and I figured we could hire a cab and take our time getting across the city to the Tower of London. On the way, we could have him stop so that I can take pictures. That way, if tomorrow is overcast, we'll already have the job done."

Gabby was fully awake now and knew everything Jarod said made perfect sense. He took his assignment seriously; she had to give him that much. "Let me change my clothes and brush my teeth. I'll be downstairs in ten minutes."

"I'll be there."

She hung up the phone and looked around the room for her bags. Further search revealed that Janice had thoughtfully put everything away. This made Gabby feel foolish for her anger at Janice's desertion. She loved her sister almost more than anyone in the world, and if Janice was having fun with Breman Butler, who was she to interfere? Still, there was a nagging sensation of worry, and with Janice's every move it seemed to build.

Against her better judgment, Gabby did something she'd never, ever done before. She opened Janice's drawers and leafed through each article. She had no idea what she was looking for. Evidence? But of what? All she knew was that Janice was desperate to have her as a companion on this trip and so far had managed to spend less than a couple of hours with her. Spotting Janice's tour folder, Gabby flipped through the pages as though hoping to find some glaring indication of what her sister was up to.

But Janice's folder looked the same as Gabby's. Nothing seemed to be added or deleted and nothing appeared to be any-thing less than it was. Putting everything back in place, Gabby wondered if Janice's need for cover might be related to something back home. Maybe the entire matter was already behind her simply by the fact that she'd come to England. Maybe a pesky boyfriend had insisted on being Janice's tour mate and Janice had refused, saying that her sister was going along. Maybe her words on the telephone had been to a sympathetic travel agent to whom Janice had already told her tales of woe. Gabby smiled. That sounded exactly like Janice.

Noticing the time, Gabby knew she was already late for her rendezvous with Jarod. Taking out jeans and a sporty navy-and-white-striped top, Gabby quickly changed and put her hair up in a ponytail. After brushing her teeth, she applied a new layer of makeup and pronounced herself fit for public viewing.

"God," she said, pausing at the door to roll her eyes heavenward, "please don't let me make a fool of myself. You know how I feel about this job. I just want the article to come together well, and I want to have fun doing it. Let me stop worrying about Janice, too. Oh, and please give me strength to endure because I don't think I've ever had a worse case of jet lag. Amen."

Seven

By the time Gabby and Jarod walked through the main gatehouse to the Tower of London, Jarod had already shot two rolls of film. He was loading a third into his camera as Gabby paid the entrance fee.

"If we go in the direction of Bloody Tower," Gabby said, looking at some notes she'd written before even leaving for Great Britain, "there's a tower history gallery. It has models, pictures, and text related to the entire complex. Maybe we could decide what has to be experienced and what can slide." She looked up at the high stone walls lining the walkway. "I had no idea it was this big."

"Too bad we don't have more time." Jarod looked at her squarely. "How are you holding up?"

Gabby grew self-conscious. "I'm tired, but I'll make it. I know what the job requires."

Jarod grinned. "I'm sure you do."

~

Gabby presumed by the reaction of other tourists that Jewel House was probably the favored exhibit of the Tower of London. It was here where the crown jewels were kept and displayed. Gabby found herself almost more interested in eavesdropping than in paying strict attention to the vast, and frankly unfathomable, wealth held in this room. People were funny in the way they reasoned, and Gabby had always loved to listen in on conversations.

"If they'd sell off just half of this stuff," one woman said to her pudgy husband, "they could wipe out poverty and house the homeless."

"Maybe they're trying to do that with the exorbitant amount of money they charge for admissions," he grumblingly replied. The woman laughed and followed the man from the room.

"I'll bet these aren't even the real thing," another man was telling a bored-looking teenager. "They've probably stashed the real ones away in some crypt."

Gabby smiled to herself and jotted some notes about the piece in front of her. The world's largest diamond, housed in the magnificent Scepter with the Cross from 1660, glowed from the staff's headpiece. Gold and rubies, along with a variety of other stones, trimmed the scepter quite nicely and made a most impressive display.

Moving throughout the exhibition room, Gabby knew there was far more than she could take in and decided to pace herself. It seemed logical to pick out two or three main objects and report their statistics rather than try to take in everything at once. An eight thousand-ounce punchbowl and jewel-adorned coronation robes vied for her attention until she finally settled on the 1841 royal christening font. The last item she wrote about was the Imperial State Crown. Designed for Queen Victoria in 1837 and used for every subsequent coronation, Gabby tried to imagine what it would feel like to wear this piece upon her own head. Rich purple velvet was the base for the jewel-encrusted crown. Ermine fur trimmed the bottom, giving it a fairy-tale appearance, but it was the large diamonds, rubies, and sapphires that caught her eye.

"Most impressive, don't you think?" It was Jarod.

Gabby looked up at him and nodded. "I can't imagine being a part of such wealth. Frankly, I'd be afraid that someone might steal it away from me."

"It's like that with most possessions." Jarod glanced at his watch. "We've got just enough time to make it over to White Tower. I understand the Chapel of St. John is not to be missed."

Gabby put away her notebook and nodded. "Lead on."

An hour later, Gabby waited while Jarod took several final photos of the "Beefeaters." These were the Tower guards who were clad in black-and-red uniforms that replicated those of the Tudor era. Gabby had learned that there were a total of forty-two guards who actually lived on the premises. It was the most coveted, prestigious job, and the subject of Jarod's attention was quite proud of his position.

Finally they exited the Tower grounds with many other tourists. They'd managed to cover a great deal of territory and Gabby, in spite of her jet lag, was beginning to get excited about the article.

"There's so much to write about," she mused. "I don't believe a single article can begin to do it justice."

"No, I'm sure you're right. Didn't Sandy say she'd have some accompanying historical pieces when your feature is published?"

"Yes, and she can have a heyday with this one. Just imagine having someone do a piece on the little princes. That would be of tremendous interest to people in America; after all, it's mystery and intrigue. People back home love that kind of thing."

"The boys were imprisoned by their uncle Richard, who would later become King Richard III, after their death. Not a lot of speculation there."

"There's all kinds of room for speculation," Gabby protested. "Edward IV's sons mysteriously disappeared after their father died in 1483. Royal children don't just disappear without a fuss. Richard was crowned later that year, and I have to wonder what the atmosphere was surrounding his becoming king. Didn't anyone stand against him? Did he just keep his nephews locked away until they died? Or was he really framed? It's possible that he had nothing to do with their demise. I think the article could be great."

"You do realize they found the skeletons of two children in 1674? They no doubt belonged to the princes."

"I doubt everything until I have proof. It's the writer in me. I accept nothing at face value, and I question everything. Facts, feelings, facades — I dig through it all."

They walked amicably together, neither one wanting to break the mood of the moment. "The light's still good. Let's walk over to Tower Bridge. If I remember right, the walkway is open to the public."

Gabby sighed wearily. "I suppose I have enough time for that, and it *would* look great for the article. Everybody recognizes the London Tower Bridge."

Tower Bridge, the design of Sir Horace Jones, was completed in 1894, and nothing else in the city seemed to symbolize London as well as that.

"Well, it's not falling down," Gabby teased. "You know, I read a book on children's nursery songs, and the London Bridge rhyme is actually quite ancient and widespread. Germany has its version for the Magdeburg Bridge, and France and Ireland both have versions of the song that seem to imply a relationship to the devil. Some scholars even think the rhyme celebrates ancient rituals of sacrifice at the building of a bridge."

"I doubt there were too many sacrifices offered in 1894," Jarod countered.

"Probably not in a human or animal way, but just imagine what it might imply. Perhaps more of the crown jewels are buried inside the bridge."

"You do have a wild imagination."

To Gabby, London Bridge looked just as

she'd imagined it might, only dirtier. The twin towers, connected by a public walkway, made a far more ornate bridge than any she'd seen in America. It spoke of a bygone era and of a people who admired beauty in their work and devoted themselves to quality. She walked onto the bridge with Jarod and tried to memorize every detail of the fading day. In the west, the sun slipped slowly behind the outline of ancient buildings. Dusk rapidly came upon them as the sky took on violet and mauve shades. They'd have to hurry if Jarod was to get any decent pictures.

But Jarod was already at work, and Gabby found it easier to remain silent and consider the day. It was hard to imagine herself an ocean away from home. A light breeze blew across her face, and the sights and sounds of London seemed to fade into memories of a day at the beach with her father. It was at times like this that she missed him most. Pat Fleming had exuded such a love of life. He was always captivated by the world around him and had shared that captivation with his children. He also saw things that other people missed, and the art of this was something that had passed itself along to Gabby. She saw everything, and sometimes that even worked against her. It was annoying not to be able to ignore things the way some people did. Many times Gabby had found herself up against a situation that she couldn't just cast aside, yet Janice seemed to have little trouble with such a concept. The fact that Janice was out with Breman Butler instead of Gabby was a good example of this. Gabby would never have dreamed of deserting Janice, especially if she'd been the one to beg the other to come along on the trip.

"Penny for your thoughts," Jarod whispered against her ear.

"Shouldn't that be a *pence* for your thoughts?"

He laughed. "Come on, I want to get some pictures from the walkway, and they'll be closing up soon."

"We don't have to climb up there, do we?" Gabby questioned, looking up at the glassed-in walkway some one hundred forty feet above the river.

"Nope, they have an elevator. Of course, you could take the three hundred steps and boast about it on the tour tomorrow."

"No thanks, Jarod. I've never been one to boast or brag. But be my guest if that kind of thing appeals to you."

He looped his arm through hers. "Come on, I'll drag you to the elevator."

After getting what he hoped were some great panoramic shots of London and the Thames, Jarod hailed a cab and slid in beside Gabby. "How about I buy you dinner?"

"No." She shook her head. "I have to get ready to go out. I'm in dire need of a bath and a bit of rest."

"You have to eat. You didn't have lunch. Why don't you get ready, then let me take you to dinner? I know this great restaurant called Manzi's. It's very down-to-earth and serves the best cooked-to-order seafood you've ever put in your mouth."

"I didn't realize you were familiar with London."

"I've been here a few times," he said as though it was no big deal. "So how about it? Manzi's is just waiting for you."

"No. I promised Janice I'd go to dinner with her."

Jarod let the conversation drop until they'd arrived at the hotel. He walked her to her room and was about to leave when Janice came bursting out, nearly knocking Gabby to the floor. If Jarod hadn't been standing behind her, he had little doubt that Janice would have run right over her.

"Oh, good!" Janice exclaimed as Jarod set Gabby right. "I was worried that I'd have to leave a message with the front desk."

"What's wrong?" Gabby asked. Jarod thought she sounded almost fearful of the answer.

Janice flashed a smile at them both. "Well, Breman has offered to take me to a really special place for dinner, and afterward, well, he said it was a surprise but promised me I'd be sorry if I said no."

Jarod saw the color drain from Gabby's face. "But *we* had plans."

"I know and I'm so sorry. Maybe Jarod wouldn't mind going with you to see *Phantom*. How about it, Jarod?" He nodded at Janice, but Gabby couldn't see this, and before she could answer, Janice was pulling tickets from her purse. "I picked these up from the front desk earlier. You two have a great time!"

Janice was gone before Gabby could even open her mouth. She stood staring at the retreating form of her sister and then to her hand, where two tickets for *Phantom* promised a night of unrivaled entertainment.

"I can't believe she did that." There was genuine hurt and disappointment in Gabby's voice.

"I promise I can be a fun dinner and theater date," Jarod said, trying to ease the situation.

"It's not that." Gabby closed her hand around the tickets. "Janice isn't acting at all like herself." The old worries were resurfacing.

He grinned. "Maybe she's attracted to our tour guide in a way that she just can't help herself. Maybe she even used his shoulder for a pillow on the flight over."

Gabby looked up at Jarod, flashing teal blue eyes and reddening in embarrassment. "I thought it was too good to be true that you'd actually behave yourself all day. Look, I think I'll just skip it all. I'm going to take a nice hot bath and go to bed."

"Oh no, you're not!" Jarod declared. "You're just disappointed, but that's no reason to give up on the evening. Clean yourself up and get into something nice. We're going to dinner and then to *Phantom*, and I promise I'll behave myself and act the role of perfect gentleman."

"*Act* the role, eh?"

"Well, I'm not always perfect."

She smirked. "And I'll wager not always a gentleman."

"Well, there you lose. I'm *always* a gentleman where it concerns a lady. Just give me a chance to prove it. We can talk shop all night if that's what you want. Hey, I even brought a suit along so I won't look too shabby."

Gabby smiled at this and opened her hand to look at the tickets. She'd wanted to see *Phantom* in London for as long as she'd known they were coming. Something about it just struck a chord in her and sounded incredibly wonderful. She had little choice but to make up her mind. There was no figuring Janice and what had gotten into her, but there was still the problem of deciding about the night and how she would spend it.

"All right. But dinner will have to wait until after the show. I'll need an hour to get ready. You want to pick me up here or meet downstairs?" She sounded reserved and reconciled to the matter.

"Well, don't sound so enthusiastic," he teased. "I'll pick you up here in exactly one hour."

Gabby nodded and went into the room, leaving Jarod to stare at the closed door.

Jarod liked Gabby a great deal, but he couldn't let his feelings get in the way of work. Gabby had made it clear that she was struggling to work with him, but what *she* didn't realize was how his *own* feelings were causing him to waiver from his normally rigid and sound judgment. *Keep it under control,* he thought. There'd be time enough for falling in love after the work was done.

Whistling a tune from *Phantom of the Opera*, Jarod thought he'd never looked forward to an evening out as much as he did this one.

Eight

Stifling a yawn the next morning and listening only halfheartedly to Breman's tour discussion, Gabby's mind kept drifting back to the night before. An evening out with Jarod had been everything she'd imagined it capable of being. Jarod had remained a perfect gentleman, and *Phantom* was just as magical as she'd expected. They'd delayed dinner until after the theater, which by that time left Gabby feeling close to starvation. Jarod had laughed at how much food she'd been able to put away.

"You said you were only a *little* hungry," he'd teased and watched as she dug in with the zest of a starving lioness.

"Well, maybe more than a little hungry," she'd admitted, trying Yorkshire pudding for the first time. It had soaked up some of the roast's juices and melted divinely in Gabby's mouth.

Even remembering it now made Gabby's mouth water. The Continental breakfast they'd been served at the hotel was enough to stave off hunger but certainly did nothing to impress her. Dinner, however, had been enchanting and Jarod had stuck to his guns, discussing only business and the article they were to create. Now in the light of day, with Jarod sharing the seat beside her and Janice not far from Breman's side, Gabby decided things could be a lot worse. Just spending time with Jarod had helped her to relax a great deal. His commanding looks were still impressive, but his personality had put her dangerously at ease. Warning bells continued to go off in her head every time he smiled at her, but it was almost as if her heart quickly silenced those alarms in lieu of a closer look at the dangers.

"If you get a chance to tour St. Paul's this afternoon, you won't be sorry," Breman said with a smile. "You may already be familiar with the interior. If you remember, this is the church where Prince Charles and Lady Diana Spencer were wed. The television coverage, of course, couldn't possibly do it justice, and I highly recommend embarking on one of their guided tours."

Breman looked at his schedule, then glanced at the passengers. "I nearly forgot. You will notice that we have four additions to our group. They've joined us from France."

Gabby glanced up at the four newest members and wondered if they spoke English. Two of the men were dark headed, with deeply tanned complexions. They seemed intent on Breman's words, even though they never so much as cracked a smile at his bad jokes. The other two, a man and a woman, were fairer and seemed intent only on each other. *Honeymooners*, Gabby thought to herself with a smile.

"You'll get to meet everyone tonight at our get-acquainted party. But for now our next stop is Westminster Abbey." Breman announced and took his seat.

The tour bus made its way through London with the rest of the traffic. It seemed to Gabby that the town was never ending, and people seemed to rush out from every nook and cranny, almost like scurrying mice in a maze. She jotted this note in her book and realized with a start that Jarod was reading as she wrote.

"Don't do that!" She tried to keep her tone quiet.

"Sorry."

"You don't sound sorry," she said, snapping her notebook closed.

Jarod grinned and narrowed his green eyes only slightly. "Well, I'm sorry I got caught."

Gabby nodded. "That much I believe." Her defenses were once again in place.

As the bus slowed and came to a stop, Breman again got to his feet. "Inside, I'll turn you over to another guide, and we'll meet back on the bus in one hour. If you get lost for any reason, we'll meet the motor coach here at this exact position."

Gabby listened with little interest. She was already overwhelmed by yet another London landmark. The rich wonder of the architectural styling made Westminster Abbey an impressive sight. Drawing on her history, Gabby thought of how in 1066, William the Conqueror had been crowned King of England in this very building.

"Kind of impressive, eh?" Jarod remarked.

"Very." She forgot her earlier agitation. "I keep thinking, if only these walls could talk. Can you imagine? My tour book says the Abbey has been the setting for coronation ceremonies since William the Conqueror. Imagine that. Queen Victoria, Mad King George, Henry VIII."

"Like I said, kind of impressive." He smiled at her warmly, causing a shiver to run up her spine. Jarod would have made an impressive royal figure.

They followed the group inside and

joined up with another large group of tourists, while the distinctive voice of their English guide announced very calmly that the tour would now begin.

Gabby tried to ignore the man at her side. In light of the centuries-old building surrounding her, it didn't seem that it should be such a difficult feat, but it was. Walking down the long, majestic nave, Gabby wrote notes while the guide, a very petite and serious-looking Englishwoman, spoke of the Abbey's wonders in a high-pitched nasal voice.

"This nave is the highest in England. It stands thirty-one meters high, which calculates out to one hundred two feet for you Americans. The flying buttresses overhead are a remarkable display of architectural ingenuity and master craftsmanship. You will note that the arch styles of the nave are French Gothic. . . ."

The woman's narrative continued, but Gabby found herself caught up in the moment. She tried to imagine the various weddings and coronations that had taken place in this austere setting. In her mind, she pictured Queen Victoria, regal and beautiful and so very young. Had she worried about the future? Did she question whether or not she would make a fitting queen?

The enormity of the nave dwarfed her and left her feeling like a small, inconspicuous mote of dust. How wondrous it all was! Gabby was mesmerized as she walked slowly behind the others. Did she walk in the footprints of Victoria? Could she ever hope to accomplish in life even a particle of what that grand old woman had accomplished in hers?

"You're lagging behind, madam," Jarod's voice whispered in amusement.

Gabby looked up at him and opened her mouth to reply, but there were no words. Her conscious thoughts were absorbed in a running medley of the church's history. At least that was how it started. But then, as if her mind simply exchanged one resplendent view for another, Gabby lost herself in Jarod's dark green eyes.

"Yes?" he questioned, waiting for some caustic retort.

The spell was broken, and Gabby simply shook her head and hurried to catch up with the group.

~

After a day of rushed tours and London traffic, Gabby was glad to retreat to the privacy of her hotel room. She'd run down a mental list of all that needed to be done before their departure in the morning. She'd have to pack, of course, but more important, she needed to compile her notes and make certain she had all the imperative information for her article on London.

"Are you taking the river cruise tonight?" Janice asked as Gabby deposited an armload of paraphernalia onto the bed.

"No, you go ahead. I have to get these notes put into order."

"You *will* join up with the others for our complimentary evening drink, won't you?"

Gabby sighed. "I suppose I should. I'd like to get a little background on each of the people in our group."

"That sounds good." Janice moved around the room, completely absorbed in what she was doing. "Hasn't this trip been fun so far?"

"Fun isn't exactly how I'd sum it up." Gabby felt strangely reserved. It was really the first opportunity she'd had to approach Janice on her activities of the night before. "Why'd you cancel on me last night?"

Janice looked at her blankly. "I wanted to be with Breman. He's such an exciting man. Don't you think so?"

"I really don't have much of an opinion of him." Gabby slipped out of her walking shoes and stretched her toes. "Are you falling for this guy or something?"

"Or something," Janice said coyly. She smiled rather like a cat with cream and slipped into a black-and-white-striped sweater.

"Janice," Gabby thought to approach the subject of her concerns, "you aren't having problems back home are you? There isn't anything you want to tell me about, is there?"

"What in the world are you talking about?" Janice stopped fussing with her hair and stared at Gabby.

Gabby shrugged. "I just get this feeling that something's going on with you and you're not telling me about it. I've had it for some time, but it just seemed like when you asked me to come on the trip —"

"I'm a grown woman, big sister. You don't have to worry about me," Janice interrupted, trying to sound nonchalant.

But when Janice exchanged her blue jeans for a snug black miniskirt, Gabby thought maybe she should give more time to worrying about Janice than she already had. "You're going out in that?"

Janice shrugged and completed the outfit with black panty hose and flats. "I should have brought my heels, but I suppose I'll be doing plenty of walking tonight."

"Where are you two going?"

"After our get-acquainted drinks, Breman promised me London theater and dinner. Hey, that reminds me" — Janice's voice dropped an octave — "how did things go between you and the gorgeous Mr. Walls?"

"We're just working together. The show and dinner was your idea, remember?"

Janice seemed nonplused. "My idea? I thought *Phantom* in London was something *you* always wanted to do. How much fun could something so romantic be with your sister for a date? I figured you'd have twice as much fun with Jarod as you would with me."

"Well, you were wrong," Gabby said, not really meaning it. She found it odd to all of a sudden have to force her protest. "I wanted to spend time with you on this trip. Look, you worked me over for days to get me to agree to coming with you, and now you've hardly said two words to me the whole time we've been in London." She wanted to remind Janice that she'd needed her for "cover," as well, but held her tongue.

Janice's elfish features softened. "I'm sorry, Gabby. I didn't mean to leave you high and dry. Listen, I can't tell you why this is important to me, but I am asking you to be understanding about it. I still love you the best!" Her little-girl smile won Gabby over.

"And I love you the best," Gabby echoed. It had been a long-forgotten ritual of childhood. When Gabby had begun to run around with girl friends, Janice had felt the void quite severely. Gabby could nearly hear the childish wails of, "You always go away with them. Don't you love me anymore?"

"Of course I love you," she would answer. "I love you the best." It was their game.

"Have fun tonight," Gabby called out through the memories. "I'll be here, and I'll be just fine."

Janice picked up her purse and opened the door. "Don't forget the get-together. And why don't you get Jarod to take you out and about? You shouldn't stay cooped up here all night and miss your last night in London."

"I think seeing Parliament, Buckingham Palace, Harrods, and the Victoria and Albert Museum was more than enough of London for a day. Don't you?"

Janice shrugged. "If you say so."

Janice left Gabby to sort through the debris of her day. Making her way to the elevator, Janice mentally calculated her plans for the evening. First she'd go to Breman's room. What progressed after that would depend entirely upon Breman Butler.

The elevator doors opened and she joined a half dozen other people. "Four, please," she announced. She caught the appreciative once-over of the man to her left before he reached up to punch in the number. The numbers began to click by, and soon Janice was deposited on the fourth floor.

Glancing first to the left and then to the right, Janice was happy to find the hall deserted. She walked quickly to Breman's room number, slung her black bag over one shoulder, and gave a loud knock at the door.

Breman opened the door and smiled. He'd taken time to change out of his customary tour clothes, a combination of casual slacks and embossed tour windbreaker, and now wore a dark business suit and red tie.

"Welcome, Ms. Fleming," he said in a rather formal tone. He pushed open the door to reveal a large suite. In the middle of the room stood a round oak table and four chairs. Two of which were already occupied. One by Roper Davenport and the other by a man with whom Janice was unfamiliar.

"I do hope they've sprayed for bugs," Janice said in a simpering mixture of southern belle and New York debutante.

"I assure you the room is quite clean, and I've seen to any infestation problems myself." Breman motioned her in.

Once the door was closed behind her, Janice's facade instantly changed. "Can we finally get down to business?"

Breman smiled tolerantly. "First things first. Janice Fleming, these are my associates. Mr. Davenport you already know. He's my right-hand man." Roper Davenport appeared to be in his upper twenties. His broad shoulders seemed to strain at the navy blue jacket that contained them. Blond and mustached, Roper's looks were quite appealing, but it was icy blue eyes that caught Janice's attention.

"Mr. Davenport," she said with a nod. Roper smiled and saluted with his drink.

Breman continued. "This is my other right hand. You'll only know him by his first name, which is Ralph. He's my London help."

"Two right hands? No lefts?" Janice knew she sounded sarcastic.

"Left hands have always been associated with bad luck." Breman's green eyes seemed to darken.

"Well, hello then, Ralph," she greeted the overweight, middle-aged man. Ralph seemed about as useful for this project as her mother might have, but she held back her retorts and continued with business. "Well, now that we all know each other, I for one would like to get to work. I have the entire Irish Republican Army wanting to know what in the world you've done with their weapons?"

Breman seemed unconcerned. "Have a seat, Janice, and we'll discuss the terms of our agreement. Perhaps we can negotiate. this into a successful settlement before the night is over."

Janice tossed her purse on the table and took the seat offered her by Roper. "I believe our arrangement was already set into motion before we left the States. Now, if you don't mind, I have people to answer to, and those people want to know where their guns have gotten off to."

"I assure you," Breman said, taking the empty chair, "the weapons are secure and ready for shipment to your people. First things first, however. Have your people agreed to my price?"

"I'm prepared to offer you two million dollars," Janice said coolly. "It's a fair price, and you know it. No one in his right mind is going to give you a cent over that."

"Ah" — Breman rolled his ink pen between his fingers — "you are presuming that

I deal only with the sound of mind. Presumption will get you killed, my dear Janice."

He smiled in a rather leering way, making Janice's blood run cold. It wasn't the first time she'd had to deal with his kind, and of course it wouldn't be the last. Putting on her best act, Janice licked her lips rather seductively and seemed to consider his words for a moment.

"I don't presume on anything." Her words were unemotional and very calculated. "If you deal aboveboard with us this time, the IRA will be very willing to negotiate future deals with you. Perhaps once you've proven yourself in this, we would consider upping the price next time."

"There isn't going to be a next time," Breman announced. "I'm retiring after this, and that is why my price stands at ten million. This business is getting much too difficult and risky."

"But two million dollars for a minuscule load of weapons is more than reasonable."

"This isn't a 'minuscule load,' as you put it. There's more to this than just the armory M–16s. Your people realize that, whether they've tuned you in to the facts or not."

Janice fixed him with a stare. "Let's see, we can expect M–16A2s, 5.56mm ammunition, along with M–203 40mm grenade launchers. These fasten under the M-16. Together they are called M–203/M–16." She flashed him an amiable smile. "Then there are 40mm grenades for said launchers. These are to be both high-explosive and fragmentation grenades." Janice started counting on her fingers. "Then we have the Beretta 92F, .9mm handguns — U.S. issue. They hold 15-round magazines and because .9mm ammunition is common in Europe, my people need not feel the squeeze of seeking the 'Made in the USA' label. Oh, and of special interest to my friends in Belfast is the highly coveted M–249. The U.S. Army calls it the S.A.W. It takes 5.56mm ammunition using a 200-round drum. However, it's also designed to take clips from the M–16. A brilliant little toy made in Belgium." Janice clicked off the items easily as if it were nothing more than a grocery list. "Shall I continue? I haven't even mentioned the rocket launchers and —"

Breman interrupted, "If you know what's involved, why do you insult my intelligence by offering me two million when you know the stuff is worth ten?"

"To the IRA, Mr. Butler, 'the stuff,' as you call it, is worth much more than ten million dollars. However, ten million is completely out of our league, and you know it. Further, while you have a nice assortment of weapons to trade, there isn't enough in quantities to make your cache very appealing to the bigger players. So I find it very doubtful that anyone else in our league is going to offer you more than we have. Now, are you prepared to cut through this bunk and deal with me, or shall I call my people and tell them you've reneged on a deal already agreed upon? Oh, and I might add, if the latter is the case, you might want to put extra security in place." She glanced first at Roper. His blond mustache twitched briefly, but his eyes remained fixed. Ralph fidgeted nervously as Janice's gaze fell to him. He was at least forty pounds overweight and seemed to fall into the description of a typical thug. Janice wasn't impressed. "I don't think these two are capable of protecting you against the retribution that will come your way."

Breman seemed to consider her words for a moment. The silence was deafening as the four exchanged unspoken challenges. Janice picked up her purse and got to her feet. "When you're ready to deal, you know where I'll be."

Breman looked at her oddly. "You seem

awfully self-assured. What makes you think I won't put my people out there to take care of you?" His voice was cold and his eyes narrowed ominously.

Janice returned his hard stare. "You have no idea who you are dealing with, Mr. Butler." She pulled the facade of a warring general around her tightly and held her ground. Experience had proven time and again that eighty percent of a successful negotiation was bluff. Breman seemed to pale ever so slightly. Janice pushed her advantage. "You think I'm just a common lackey. A message runner for the IRA. Well, Mr. Butler," she said, her voice lowering to a bare whisper, "in America, I have affiliates so close to your organization, you'd be hard pressed to trust your own brother. Don't threaten me, and never, ever underestimate me. I'm in this to benefit myself. If you think I'd come play tourist on your little expedition without backup and reasonable protection, you're crazier than your dossier suggests."

"I don't think we should be hasty in this," Breman said, getting quickly to his feet. "Come on, Janice, relax. Up until now, you and I have had some fun. We don't need to settle this thing tonight. Think about it. Consider the full list of what we're offering and see if your people won't consider coming up to at least, say, five million? That's half my asking price." He gave her a smile the likes of which Janice was certain had caused more than one woman to forget her resolve.

"Maybe we can work together. We want those weapons, and you want our money. Maybe, just maybe, we can do business."

Breman seemed to start breathing again, and Janice felt assurance course through her veins like lifeblood. He was purely an amateur, she decided, but this made him both unpredictable and uncertain. And Janice knew those two things could add up to a deadly total more quickly than anything else.

"Would you want to see our list?" Breman asked hopefully. "Maybe double-check it against what the IRA has asked for?"

"Of course," Janice fairly purred. "I'd like to see whatever you'd like to show me."

Nine

Jarod's first thought at seeing Janice Fleming enter Breman Butler's room was that Gabby was alone. His second thought was to wonder just what Janice had planned for the tour director. Thoughts of Gabby won out, and with little attention as to what he was doing, Jarod hurried through a shower and shave and made his way to Gabby's room.

He knocked twice before Gabby called out, "Who is it?"

"Jarod. I came to escort you to our get-acquainted party, and then to talk you into dinner."

Gabby opened the door, and Jarod whistled at the sight of her in a thick bathrobe with a towel wrapped around her head. "Say, you'll be the hit of the party. Bet no other woman shows up in that outfit."

Gabby smirked. "Ha, ha, ha. Very funny, Mr. Walls. If you must know, I don't plan to go out this evening. I have too much work to do."

"Work can wait," Jarod insisted. "Look, I got cleaned up and shaved." He ran a hand under his chin. "I even put on one of those cheap yet maddeningly alluring after-shave scents." He winked and leaned closer. "Just smell me."

Crossing her arms, Gabby refused to be drawn in. "I just took a shower myself, Mr. Walls, and I have my own perfume to enjoy, thank you."

"And a very pleasant scent it is," Jarod remarked. "But seriously, we're suppose to be there tonight. It's good for the morale of the group."

Gabby glanced at her wristwatch. "But it's already a quarter of seven. I don't have time to do anything with my hair and makeup, much less dress to kill."

"You don't have to kill anyone or anything. And given the fact that I saw your sister go into Butler's room less than a half hour ago, I doubt we'll be the only late arrivals to the party."

"You saw Janice where?" Gabby questioned with a frown.

"She was going into Breman's room."

"How do you know it was Breman's room?"

Jarod smiled. "He answered the door and invited her inside. I was just getting off the

116

elevator, and my room is two down from his."

"And you're sure it was Janice?"

"Black miniskirt, legs up to here," Jarod replied, drawing a line at his neck. "All this time I thought your sister was short."

"She is, but, unfortunately, so was that skirt."

"So you're satisfied that I actually saw your sister?"

Gabby's frown deepened. "No, in fact, I'm very unsatisfied. Janice should know better than . . . oh, never mind. She's a grown woman, as she keeps reminding me."

Jarod noted her agitation and sought to offer her some kind of comfort. "Look, why don't you just get dressed and come out with me. I promise to show you a good time." He noted her expression changing to one of sarcastic disbelief. "We had fun last night, didn't we?" he questioned without giving her time to answer. "And I was a perfect gentleman, just like I promised."

Gabby seemed to relax. Her blue eyes, enormous beneath the white swathing bulk of the hotel towel on her head, searched his face for some further reassurance.

"I promise to be just as much fun and just as wonderful as last night." He smiled and gave what he hoped was a look of pleading expectation.

"But I have work to do. Notes to catch up on and thoughts to put down on paper." She didn't sound like it would take much to convince her to leave it behind.

"It'll wait. You'll have plenty of time on the bus tomorrow, and we don't even leave until eight-thirty tomorrow morning. You could get up early with a fresh, clear mind and write for a couple of hours."

"That sounds reasonable. I suppose I should at least meet the others," Gabby said with a sigh. "All right. I'll meet you in the lobby in fifteen minutes."

"Good."

True to her word, Gabby appeared in the hotel lobby fifteen minutes later. She'd fussed over her hair, finally deciding to pin it up with an elegant clasp. Her simple black dress would take her through any occasion from casual to formal, all depending on the accessories. Tonight Gabby had opted for modestly elegant. Around her neck hung a single strand of faux pearls, and drop-shaped pearl earrings were clipped neatly to her ears.

"You look wonderful!" Jarod declared, admiring her from first one angle, then another. "I must say, you can certainly accomplish a lot in a little bit of time."

"Daddy always said I was a doer," Gabby said, beaming a smile.

"I guess he was right." Jarod motioned to the far side of the stately lobby. "We're in a room just over there."

"Has Janice come down yet?" Gabby hated to ask the question but knew she couldn't stay silent on the matter. She'd grown more and more apprehensive about the evening. She had decided that she'd rather do just about anything else than spend the evening watching her sister and drawing conclusions about her activities in Breman's hotel room.

"Yes, about the same time I arrived here."

"And Mr. Butler?"

"Yes, he was with her."

Gabby drew in a deep breath and sighed. "I'm not sure I want to see them. I can't believe Janice is acting this way."

"You mean going to his hotel room? Hey, I didn't hang around. Maybe all she did was wait for him to grab his coat. Don't judge her without the facts. I was just teasing you earlier about them being late to the party."

Gabby felt ashamed for the thoughts that had already invaded her quiet moments alone. "Janice isn't like me. She's much freer about what she does and who she does it with."

"Whereas you have to calculate each and every relationship until the surprise and spontaneous elements are all washed away?"

Gabby frowned. "Well, I wouldn't exactly say that."

"What would you exactly say?" Jarod asked softly. Gabby didn't answer, so Jarod continued. "Let's just forget about the party. I suggest we go out to dinner and maybe take a cab through Piccadilly and then go on the river cruise."

Gabby's heart wasn't in it. "Maybe just the dinner?" she asked hopefully.

"It's a start."

They left the building and slipped into a cab before Gabby had time to change her mind. More than a little aware of the dashingly handsome man at her side, Gabby still couldn't help but worry about her little sister. Janice was far more carefree than would ever do her good. Hadn't Mother said that at least a million times? Where Gabby feared to tread, Janice moved in with all the zeal and enthusiasm of a professional cheerleader. It was probably this very attitude that had gotten her in trouble back home. If, indeed, her trouble *was* back home.

"You shouldn't spend the evening worrying about Janice," Jarod said, disturbing her thoughts. "She seems to have a good head on her shoulders."

"I guess she does. She's just always been more adventurous than me."

"But you're a travel writer. You go all over the U.S. I know because I asked to see some of your work before I agreed to team up with you."

Gabby glanced across to find Jarod's serious expression. "I guess I must have passed muster or you'd still be in the States."

"I enjoyed your way with words. You made those places come alive. I found myself wanting to go experience every detail. It takes a good writer to do that, and you couldn't have written so enthusiastically about those places if you hadn't gone to explore them. I'd say that's very adventurous."

"Those trips are all planned out well in advance. I know exactly where I'm going and who I'll interview. I know everything down to the last detail about my transportation, my room, my budget. But Janice isn't like that. Janice will go off on a whim and does so quite frequently. I don't know how she manages to keep up her grades at college."

"Guess she's one of those enthusiastic life-lovers."

"Maybe she just craves the unexpected," Gabby remarked.

They came to a stop outside a quaint little French restaurant. Gabby had enjoyed French cuisine "American-style," and now she hoped that perhaps English-style French cuisine would be even closer to the real thing. Jarod paid the cab without allowing a word of argument from Gabby. Then with a dazzling smile and a quick wink, he looped his arm through hers and led her into the restaurant.

When they were finally seated at an out-of-the-way table and had placed their dinner orders, Jarod surprised Gabby by posing some personal questions.

"I'd really like to know more about you, Gabby."

"Such as?" she questioned suspiciously.

"Where do you live and what do you like to do in your spare time?"

Gabby studied him for a moment. He was dressed conservatively in the same dark suit and tie of navy blue and red that he'd worn the night before. His reddish brown hair seemed darker, but Gabby could see the blaze of emerald fire in his eyes against the lighted candles on their table.

"You want to know about me?"

"Sure," he answered casually, as though

122

the answers weren't really all that important.

Gabby played with the linen napkin on her lap while trying to formulate safe answers to Jarod's questions. "I live with my mother and sister on Long Island, not far from Southampton. And what constitutes spare time?"

Jarod laughed. "Touché. I often wonder that myself. So writing travel articles keeps you pretty busy, I take it?"

"It keeps me on a perpetual deadline, that's for sure."

"But surely there's some time out for fun. What about a boyfriend?"

"No, there's no one," Gabby admitted. Turning the tables, she asked, "How about you?"

"No. There's no one."

Gabby couldn't judge from his response as to whether it was disappointment or reconciliation he felt for his situation. She waited until the waiter arranged drinks and bowls of soup on the table before continuing the conversation. "I don't really plan out my spare time, what little there is of it. It just sort of happens, and when it's over and gone I wonder where it went and why I was so foolish as not to plan it more wisely."

"I know what you mean," he answered,

and Gabby felt as though he was most sincere.

She looked down thoughtfully at the table and contemplated the moment. It should have been Janice sharing this intimate conversation, but instead it was a total stranger. Well, not a total stranger, but very nearly. Gabby only knew Jarod from Sandy's word that he was the best. She knew him also from what little time they'd shared together on the trip, which by last count was gradually amounting to more than just a little time. The only other thing of which she was absolutely sure was that Jarod Walls was clearly the most handsome man she'd ever met, and he made her feel very self-conscious.

She was unaware of Jarod's gaze upon her, yet in some way she couldn't explain, Gabby knew she had his undivided attention. A part of her liked that sensation of being the whole diversion, while another part screamed out for her to take cover. Moments like this usually lent themselves to reflections of the past. Quiet, intimate moments had never been her forte, and now with this intense man sitting directly across from her, the past was the last thing on Gabby's mind. She didn't think about Dustin and what might have been. She didn't think about the passing of time and her concerns about whether or not she'd ever be a wife and mother. What possessed Gabrielle Fleming's mind at that precise moment was an insatiable curiosity of what it might be like to kiss Jarod Walls.

"Care to share the thoughts behind that Mona Lisa smile?" Jarod asked.

Gabby's head snapped up. She felt her face grow hot. Swallowing hard she grabbed for her water glass and took a long drink. Jarod's quiet chuckle only made matters worse, causing Gabby to linger over the water a bit longer.

"I'm afraid my thoughts wandered," she finally said. "You were asking about my spare time. I like to walk on the beach and I enjoy looking around antique shops."

"There, that wasn't so hard, was it?"

"Depends on how you look at it," she replied and was grateful for the arrival of their main course.

They ate in a casual manner, as though they'd known each other for years. Gabby wasn't even surprised when Jarod offered her a bite of his rosemary chicken. She took it, savoring the flavor and applauding the cook, then offered Jarod a bite of her foie gras torte with asparagus.

"I didn't think I'd like this," she admitted,

"but I'm glad I took your suggestion and tried it. I'll definitely write it up." She hoped they'd keep the conversation professional for a time.

"Maybe in the future you'll take my advice more often," he said with a challenge in his expression and raised brow that made Gabby intensely nervous.

"If it has to do with food, maybe I will."

Jarod pushed his plate to the side and eyed her seriously. "So you live with your mother and Janice and you write magazine articles. What else is there to know about you?"

"Nothing at all."

Jarod was undaunted. "Nothing? I find that hard to believe. You appear to me to be one of the most complex persons I've ever known." She kept her face down and toyed with her fork. "What about your father? You told me on the plane that he was dead."

"Yes. He died three years ago."

"I'm sorry."

"Why? It wasn't your fault." She realized how flippant the words sounded.

Seeming to sense her feelings, Jarod changed the subject. "You said there was no one special in your life right now. Has there ever been?"

"What a personal question," she snapped.

"Of course there've been men in my life. There just doesn't happen to be one right now."

"Sorry, I guess I touched a nerve. Usually women love to discuss the men they've gone through. I can't tell you the number of times I've been compared to some lost love or at least heard horror stories about such men. I think it must be a part of the process for most women."

"Well, you'll get none of that from me." Gabby put her walls of defense into place. She wasn't about to discuss her past love life. The nature of such a beast would probably lead her into the present, and that was definitely an off-limits subject as far as she was concerned. She couldn't even explain to herself the foreign feelings Jarod stirred — how could she dare to be honest with him about it?

"Pity," Jarod said in a lighthearted manner, "I would have enjoyed a more in-depth understanding of the men who let you get away."

Ten

The next morning, the tour bus stopped just outside of London at Hampton Court Palace. Home to Henry VIII, the brick structure stood just off the banks of the River Thames and was surrounded by magnificent grounds and strange triangular-shaped trees. The sight held the tour group spellbound.

"The estate was a gift from Cardinal Wolsey to Henry VIII in 1528," Breman announced. "The Cardinal, finding himself and his home to be at the center of Henry's interest, turned the palace over to his king in the hopes of retaining favor with him. Henry instantly took a liking to Hampton Court and it quickly became his favorite country residence. Actually, Henry enjoyed a hearty game of tennis here and you'll get a chance to see the indoor courts. He also liked to joust in the gardens. It's hard to imagine the obese man we've come to think of Henry as running about on a tennis court, but I assure you he was quite fond of the game and didn't become his heaviest until his latter years. There is a tremendous amount of English history symbolized here, so pay close attention to your tour guide and give yourself a special treat by taking in the gardens." He looked at his watch as Roper brought the minibus to a stop. "We'll have two hours here, so enjoy."

Gabby gathered her bag and pulled out her notebook. She was still putting down some of Breman's comments when Jarod asked, "Are you going to make this a focal point of your article?"

"I don't know," Gabby replied. She looked up and instantly felt a kind of shyness that she couldn't explain. Feeling confused, she quickly lowered her gaze to the notebook. "I'm not that familiar with Hampton Court, and so I suppose I won't really know until after we've toured it."

"I'll take whatever pictures they'll allow. It'll probably be mostly exterior shots."

"That's okay," Gabby replied. "I'll take good descriptive notes and if you have something impressive, say with the gardens and flowers for color, I'm sure it will be most complementary."

Jarod nodded and checked the 35mm he'd slung over one shoulder. "Why don't I wander around the grounds while you do the tour?"

Gabby felt instant relief. "Yes. I think that'd be wonderful."

Jarod nodded again and made his way from the bus. When Gabby joined the group, she noticed Jarod slip away to photograph the river.

Their guide was a well-dressed older man who introduced himself and quickly led them on their way. Gabby was dumbfounded by the intriguing murals along the walls and ceilings. Someone had gone to great pains to detail the room in a way that a person could spend an eternity studying and still never completely comprehend it all. The black iron railing of the staircase made an impressive contrast, and Gabby found herself wishing she could slip away as Jarod had for a look on her own.

"Hampton Court was home to Henry VIII, as well as five of his wives. Catherine of Aragon was held prisoner here with her baby, Mary, after falling out of Henry's graces. When he finally decided how to go about dissolving the marriage, declaring it annulled on the grounds that Catherine had first been his brother's wife, he had Catherine removed and married Anne Boleyn."

Gabby wrote notes as quickly as she could, all the while taking in the majestic rooms. They were guided down a long walkway with wooden floors. On one side, multiple white-framed windows lined the wall at regular intervals, while paintings of long-dead ancestors to the throne and numerous other questionable folk lined the other.

"Anne, you will remember, gave Henry another daughter, Elizabeth. Henry claimed Elizabeth to be his only legitimate heir, and Anne his only queen. He declared by punishment of death that no one was ever to refer to Catherine as queen, and she was put from the hearts and minds of the people most thoroughly. Although, there were those few loyalists who no doubt kept their feelings to themselves. It was probably a great joy to Catherine when Henry beheaded Anne for adultery and treason.

"Henry then married Jane Seymour, who promptly gave Henry the son he so longed for. She died only days after the birth of Edward VI, and it is said that her ghost, as well as that of Catherine Howard, yet another of Henry's executed wives, haunts Hampton Court."

Gabby tried not to be saddened by the thoughts of such a young mother dying.

Mortality for mothers and infants was tremendously high in those days, and many a woman died before even having a chance to give birth to her child.

The bedroom they were shown was said to have been a favorite of Jane's, and Gabby made notes about the huge bed with the ceiling-to-floor canopy of heavy brocade and the ornate wood headboard. Then before she could dwell too long here, they were off and moving to another part of the palace.

When at last they were taken outside to the gardens, Gabby had lost all track of time and hadn't even thought of Jarod. They were allowed to spread out and enjoy the gardens and grounds at their leisure, and after Gabby made notes about flowers and graveled walkways, arched entryways and patterned shrubbery, she put her notebook aside and decided to simply soak up the ambiance of the regal estate.

She wandered for a ways before thinking of Jarod and wondering what kind of pictures he'd managed to secure. Overhead, the clouds were gathering and it looked as though it might drizzle rain on them soon. She hoped Jarod had managed to beat the clouds and looked around for a moment trying to spot where he might be. Seeing

Janice and Breman deep in discussion as they wandered toward the far end of the garden, Gabby quickly forgot Jarod and picked up the pace to walk after her sister. Perhaps there was something more to Janice and Breman than what met the eye. They seemed terribly preoccupied with their discussion, and from the expression on Janice's face, Gabby wasn't convinced that the conversation was at all pleasurable.

Hampton Court was famous for its intricate garden maze, and it was this that provided Gabby with secluded protection. As Breman and Janice chose to walk outside the labyrinth rather than inside, Gabby picked up the pace and quietly made her way along the narrow path. The tall, heavily leafed shrubbery offered her the perfect cover and allowed her to parallel them without being seen.

"I told you, I'm not a patient woman, and I don't care for the way you're trying to manipulate this situation." It was Janice, and Gabby frowned at the intensity of the moment.

"You knew what you were in for when you came on this trip. I want five million, and I won't settle for less. If you know what's good for you, you'll see to it that the money is —"

"Don't threaten me, Breman," Janice interrupted in a very calculated manner. "This deal either benefits us both or it benefits no one. I won't be treated like a rookie child."

"Oh, Breman!" sang Ginger Applegate from a distance.

Gabby bit her lower lip and moved ahead, following the voices.

"Mrs. Applegate, what can I do for you?" Breman was asking.

"Can you direct us to the Fountain Garden? I'm afraid we've lost our way."

Gabby waited while Breman gave directions. She was trembling and terribly afraid for Janice. What kind of trouble was she in, and what in the world was costing her five million dollars? She instantly felt a burning anger for Breman. Was he blackmailing Janice? And if so, why?

"Thanks *so* much," Ginger was saying, her husband grunting a similar reply. Gabby held her breath and moved deeper into the maze as Breman seemed to pick up his pace with Janice.

"You'll have to give me your decision by tomorrow," he told Janice in a low voice.

Gabby tripped and nearly fell to the ground. The noise was apparently enough to cause Breman some caution because he didn't say another word, and Gabby could hear their footsteps hurrying off in the distance.

Looking up, she could see nothing but the maze — well manicured and gloriously green. Gabby might have enjoyed the walk if the circumstances had been different. She looked behind her and then to the side but realized she was hopelessly lost. Panic filled her, especially when she thought of Janice being helplessly manhandled by Breman Butler.

Gabby started to walk and then to jog, but her steps only seemed to take her deeper and deeper into the maze. It started to sprinkle, and she thought to call out but changed her mind. She'd only sound like an hysterical child if she opened her mouth to say anything. She was near to tears and her anxieties for Janice were clearly taking control.

"I knew she was in trouble!" Gabby panted. Coming to another dead end, Gabby thought to try to penetrate the shrubbery for a look on the other side, but the thickness of the brush instantly changed her mind for her. She backtracked her steps and took another turn. This one seemed to go on for a ways, and when given the choice of a right or left path, Gabby chose the right and found herself, within six feet, to be again at a dead end.

Biting her lip, she struggled to draw a decent breath. Her side ached and her lungs seemed to burn from the exertion. It wasn't that she was out of shape, but rather it was the terror of concern for Janice and the closing in of the maze walls. She struggled to listen, hoping to hear that Breman and Janice had returned, but she heard nothing. She glanced at her watch and saw that they were to meet at the bus in less than ten minutes. *Good,* she thought. *They'll realize I'm missing and come looking for me.*

Then a terrible thought filled her mind. *If Breman learns that I'm the one who made the noise in the maze, he'll presume me to have overheard the conversation. It might well endanger Janice's life,* she reasoned. This gave her new incentive to find her way out of the labyrinth. She started to hurry through the corridors again and, without meaning to, began to cry. She was scared, and she hadn't felt like this in years. It reminded her of a time she'd accidentally locked herself in the basement. It had taken hours before someone returned home to find her pounding on the door and crying. Her father had rescued her then, she remembered. This thought only made her cry even more. Her father could never rescue her again.

Trying hard to concentrate on the maze

through the blur of tears, she focused on each turn, but they all appeared to be the same. A sob broke from her lips. "Janice! Oh, God, please let Janice be all right. If Breman's hurt her, I'll . . . I'll . . ." She rounded another turn just as despair was overtaking rational thought and plunged headlong into the arms of Jarod Walls.

"Hey, what's the hurry!" he exclaimed with a laugh.

Without thinking, Gabby wrapped her trembling arms around Jarod as though he might disappear. She struggled to draw a decent breath and could have cared less that the drizzle was steadily increasing and that Jarod was now stunned into silence.

"What's wrong? You're shaking."

Gabby forced herself to let go. "I'm . . . I'm . . . sorry," she gasped. Her heart was racing and her breathing labored, but she was so very glad to see him.

He reached down to lift her chin and immediately frowned. "You were crying. Why?"

She shook her head, suddenly feeling very foolish. Here was the one person in all the world to whom she wanted to appear competent. She couldn't explain the circumstance with regard to Janice, however, so she would make herself out to be a ninny in Jarod Walls' eyes.

"I got lost. I guess I got a little claustrophobic, too. I'm really . . ." She stopped talking because he was looking at her with such tender concern that it made her heart skip a beat. Swallowing hard, she blinked away the mixture of rain and tears and didn't think it so very terrible at all when Jarod lowered his lips to kiss her.

His kiss was unhurried and gentle, almost as though the only way he could offer her complete comfort was in this gesture. For a moment, Gabby forgot about everything. Janice. Breman. The article. Nothing else seemed quite as important as this one single moment with Jarod.

When she pulled away, he refused to let her go. Gabby, wishing to do nothing but hide from her feelings, would not meet his eyes again. Of course, she'd have to say something, and she couldn't just put this off on Jarod, even if he had been the one to initiate it.

"I've been wanting to do that ever since you brought up the subject of baby-sitting me." Jarod's tone was lighthearted and teasing. "I hope you aren't angry with me again. I mean, we have a lot of work to do and —"

Gabby pushed away, her head just starting to clear. Rational thought was re-

138

turning. "I'm sorry. You aren't to blame, and of course I'm not angry. I was just upset and scared. Look, if we don't get back to the bus soon, they'll leave without us."

Jarod looked at her strangely, and Gabby was already backing away. "How do we get out of this?" she asked, suddenly realizing she was just as lost as ever. The question held double meaning, and Jarod's face broke into a mischievous grin.

"I'm not sure I want out."

"Oh, Jarod," she said with a sigh, "they'll all be waiting for us."

"Let them wait. I want to know what has you so upset. It can't be just the maze."

"Why can't it?"

He walked toward her, and Gabby found herself backed up against the leafy wall of the shrub. "You wouldn't be so upset if it were that simple."

"I got scared, okay? I try hard to be strong, but as you can now see, I fail at times." As usual, she stood on the defense of her anger. "I suppose you'll ever be throwing it in my face and treating me like a helpless woman, but I'm not. I just let things get to me, and on top of everything else I still have jet lag."

Jarod shook his head. "You might as well name world hunger and the threat of wars to come as reasons for being upset. None would be any more true than what you've just dealt me."

Gabby, afraid he might take her in his arms again, pushed him away and walked past him. If it took tearing down the hedges around her, she was not going to let Jarod touch her again. "I'm through talking. By my watch it shows that we should be at the bus in one minute."

Jarod raised his arms in surrender. "Fine. You don't want to tell me the truth, that's just great. We can tell lies until our noses grow as long as this maze, but you know what, Gabrielle?"

She stopped at this and turned as if to respond. His jaw was set in that determined way that told her he was plenty put out but still under control. "What?" she finally forced herself to ask.

"It won't change the fact that we have feelings for each other." He walked past her and turned. "Feelings that, I might add, run deeper than whether or not I take any good pictures of the local tourist traps." With that, he took off, and Gabby had to hurry to keep up. There was no sense in denying what he said, and there was certainly no sense in taking too much time to follow after him.

"*We have feelings for each other,*" he had said. *He has feelings for me.* It was a sudden but very interesting revelation. Gabby almost smiled until she thought of Janice. Poor Janice. She was trapped in some kind of blackmail scheme, and Breman Butler was threatening her. Whatever the problem, it had obviously started back home, given Breman's reference to Janice coming on the trip. Gabby decided from that moment on, no matter what happened, she was going to get to the bottom of Janice's problem and help her through it. Jarod Walls could wait, but Janice clearly couldn't be put off.

Eleven

Dinner that night was on their own in the city of Exeter. Gabby insisted Janice remain with her that evening, but Janice declined.

"I have plans already made. Look, I spent the afternoon with you," she protested. "I thought you'd lost your mind the way you nearly hung on my arm."

"I came on this trip to spend time with you. At least that's what I *thought* we were supposed to be doing. You know, 'Come with me to England and we'll have a blast together'? I do believe those were nearly your *exact* words. If there's something else about this trip that I should know, I'm open to explanation."

Janice shrugged. "I can't help it. I like Breman's company. In less than two weeks, this trip will be over, and, well, if I get our relationship established here, then maybe it will go on when we get back home."

Gabby eyed her sister suspiciously. "I

thought you and Breman looked a little angry with each other at Hampton Court."

"We just argued over whether I'd stay in his room tonight or not."

Gabby's mouth dropped open in stunned surprise. Janice was lying to her. At least she hoped it was a lie. She already knew about the threats, but what if Breman was demanding more than money?

"And what did you decide?" Gabby finally forced herself to ask.

Janice laughed. "I told him I wouldn't be tied to any absolutes. I told him we'd see what happens."

"You can't be serious. Janice, you can't be that irresponsible. Even if you don't have any moral values or spiritual faith —"

"Who says I don't have moral values or spiritual faith? Just because I don't think like you and hold my head 'just so' when we stand in church with Mom, you think I don't have any values?"

Gabby heard the anger and hurt in Janice's voice. "Look," she said, trying to calm Janice, "I'm just worried about you. I thought Breman was acting a bit strange around you, and it worried me."

"Breman wasn't the only one acting strange. What did you do to poor Mr. Walls? He hardly said two words when we stopped at Stonehenge. He just went around snapping pictures and muttering."

Gabby felt her face grow hot. "He's just having a hard time taking orders from a woman."

"I'll bet he is," Janice said with a laugh. "He doesn't seem like the type to let *anybody,* much less a *woman,* push him around."

"No, I suppose not." Gabby fell silent for a moment. She wanted so badly to confide in Janice, but Janice's obvious lack of faith in her, and the fact that she was keeping Breman's threats a secret, made Gabby apprehensive. Something just wasn't right, and until she could get to the bottom of it and figure things out, she'd just have to keep her mouth closed.

Janice finished pulling on a sweater and picked up her purse. "Look, don't worry about me. I'm a big girl, as I've said before. I love you for caring, but don't interfere." These last words were uttered with such a severe tone of insistence that Gabby didn't say another word.

When Janice had gone, Gabby sat down on the bed and wondered if she should follow her. The idea of spying on Janice and Breman wasn't new. In fact, she'd considered it all day. The only problem was, Gabby worried she might not be any good at it, and if she got caught, it might spell disaster for Janice.

~

Janice looked across the table at Breman and Roper Davenport and smiled. "My people have agreed to go four million."

"I said five," Breman replied, but he didn't sound overly insistent, and Janice felt confident that she'd have the entire matter sewn up in a matter of minutes.

"Look, we've already done our homework," Janice said, leaning back in a nonchalant manner, a lazy smile hinting at her lips. "No one else is prepared to pay you that much, and no one else is available to even *consider* the matter at this moment. Not unless you count those two buffoons who joined our tour group. I believe my sources said they are Croats and are prepared to go one point five million, but no more."

Breman stared at her in stunned disbelief. "Who told you that?" He looked at Roper, who simply shrugged his shoulders.

"Does it really matter?" she asked sternly, all pretense of a smile vanishing. "I've told you before, Breman, I know my job and my organization. I knew they'd go up to four million, and I know they'll go no higher. Take it or leave it, but I do promise you this —" she paused and knew by the rapid blinking of

Breman's hazel green eyes that she was accomplishing just the right effect — "if you do not sell those arms to the IRA, your entire project could meet with a terrible demise."

Breman seemed to recoup some of his strength and with it came his anger. "How *dare* you threaten me!"

He leaned across the table, and for a moment Janice grew concerned. Under the table she put her hand inside her purse, feeling for the small-caliber pistol she recently managed to acquire. Guns weren't as readily available in England as in the U.S., but never before had she felt the need of one quite as much as she did just now. Comforted by the feel of cold metal against her fingers, Janice relaxed a bit.

"I like you, Janice, which is the *only* reason I haven't tired of this little game. Now, we can go on having fun together and make a profitable trade, or I can call this whole thing off and sell the weapons to the Croats, whom I believe will happily come up with as much as you're offering, if not more."

Janice toyed with several alternatives. She could call his bluff or she could pull her gun and make a very nasty confrontation of power and totally humiliate the man. Or better still, she could back off, give him the sensation of running things, and promise to see if her people couldn't squeeze out just a little bit more money. The latter seemed the best solution.

"I suppose you're right," she said, her voice as thick as honey. "Why don't you give me another day or two, and I'll get word to my contacts and see what can be done to come a little bit closer to your asking price. After all, I like you, too."

Breman smiled and sat back. "I thought we could deal amicably with each other. You really are a very enchanting woman, Janice. Maybe you'd like to join forces with me when this is over?"

"But I thought this was to be your last deal. What happened to your plans for retirement?" She smiled coyly. He was such a stupid man. His greed would be his undoing.

"Well, with someone like you, I could probably be convinced to come out of retirement." Breman looked quite serious, but Roper appeared bored and restless.

Janice smiled. "You forget that I'm quite devoted to my cause."

"Ah yes. The Irish Republican Army," he murmured.

"Not at all. *My* cause is Janice Fleming, and I go where I'm most profitably re-

147

warded." She released her hold on the gun and calmly got to her feet. "Perhaps if you showed me how you could profit *my* cause, I'd give it some greater consideration."

Breman stood and extended his arm. Janice let his hand close over her fingers. He kissed her hand, as she knew he would, and flashed an expression of pure seduction. "I'm sure that I could profit your cause in many ways, my dear Janice. Maybe later this evening you'll allow me to show you some of my ideas."

"Maybe." She drew her hand back slowly.

"But for now, you'll call your people?" he questioned, looking hopeful.

"In time. In time." She clutched her purse under her arm and went to the door. "Now I must go. You have your Croats to deal with, and I have my sister. Both parties, I have noticed, are feeling rather left out. Good evening, Mr. Davenport."

Roper nodded but remained silent.

Janice left Breman's room feeling both a charge of excitement from the clash of wills and a sensation of dread. There was no way she could explain any of this to Gabby. Even though Janice was heading into her senior year of college, Gabby would never concede that she had grown up. Her big sister always saw her as being a bit airheaded and addlebrained. Gabby would positively pass out cold if she knew even the half of Janice's exploits.

Taking the stairs, Janice contemplated what she would tell Gabby. It seemed best to keep the distance between them in place. If she apologized now, Gabby would suggest they make up for lost time, and Janice couldn't be tied down to that. If only she hadn't needed Gabby's presence at all! She really resented having to put her sister at risk, but there hadn't been any other way. She needed Gabby to keep up her cover and to protect the rest of the operation. No, she'd have to keep Gabby off her back and under control without any lengthy explanations. She'd make Breman appear for all the world, but especially Gabby, to be the love of her life. He'd no doubt relish every minute of it, but Janice already felt the need for a bath to wash off the memory of where his lips had touched her hand.

She reached the bottom of the stairs and squared her shoulders. Gabby would just have to understand, and someday, though probably not very soon, Janice would try to explain her underhanded dealings. With new determination, Janice went in search of a telephone. She had to check in with her contacts, and she would have to see about upping the price of the arms. Crossing the lobby, she saw Jarod Walls coming toward her and smiled. Jarod, however, was oblivious to her greeting. He seemed very preoccupied, almost angry, and Janice couldn't help but laugh to herself and wonder what Gabby had done to him this time.

~

Breman Butler smiled at the two dark-headed men. Having them join the tour group as brothers from southern France had been a stroke of genius. In truth, they represented the Croatian government, and they'd just made their final offer on the weapons he held.

"One point five million?" Breman stroked his chin, then leveled his eyes to meet theirs. "It's a tad short of what I'd hoped for, but since I'm in agreement with what you fellows are trying to accomplish, I'll take a chance on it."

The two men exchanged a veiled look of elation. "You won't be sorry," one man said in a heavily accented voice.

"No, I don't suppose I will be," Breman replied. "Now what I need for you to do is have that money transferred into this Swiss account by midnight tonight." He handed them a slip of paper with several numbers written on it. "If the money isn't there by 12:01, I'll

150

sell them to one of my other buyers. Understand?"

"Transferring the full amount before we have receipt of the goods would be foolish. We are prepared to show good faith by wiring in half of the money now and half when we are in control of the weapons."

"That's not the way I deal," Breman said, feeling a trickle of sweat run down his back.

"Our people will never agree to it any other way," the man assured him without even a hint of emotion.

Breman weighed the matter. He could accept their proposition and have at least that much more money in the bank, or he could fold up on the entire deal and back out. It didn't seem reasonable to do the latter, yet Breman hated allowing terrorists dictate the terms of his deals.

"I have other parties interested," Breman said, staring thoughtfully at the ceiling. "I don't like to break with operating procedures." He scratched his chin as though contemplating his next move.

"We understand your concerns," the bigger of the two men began, "but you must also understand that we aren't very well financed. There have been questionable dealings in the past that have left us victims of, shall we say, less than honorable men."

151

Breman nodded. The man's words made up his mind. "If you will deposit one million by midnight, I will hold off on receiving the other half a million. Otherwise, I must put an end to this deal. You, too, must understand that as a businessman I have to look out for my own best interests. I alone have to be responsible for getting the weapons unnoticed into Istanbul. This will be no small feat, as I'm sure you are well aware."

The men muttered to each other in their native tongue, then nodded at Breman and got to their feet. One glanced at his wristwatch and nudged the other. "That barely gives us two hours, but I'm certain we can do as you ask. One million — no more. When we receive the weapons, we will have the rest of the money with us and give it over to you then."

"Good. We can meet again tomorrow and discuss the transfer."

With that the men dismissed themselves and hurried from the room. Roper Davenport looked across the table where he'd sat in silence for the last half hour. "Well done, boss," he said in a congratulatory offer. "You've managed not only to sell the arms to the IRA but to the Croatians, as well."

Breman laughed. "Don't forget the Americans."

"What Americans?" Roper asked with a puzzled expression.

"I sold them to a paramilitary group in the U.S., as well."

Roper shook his head. "You've sold the same cache of weapons to three different players? How much did you get out of the Americans?"

"Two and a quarter million."

"So who'll really get them?"

Breman threw him a look of disbelief. "The Americans already have them, my friend. I couldn't sell them abroad without a great many problems. The transfer would be too risky, especially in light of the fact that half the shipment was just stolen a month ago. No, it was best to dump that load as quickly as possible. The nice thing is, it's not like the Americans are going to open their mouths and admit to having bought them. Once everything is said and done, neither the IRA nor the Croats are big enough to hunt me down. Not with my preparations in place."

Roper looked rather confused, as though trying to take it all in. "I suppose that makes sense. Are you really going to make this your last trip? I have to say, I've rather enjoyed the good pay. Driving tourists around can be kind of entertaining."

"The travel agency has provided the perfect cover for our business, but I want to get out, not get caught. I've felt the noose tightening on our organization several times, and I think I've risked about as much as I dare. I'll sell my agency and pocket the money as an honest business transaction. After all, it's served its purpose. Butler Travel will cease to exist — as will Breman Butler. I have a nice collection of foreign accounts and a home waiting for me on a rather secluded Caribbean island."

"And Miss Fleming? Is she a part of that?" Roper leered a smile.

"Perhaps. I can't say that I would mind her companionship. She knows the rules of the game and the importance of keeping her mouth shut. Besides, we'd have the goods on each other. It might well make for a most amicable relationship. After all, man cannot live on bread alone."

Roper laughed. "You beat all, Breman." He got to his feet and ran a hand back through his straight blond hair. "What I don't understand, however, is why you didn't dicker with those Croats for more than one point five."

Breman shrugged. "Janice said they wouldn't go over that, and she's proven herself to know everything else about my business."

154

"Doesn't that worry you?" Roper questioned. "I mean, how does she know so much?"

"I can't tell, but that only adds to the incentive to keep her under control. I must make her so desirous of my attention and companionship that she forgets her other connections and ties. It might well be that, given her propensity for information, I can make her a deal that will sweeten the pot."

"Her own Swiss account?"

Roper was only joking, but Breman nodded. "Maybe. She said Janice Fleming was her only real cause. Maybe she won't be all that hard to entice."

Twelve

Gabby spent the morning in sheer misery. Both Janice and Jarod were angry with her, and neither one seemed inclined to talk to her. She just couldn't figure it all out. Janice seemed to be in some kind of trouble with Breman Butler, yet she wanted to spend all of her time and energies on him. When Janice had returned from dinner with Breman the night before, Gabby had tried again to approach the subject of her concerns for Janice. But it was all for nothing. Janice was deeply offended that Gabby was playing mother to her and in no uncertain terms told Gabby to mind her own business.

Jarod was an entirely different matter. He hadn't spoken much more than half a dozen sentences since their time together at Hampton Court, and then it was only to ask about photos she wanted and whether a certain thing should be included in the article. He had stopped referring to it as "our" article and simply called it "the" article, as though he was putting as much distance between them as possible. And he had chosen to sit at the back of the bus across from Ginger and Fred and was even now engaged in a lively conversation with them.

Gabby felt a deep sense of loss and a terrible ache of loneliness. She'd alienated the only two people she cared about on this tour, and now neither one was speaking to her. She stared out the window at the passing Cornish countryside. They'd made a short trip to Torquay, where subtropical plants and palm trees gave credence to the nickname "English Riviera." Gabby faithfully took down notes and descriptive information but remained behind on the bus when Breman gave them a five-minute stopover to snap pictures. Pictures were not her job, and even though she had her own camera, her heart wasn't in it.

Next they pushed west to Plymouth, where they discussed the Pilgrims' escape to America, and finally after chilling tales of Cornish smugglers and secret coves, they were headed north to Bath.

As Roper parked the minibus, Breman was already making announcements about the tour of Bath. Gabby listened only half-heartedly. She felt like she already knew everything there was to know about Bath. It was a city built around a hot springs. The Celtic people had discovered the curative properties of the heated springs in 860 B.C. Then around the first century, the Romans had built the baths and temples around the springs and dedicated the entire thing to the goddess Minerva. The Celtic water goddess Sulis was also honored because the Romans didn't want to offend any gods or goddesses who might be connected with the place.

"Of course," Breman was saying now, "the popularity of the spa was probably reached in the early years of the 1700s. Bathing took place both in clothed and un-clothed states, and of course was mainly en-joyed by the wealthy and those of noble birth."

Gabby sighed. She couldn't stand having anyone mad at her, and she could very nearly feel Jarod's heated stare on her back. It was then that she decided to skip the tour of the Roman baths and just walk around the area. Maybe she'd talk to some of the lo-cals for her article. This would be far more preferable to the cold shoulder she'd get from Janice and Jarod. Feeling a little better, she noted the time they were to be back on the road for Liverpool and put her notebook away.

Just as she'd suspected, no one seemed to notice her lagging behind the group. Pulling out a little map, she waited until everyone was out of sight before slipping off toward the Bath Abbey and Cheap Street. She walked in silence, enjoying the unusually bright, sunny day.

Needing to cleanse her conscience, she prayed. *Lord, I've really made a mess of things, and I know that my emotions and attitude are the cause of the damage. Jarod is angry at me because I don't want to talk about my feelings for him. But how can I talk to him about these things when I don't understand them myself?*

She moved down the road, past the abbey, and noticed what looked to be a park across the busy street. Crossing, she picked up her prayer as she lost herself along the flowered walkway.

"I didn't come on this trip to have a summer romance, like Janice suggested. I like Jarod . . . a lot," she admitted in a whisper, "but I'm worried about Janice, and I can't allow Jarod to take me away from keeping an eye on my sister." Yet what about now? her conscience pricked. Here she was, *avoiding* contact with Janice and Breman. They're well supervised, she reasoned, but hadn't they also been supervised at Hampton Court? Her mind was a mass of questions, and there seemed to be no easy answers. Perhaps she should heed Janice's advice and mind her own business.

The breeze picked up ever so slightly, and she instantly wished she had thought to bring her sweater. *I'm making a mess of everything,* she thought and wondered if it might be possible to just get on a train and go back to London and then fly home. Of course, she couldn't consider it seriously. She honored the responsibilities of her job and knew that it had only been at her insistence and enthusiasm for the project that Sandy had agreed to send her to England in the first place.

She crossed her arms and moved toward a placard that told about the park. This had been a popular place for courting couples during the eighteenth century. Tucked next to the river, it made a lovely setting for secret meetings and clandestine love affairs. She sighed again and wondered what it might be like to come here with someone she loved. Catching sight of several couples walking hand in hand, she grimaced. Maybe she'd never know what true love is. Maybe she'd always push it away in fear. This made her frown even more. Was she just using Janice as an excuse to not have to deal with Jarod? Like Janice said, she was a big girl and she clearly didn't want Gabby's interference. Still, Gabby couldn't forget the demand of five million dollars and the fact that Janice had included her on this trip to provide some kind of cover to her own travels.

Dear God, please show me what to do. How can I help Janice when she keeps insisting that nothing is wrong? How can I help her when all she does is lie to me?

She walked on toward a lovely stone bridge. The closer she drew to it, the more charming it grew. It seemed to house shops on each side. Reaching a plaque, Gabby read that this was Pulteney Bridge built 1769–74 and designed by Robert Adams. People seemed intent on swarming in and out of the stores like bees gathering nectar. She watched the tourists with a writer's eye. They fascinated her with their animated talk and gestures.

They all seem to be searching for something, she mused. And, indeed, this had been the reaction she'd had to many of the other tourists she'd run across in England. Were they looking for some type of ancestral roots? Or was it even more self-centered? Were they searching for some kind of personal identity? She took out her notebook and leaned against the wall in order to remain out of the flow of traffic.

The people, she wrote, *are like pilgrims on a mission. Each person, even the very young, seem to be looking for something. It's almost as if they've lost something and have come to England to find it. I can't really put my finger on it, but even in their discussions and comments, it appears a kind of introspective awe marks them. Do they feel as kindred spirits?* She shivered from the chill of the wall and added, *Are they seeking to touch a history they can have no part of?*

"I thought you might need this," Jarod's voice said in a low, barely audible tone. He handed up her navy blue sweater and smiled rather sheepishly. "It's my truce offering."

Startled, Gabby tucked her notebook in her bag and matched his smile hesitantly. "I'm really sorry for the way I acted," she said, allowing him to help her into the sweater. "I've got a lot on my mind and —"

"I know, you're focused on the article, and you always get this way when you're working."

She shook her head. "No, it's more than that. I can admit it . . . now that I've prayed about it."

"Oh?"

Gabby swallowed and took a deep breath. "You've really rattled my cage, Mr. Walls."

His brows raised as he cast her a ques-

162

tioning look. "I've done *what?*"

His eyes were so green, and for a moment she wasn't sure she could — or should — continue with the conversation. She swallowed her pride. "You've upset my plans. You came into my life and disturbed my very neatly ordered world."

"Oh, I see. And you think you are innocent of the effect on *my* world?"

"No, you made it clear in that awful maze that you had some of the same feelings on the matter."

"That's a unique way of putting it," he said, taking hold of her arm. "How about we talk while we make our way back to the bus? There's only about fifteen minutes before they pull out."

She looked at her watch and gasped in surprise. "I had no idea. I mean, I just started walking, and then the people all started grabbing my attention, and I began to write about their search for whatever it is that seems to elude them."

She allowed him to maintain his hold. She wanted to be companionable. After all, he had come all this way with her sweater.

"I'm not sure I understand," he replied, looking down at her intently.

"The people, these tourists, they all seem to be looking for something. I've noticed it before, but I just haven't been able to put my finger on it. They seem almost lost, and I know it sounds ridiculous, but I'm beginning to suspect they think that England is somehow their pathway back. Like being here can give them back what they've lost."

"Or never had to begin with," Jarod replied softly. He dropped his hold on her arm and slipped his arm casually around her instead.

Gabby stopped walking and stared up at him for a moment. "Yes, I think you're right."

"They're rather like a legion of lost souls looking for something spiritual to make them whole. They're making their pilgrimages as people did in the days of old, and they are hoping to find what is missing down deep in their souls."

"Yes. That's it!" she exclaimed. "They have that rather vacant, yet hopeful, look in their eyes. Too bad they can't realize that what they need isn't a place or a thing, but God."

They started walking again and Gabby didn't protest the protective way Jarod continued to hold on to her. She wondered instead how he felt about spiritual matters. "God is a very important part of my life, and I know without Him I'd be searching for something more. I can't imagine what it must be like not to have the peace of knowing Him personally."

"You can't believe that all these people are unsaved, however," Jarod said good-naturedly. "Even Christians go on vacation. Look at us."

He said "us," she thought silently. *He's saved, too!* He must be or he'd have never included himself in the count. For some reason, this gave her more joy and peace than she'd had the entire trip.

"We're *all* looking for something," he added, gazing directly into her eyes. "It's better to fill an empty soul with God than to seek to fill the void with a nation or history of lost ancestors. And," he added with a tenderness that melted away Gabby's apprehension, "it's better to fill a heart with love than to put up walls of fear and apprehension."

"I suppose some people have a hard time trusting," Gabby replied with a smile playing at the corners of her mouth.

"I suppose *some* people could just learn to give it a try," he remarked with teasing sarcasm in his voice.

"I suppose they could." She looked at him for a moment, then looked away and started to walk again. *What am I doing?* She felt her heart racing and knew that she wanted more than anything in the world to better know Jarod Walls.

He easily kept stride with her back to the bus, and when they climbed on board, he took a seat beside her and reached for her cold hand. She looked up at him, knowing that a million questions would probably reveal themselves in her eyes. She felt him rubbing warmth back into her hand and barely heard anything else but the pulsing beat of her heart. Could she really trust him? Could he really be the one she was meant to fall in love with?

Thirteen

Janice had waited all evening for Breman to leave his room. He and Roper were going to be joining the tour group for some sort of medieval entertainment dinner, and Janice had figured this to be the perfect opportunity for action. She looked at her watch and, when she was certain no one would notice her, slipped down the hall and picked the lock to Breman's room.

Once inside, she waited for her eyes to adjust to the dark, then turned on a pen-sized flashlight and shined it around the room. Near the window was a small tablelike desk and on this was a briefcase, which Janice recognized as belonging to Breman.

She crossed the room silently, rather stimulated by the intrigue of the moment. Noting the combination lock on the briefcase, Janice smiled. Breman was such an amateur to think this constituted security. Within moments, she'd managed to bypass the combination and pop the lock from place. The sound seemed to echo loudly in the tiny room, and for a minute Janice felt apprehensive, almost fearful.

She flipped through the contents of the briefcase. Tour information was on the top, but digging deeper revealed the gold mine she'd hoped to find. There were several papers related to the weapons and even a newspaper clipping about the armory heist. Breman was no doubt the one responsible for the armory theft in South Carolina and had probably brought the clips as proof to his buyers that he actually had access to the weapons they desired. She'd remembered hearing about that debacle on the news. It only confirmed Breman's rather amateurish style, given the fact he'd left a great cache of explosives in the building next door. A cache that would have been far more valuable and a great deal more deadly. The IRA would have pledged their very souls to get their hands on that much high-grade explosive material.

She picked up a folded document and, with the penlight in her mouth, opened it and read the signed agreement between Breman and the Croatian representatives. One point five million dollars had been agreed upon, and part of the money was to have been transferred to a Swiss bank account on the night before. So he had sold the weapons to the Croats! She frowned and continued her search. It was foolish, she thought, to have so much paper evidence to pin you to your illegal affairs. It was one of the things that she hated, or in some ways loved, about the IRA. They were meticulous record keepers. For some odd reason there was always a paper record of everything. This proved both helpful and deadly, and Janice had many times seen the failure of a mission because of just such paper work.

Another set of folded papers at the bottom of the case drew her attention. Pulling them out, Janice found something she'd not expected. It was some sort of record between a paramilitary group in the U.S. and Breman Butler. But from the scant information on the document, Janice wasn't really sure what she'd found. Could it be that Breman had more than one deal going on at a time? Was he dividing his store of stolen goods with more than one organization? Obviously he'd made arrangements with the Croats, but what did it all mean? Perhaps the weapons he'd sold to them for 1.5 million were from an entirely different arsenal.

The sound of the door being opened caused Janice to throw the documents back in the briefcase, but it was too late. Breman Butler snapped on the lights and looked at her with an expression of disbelief.

"What in the world are you doing here?"

Janice knew she'd have to think fast, but for reasons beyond her understanding, nothing was coming to mind. Blinking against the blinding light, she finally shrugged her shoulders. "I wanted to know if you were on the up-and-up. I have to look out for my people, you understand."

Breman's eyes narrowed and he closed the door behind him. "And did you find what you were looking for?"

Janice swallowed hard. She'd foolishly not brought her gun with her, and with nothing more than the penlight in hand, she tried to appear nonchalant about the whole thing. "It appears that you may well be double-crossing the IRA. That won't bode well. Is it a part of our weapons shipment that you agreed to sell to the Croats?"

Breman laughed and picked up the telephone. Janice eyed him as she cautiously surveyed the room. She was on the far side with the bed, and Breman stood between her and the door. Breman shook his head even as he punched in the numbers.

"Don't even think about leaving," he warned Janice. Then to the telephone receiver he said, "Roper, come to my room." Pause. "And bring your gun."

Janice could feel a sense of sheer panic mounting inside. It was now or never. She would have to try to escape before Roper appeared. Hurling herself across the bed, she came up on the other side, just as Breman tossed the receiver to one side and threw himself in her path. He held her in an ironlike grip and slammed her backward onto the bed.

"I've tried to get you here under better circumstances," he said with a leer. "I don't suppose I have time for much fun right now. I mean, what with Roper coming to join our little party." A knock sounded at the door. "Ah, there he is now."

Janice was pinned beneath Breman's solid frame. Her mind raced for some plan of escape, but nothing seemed sensible or feasible.

"Come in," Breman called out, and Roper entered the room with a look of surprised confusion.

"You wanted me?" he asked, seeming to find that thought unfathomable.

"Yeah, it seems our friend Janice decided to do a little research." Breman got up from

171

the bed but ordered Janice not to move. "We'll have to get rid of her one way or another. She knows too much."

"Are you sure?" Roper questioned. He seemed disturbed by Breman's sudden suggestion, and Janice used it to her advantage.

"You can't let him get away with this, Mr. Davenport. He's in over his head with this one, and the IRA will kill him for the double-cross."

Roper shrugged. "He knew the risks."

Janice eased up on her elbows and switched strategies. "Look, I told you both before, I'm in this for myself. If you want to deal dirty with the IRA, that's your problem, but it doesn't have to include me. I thought you said we had a good thing going together," she said, looking directly at Breman.

He gave her a tight, cold smile. His eyes were void of emotion. "We could have had, but now you're a liability I cannot afford."

"You can't just kill me," she said, sitting up in spite of Breman's cruel expression. "I have friends, both on this tour and in the surrounding areas. You can't believe I'd be stupid enough to travel without backup. You kill me, they'll kill you. If I show up missing, they'll know something is wrong and you'll blow this deal."

"She has a point, boss."

Breman looked at Roper as though trying to make up his mind as to whether this new information was valid. Janice took the opportunity to press her bluff home. "Besides, my people were finally prepared to go to five million." She got to her feet and gave him her most seductive smile. "That's an awful lot of money to wave good-bye to, and without me, there'll be no deal."

Janice couldn't realize it at that moment, but it was this statement that cleared the indecision from Breman's mind. "If the IRA wants their weapons, they'll deal all right. I'll simply tell them that you were trying to double-cross them, and that in doing so, you managed to get yourself killed. Then I'll up the price to eight million and see how badly they want those guns."

"You can't do this!" Janice protested, feeling suddenly sick at her helplessness. She'd already alienated Gabby, so it might be hours before anyone questioned why she was missing.

Breman stepped toward her. "And why not? You stuck your nose into a place it didn't belong."

"But you talked of us working together in the future. Why does this have to change anything? I've already told you I couldn't care less about the IRA cause, and if you

173

want to deal them dirty, it's no sweat off my back. I simply was looking out for my own interests. If you don't want this thing to fall apart, you'd better rethink your strategy. If I turn up dead tomorrow, my sister, for one, will raise the roof off every hiding place in England to find the responsible party."

"She's probably got you on that one," Roper agreed. "But what if I take her out and dispose of her? I know this place near the docks . . ."

"But how do we explain her disappearance from the group?" Breman questioned.

Janice couldn't believe they would just talk about her demise so nonchalantly with her standing right there.

"She's a student, right?" Roper asked.

"Yes, but what does that have to do with anything?"

"Well, what if we let it get around to the group that she'd come across some other friends of hers from college? She could leave word with her sister that she's gone off on holiday with them and will catch up with the group in, oh, say Edinburgh or York. That would put the trip near the end, and then when she doesn't show up, we can fabricate something else like a telephone call that says she had to go home early due to injury or sickness."

"It just might work," Breman replied. "That's ingenious, Roper. Then when her contacts find her amiss in communications, they'll realize they must come to me and continue the negotiations or lose the weapons altogether."

"My sister will never believe you," Janice said, trying hard to sound convincing. "And my operatives will never buy it. They know very well I always see my job through to the end."

"You will write your sister a very detailed note and explain that you need your own space and that you don't want her interference. Don't forget, you've already confessed to me the trouble you two are having on this trip. Gabby might well be glad to see you go. As for your operatives . . . Roper, keep her alive long enough to have her make the appropriate phone calls. I want that money transferred to Switzerland before she's dead."

"I won't do it!"

"I think you will. I can be *very* persuasive," Breman said with a wicked expression that revealed he would probably enjoy the task. Breman motioned toward Janice. "Roper, bring her to the table."

Roper produced a gun from beneath his jacket and extended it. Janice recognized the .9mm Sig-Sauer and grimaced. *If only I hadn't left my gun back in the room . . . I'd what?* she thought. Have an old-fashioned shoot-out? How would that ever be explained? England had stricter gun laws than America. How could she ever explain that as an American tourist she was able to obtain a weapon for defense?

"Go on, now, be a love and do as you're told." Roper eyed her without so much as a smile.

Janice walked to the table, where already Breman had taken out a sheet of paper and a pen. "Now, write sister a nice little letter and explain all the details that you know only she would question."

"The only detail Gabby will question," Janice said, hoping to buy time, "is my absence. She's not going to believe anything I write. She knows how important this trip is."

"Then be extra convincing. Use whatever terms of endearment you must, but convince your sister that you've gone off with friends, or" — Breman lowered his voice to a deadly whisper — "I'll simply have to kill her, too."

Janice swallowed hard and nodded. She could feel her strength giving out. Picking up the pen, she wrote out several lines in shaky script. She looked up at Breman and asked, "Now what?"

"Now you make a telephone call to your comrades and get my money."

"No. I won't do it," Janice replied frankly. "They'll be on to you in a flash. No one does business this way, especially me. They'll know something is wrong, and the deal will fall through."

Breman studied her for a moment. "There must be some way to convince you," he said rather sarcastically.

"You'll kill me no matter what I do. So kill me. I won't betray the operation simply because I was stupid enough to get caught." Janice shrugged as though indifferent to the whole matter. "However, my partners already know about you, and when they learn that I'm dead, they'll in turn come after you."

Breman paled a bit but stood his ground. "Perhaps we will make an example of you, and they won't be so inclined to be rash. The IRA is desperate for weapons. When I sweeten the pot with several rather nice caches of explosives, I doubt they'll worry much about losing you. I'll simply tell them that you double-crossed us both. I'll find your cohorts and explain that you planned to leave them high and dry."

"They won't believe you!"

"I think they will." He glanced at his watch. "I have to get back to the dinner. The job of tour director requires I continue to keep my tourists happy, don't you know. Our good friend Mr. Davenport can take you for a little ride. I'm certain he can persuade you to see things our way." Janice shivered and the reaction was not lost on Breman. "I'm really sorry about this, actually." He ran a finger along her cheek. "I was truly beginning to see a future with you."

"There still could be," Janice said in a voice barely audible.

"No, I'm afraid this is the only way. I can't trust you, Janice. You've proven that tonight. I can't trust you not to inform your buddies in the IRA that I've double-crossed them, and I can't trust you not to stab me in the back the minute I let my guard down. So you see, really it's better this way." He turned to Roper. "Make certain she calls her people before you finish her off."

Roper nodded and took hold of her arm. Whispering in her ear, he said, "We'll pass down the backstairs, and if anyone sees us, you'd better convince them that we're the hottest combo since fish and chips."

Janice nodded and moved toward the door. With one final glance over her shoulder she said, "You'll be sorry for this, Breman."

After Roper had taken Janice away, Breman began to have second thoughts. What if she was right? What if the IRA refused to deal with him after this? No, he thought, shaking his head. The IRA was too hungry for weapons. They were desperate to push their cause forward and just as desperate to prove to the world that talk wouldn't make satisfactory changes in Ireland. One stupid American wasn't going to cause them to nix the entire deal, of this he was certain.

He sat down at the table, regathered his papers, then stopped. One stupid American, he thought. Janice Fleming really wasn't that stupid. Maybe she was setting him up. Maybe her people would refuse to deal with him. Her people? Just who were her people? The IRA would be the recipients of the weapons, but she mentioned having partners close at hand. Who were they? Her sister? That thought intrigued him.

Glancing at his watch he realized he'd have to get back downstairs soon. He grabbed Janice's note to Gabby, read it through, and put it in an envelope he addressed "Gabrielle Fleming." The words drew his attention and his mind again questioned whether or not Gabby might be Janice's partner. It would make sense. It would fit with the facts.

Facts like the Flemings were of Irish descent, and that Irish-Americans made up the second largest ethnic grouping in America. With 40 million people able to trace their ancestral roots back to one Irishman or another, Breman knew that sympathy for the IRA often ran high. People didn't think of them in the same way they usually thought of terrorist groups. They considered the IRA to have a nobler cause. A people enslaved, fighting for their freedom.

He sat back and sighed. Since long before he'd ever thought of dealing in weapons, Breman had known about the powder keg of IRA activists. He'd grown up seeing Belfast burning on the six o'clock news. And he'd heard stories from local sympathizers. Stories about British brutality and indifference. Stories of Catholics pitted against Protestants and the war that resulted from injustices both real and imagined. Maybe Janice's connection to them was no more than she had said. Maybe it was just one more avenue to further the well-being of Janice Fleming. But Janice had an Irish background. He'd checked it out. He knew that her father had once been a strong supporter of aid to Ireland in the form of fund raisers.

What if both Janice and Gabby were actually in the hierarchy of the IRA? Janice always seemed to have plenty of support and power in the U.S. How could this not be backed by equal amounts of respect in Ireland itself? He felt his hands tremble slightly. He'd ordered her to be executed, and by now she was probably dead. There was nothing he could do to stop that, and even if he could, it wouldn't be prudent. He'd learned early on to never put your trust wholly in any individual player. With a deep breath, he finished with the briefcase and fixed the locks once again. He'd simply wait for the next IRA representative to show up when everyone learned of Janice's desertion. If it happened to be Gabrielle Fleming, he'd cross that bridge when he got to it.

Fourteen

Gabby opened her eyes and moaned. For a moment she couldn't remember where she was, but her back ached terribly from the rock hardness of the bed and pitiful excuse for a pillow. Rolling over, she caught sight of her travel alarm and then it dawned on her that she was in England. Liverpool, to be exact. It was only six o'clock in the morning, but for some reason Gabby sensed the urgency to wake up.

Throwing back the covers, she sat up and rubbed her eyes. Focusing, she noticed for the first time that Janice's bed had not been slept in. She jumped to her feet and went to the bathroom. It was empty, just as she'd known it would be. Janice had never come back to the room last night.

Sitting down in stunned disbelief, Gabby remembered Janice's excuse that she and Breman had argued about her sleeping in his room. Apparently her sister had given in.

The thought sickened her. She had known, by Janice's own admission, that her sister wasn't saving herself for marriage. Unlike Gabby, whom Janice thought terribly out of sync with the times and very old-fashioned. But Janice's actions were frightening to Gabby, who could well understand the temptation of physical desires but could never, ever tolerate the idea of one-night stands.

Maybe her sister saw it as something more permanent. Janice had indicated her hopefulness that the relationship might become serious. "Or was that just a cover-up?" Gabby spoke aloud. Maybe Janice had only thought to throw Gabby off the right trail. If Breman was threatening her with some kind of blackmail, perhaps this arrangement was just one additional part of Janice's payment.

"What in the world can she have done that would entice her to give herself to a man like that in return for his silence?" she asked the room. Of course, maybe it wasn't Breman's silence that Janice was buying. Maybe there was something more to this whole ordeal. Determined to get to the bottom of it, Gabby quickly showered and dressed. Noting the rain outside, she pulled on jeans and a burgundy sweat shirt. She packed her bags quickly, hoping that when Janice did choose to reappear, they'd have some time to talk privately before joining the tour group. With this task accomplished, she packed what few things Janice had taken out. No doubt Janice would want to change clothes when she finally did make it back to the room, but who knew if there'd be time for anything else? At least with the bags ready, Janice couldn't put her off on the pretense of needing to see to her packing.

Pulling her long blond hair into a simple ponytail, Gabby applied a light foundation of makeup and finally put on her socks and shoes. She practiced aloud exactly what she would say to Janice.

"Look, sis," she'd begin, trying to keep it lighthearted and non-threatening, "I know you're a grown woman, but I don't like to sleep alone in strange hotels." *No, that won't work*, Gabby reasoned. *I sleep by myself in strange hotels all the time when I'm traveling for the magazine.*

She thought for a moment and took another approach. "Hey, Janice, I missed you last night. Maybe you should —" No, that wouldn't work, either. The minute Gabby opened her mouth to suggest Janice should do anything, her sister would become defensive and angry.

Taking the travel bag that doubled as her

purse and personal carry-on, Gabby made her way downstairs to the front desk. It was exactly six-forty-five, yet already the place was buzzing with people.

"May I help you?" an older woman asked. She wore the uniform of the hotel and a name badge that read "Madge."

"Yes, I'm wondering if you could tell me which room is Breman Butler's? He's my tour director, and I've forgotten where we're suppose to meet this morning."

"Sorry, dear, but I can't give you that information."

Gabby bit at her lower lip. "Well, maybe you can tell me if you've seen a young woman around the lobby this morning. She's about five three, one hundred and ten pounds, and blond. Her hair's cut in a shaggy style and —"

"No, I've not seen her. But you must understand, I've just now come to work. Is this one of your traveling companions?"

"Yes. She's my sister, Janice Fleming. We're sharing a room, but she, well . . ." Gabby felt her face heat up. "She didn't come back to our room last night and I was worried."

The woman nodded. "If I see her, I'll tell her you're looking for her."

Just then Breman Butler strode through

the lobby like he owned the place. Gabby excused herself and ran after him. "Breman!" she called.

He turned and looked at her, but Gabby couldn't read the expression on his face. It almost looked confused, yet at the same time startled.

"Good morning, Gabby."

"Look, I'll get right to the point," Gabby said, suddenly feeling a dislike for Breman that was stronger than before. "I'm looking for Janice. She never came back to our room last night. I thought maybe she was with you."

"Where in the world would you get that idea?" Breman asked with a touch of indignation.

"Janice told me she was considering it." Gabby left it at that and hoped that the better part of Breman's discretion would take control of his mouth.

He smiled and smugly leered. "I'm flattered, but honestly I've not seen her since the afternoon tour yesterday."

"What? But she said you were having dinner together last night. I thought I might catch you both at the medieval theater presentation."

Breman shook his head. "I'm afraid you were mistaken. Janice and I had no plans for last evening. I think we said our good-byes around," he looked at his watch, "maybe five-thirty or a quarter till six."

"But when I asked her to accompany me to the dinner theater, she specifically said that you two had plans."

"Was this before or after she mentioned staying the night with me?"

He was mocking her now, and Gabby hated his sarcastic expression. "Mr. Butler, if you've not seen her, then Janice is missing. She didn't return to our room last night, and no one has seen her downstairs this morning."

He shrugged. "I can't make it my concern until she doesn't show up on the bus. You yourself have walked away from tour activities, even though the tour booklet makes it clear that you should stay with the group. Maybe Janice simply found someone to keep company with and the time got away from her."

Gabby shook her head. "Or maybe she's in trouble. Maybe she got lost or —"

"Miss Fleming, I assure you a simple request for directions or a cab would have brought her right back to our hotel. I think you're overly protective of her. She is, after all, a grown woman entitled to her own life." With this, Breman glanced up to find Fred and Ginger approaching. "Ah, I must excuse myself. I promised to breakfast with the Applegates." He left her standing there and went to greet the couple.

Gabby couldn't believe the way he'd just dismissed her. She'd expected that Breman, above all others, would know where Janice was. And when he didn't know, Gabby figured equally that he, above all others, would want to know where she'd disappeared to. Especially with the sum of five million dollars being bandied about between them.

She went back to the front desk and asked Madge for the manager. A youthful man with coal black hair and blue eyes appeared. "I'm the manager. May I help you?"

"My sister is missing. She left around dinnertime last night and I've not seen her since."

"I see. And you are . . ."

"Gabrielle Fleming, and my sister's name is Janice Fleming." Gabby noted his air of indifference. "Look, I know what you're going to say. Maybe she wandered off and maybe she found somebody to stay the night with, but I'm telling you that isn't like her." But it *was* like her, Gabby argued within her own heart. Still, she felt a desperation mounting to know exactly where Janice was.

"Could you describe her?" the man asked,

and Gabby repeated the things she'd told Madge. The man shook his head. "I was on duty all night and I'm afraid I've not seen anyone fitting your sister's description either come or go."

"But that's impossible!" Gabby was quickly losing her patience. "Let me talk to your staff. Is there anyone still here from last night? Someone who was working up on the second floor?"

The man disappeared for several minutes and returned with two willowy girls in maid uniforms. "I've questioned them already, and neither one remembers seeing your sister."

"You're certain?" Gabby asked them. "She's younger than me, blond with a short, shaggy hairstyle, and usually she wears sporty, trendy clothes, although I can't remember just now what it was she was wearing last night."

"Was she at the medieval banquet?" the manager asked, appearing to be giving the matter his utmost attention.

Gabby shook her head. "No, I waited for her to show up, but she never did. Since Breman wasn't there, either, I figured they were having dinner together just like she told me she was going to do."

"Perhaps this Breman can —"

"No, I've already asked him," Gabby interrupted, knowing what the man's suggestion would be. "He hasn't seen her since our tour yesterday afternoon."

Gabby turned to the two girls. "Look, we're in room 210. Are you sure you didn't see a woman about this high?" Gabby held her hand to where it was only a couple of inches below her own height. The young women shook their heads.

"But you must have seen something. She left our room last evening about six-thirty." Again they shook their heads and Gabby couldn't help but raise her voice. "Somebody must have seen something!"

At this, Gabby was surprised by someone placing a hand on her shoulder. Whirling around she found Jarod. He seemed to immediately recognize her concern. "What's wrong?"

"Janice is missing!" she said, struggling to keep from screaming the words. "No one knows anything, and nobody has seen her."

Jarod frowned and led her away to a quiet corner of the lobby. "What do you mean she's missing?"

Gabby drew a ragged breath and fought to clear her mind of the hideous, frightening images of what might have happened to her sister. "Janice left me last night before the dinner. Remember I told you that she and Breman were to have supper together?"

He nodded.

"Well, Breman says that never took place, nor was it planned. He says the last time he saw Janice was when we arrived back here after our afternoon tour."

"But surely you saw her last night when you went to bed, right?" His voice sounded hopeful.

"No. Remember when you walked me to my room? Nobody was there, and that was midnight. I got ready for bed and wondered when Janice might show up, but I guess I fell asleep waiting for her. When I woke up this morning, I found her bed hadn't been slept in and no sign of her anywhere. I thought maybe she'd spent the night with Breman." Gabby grew embarrassed even mentioning this aspect.

"But of course Breman denies that," Jarod stated matter-of-factly.

"Yes, he does. Oh, Jarod, what could have happened? Where is she?" Gabby knew she was close to tears, and she felt a tremendous relief when Jarod put his arm around her. Then a thought came to her. "I'm going to call the police." She started to move back toward the front desk, but Jarod held her fast.

"Let's go back to your room to see if she

left anything you might have overlooked."

Gabby allowed him to lead the way, but she was certain the search would prove futile. She unlocked the door and pointed to Janice's side of the room. "I packed her things already, and I didn't find anything to indicate that she left intentionally." Wearily, she plopped down on the bed.

Jarod searched the room, even looking under the beds. He went into the small bathroom and after a brief appraisal, returned to where Gabby sat. Glancing at his watch, he said, "Look, the maritime museum tour is about to begin. Stay here, and I'll go see if Janice shows up for that. If she's not there, I'll search through the rest of the hotel."

"No!" Gabby declared, getting back to her feet. "I will not stay here while my sister's very life might be in danger."

Jarod tried to look patient, but Gabby could see that he was anxious to be on his way. "If she comes back, she'll come here. She knows we're in Liverpool for two days. You should be waiting here for her. If anything is wrong, she's going to need your support."

"I can't just sit here and do nothing. She's my sister, and she's nothing to you. I'm going to talk to the other members of the tour and find out if any of them have seen her."

Jarod shook his head. "You *have* to stay here."

"I won't!"

"Then I'll tie you to the chair," he growled and stepped toward her as if to do the job.

"You wouldn't dare!" Gabby was backing up now because something inside her told her that he would do just as he'd said.

"I know you despise someone else being in control," he stated in a low, determined tone, "but this one time you are going to do *exactly* as I say."

"But —"

"No! No buts. No arguments! Nothing but 'Yes, Jarod. Gladly, Jarod. Happy to oblige, Jarod.' Do you understand me?" He stood only inches away with a stern, resolute expression.

Gabby swallowed down her fear and nodded. "Yes, Jarod. Gladly, Jarod. Happy to oblige, Jarod," she forced herself to say.

He gave her the briefest nod and went to the door. "I'll be back as quickly as I can. Don't leave this room for *any* reason, not even the tour. Do you understand?"

"But what do I tell Breman? He'll no doubt come to inquire as to why I'm not in line for the bus."

"Tell him the truth. Tell him that Janice

193

hasn't come back and that you want to wait here for her. But, Gabby," he paused as if considering something of grave importance, "don't let on how worried you are. Make out like you're angry at her inconsideration — act like she does this all the time."

"But why?"

He shook his head. "No questions. Just do it for me, please?"

Gabby finally agreed. "All right."

"Good girl."

She waited for several minutes before gathering her things and heading to the door. "Tell me what to do, will you!" She glanced around the room, wishing silently it could offer up some kind of counsel. She hesitated for only a moment as she contemplated Jarod's rationale for her remaining behind. Janice would already have returned to the room if something wasn't wrong, Gabby reasoned. Of this she was quite sure, and because of her certainty she couldn't just sit in a hotel room and wait around.

"Sorry, Jarod," she whispered, pulling the door closed behind her, "but some things have to be done *my* way."

Fifteen

It was difficult at best for Jarod to appear calm and reserved as he searched through the corridors of the hotel for some sign of Janice. He tried to picture what might have happened, but the images made him shudder.

He glanced at his watch. It was nearly time for the maritime museum tour. At least that would keep Breman occupied. Jarod slipped down the backstairs, checking for something that might indicate Janice had passed this way. Nothing!

Sweat formed on his brow, and in spite of the warm woolen sweater he'd worn over his shirt, Jarod felt an unsettling chill travel down his spine. He sensed the danger and wondered if his imagination was working overtime, or if indeed something was about to happen. Hadn't this sixth sense kept him out of trouble before?

Reaching the bottom step, Jarod glanced around the short corridor and found himself with two choices. One door evidently led into a kitchen area, while another door appeared as a complete mystery. Choosing the latter, Jarod found himself outside in a very run-down alley. There was no sign of struggle. No telltale article of clothing or purposefully planted note to let him know she was in trouble.

Slamming his fist against the wall, Jarod went back inside and made his way through the kitchen. His presence brought quite a stir, but no one remembered seeing Janice, and they could offer him little but negative responses to his questions.

He went quickly to the public pay phone in the lobby and dialed a number he'd hoped not to have to use.

"I hear you're having pleasant weather," he said when a female voice answered on the other end.

"We're due to have rain," the woman replied.

"It rained in America the night before I left."

"One moment."

There was a terribly long pause, and Jarod felt a certain amount of relief in knowing that Breman was already on his tour and Gabby was safely staying out of trouble upstairs.

"I understand you're concerned about the weather," a male voice suddenly said.

"Yes, and I'd like to meet with someone who might be able to help ease my concerns," Jarod replied.

"We can certainly accommodate you."

"When? Where?"

"Patience is a virtue, old man," the voice answered.

"Then consider me virtueless," Jarod replied dryly.

"Perhaps you should look for seashells."

Jarod closed his eyes and pulled from memory the reference to seashells. "I'll do that right away," he replied and hung up the phone.

Hurrying outside, he caught a cab. "The Walker Art Gallery," he commanded.

The drive was fairly short, but even so, it gave Jarod more than enough time to consider a million possibilities. His dislike of these "gruesome little affairs," as he'd come to call CIA operations, had just grown to overwhelming proportions. Nothing was supposed to go wrong this time, but it had. Now the entire operation might well be blown, not to mention that he might have lost another partner.

He thought of Janice and tried not to let his anger get the best of him. She was more

197

headstrong than her sister, but she was one of the best agents he'd ever worked with. After losing his partner, Barrett Devader, in a nasty cross fire last year, Jarod had nearly quit the agency then and there. But as he was amply reminded, no one ever really *quit* the agency. He was offered an extended leave, but then there was an unexpected break in the case, and the people responsible for Barrett's death were close to being put away for good. Jarod couldn't bring himself to leave at that point, and once Barrett's killers were caught and the initial crisis had slipped by, he was once again wrapped up in a whirlwind of espionage and clandestine meetings.

Janice was a fairly new agent, recruited on campus only the year before. She was perfect agent material. Young, athletic, single, and very intelligent. She had few misgivings about using whatever was at her disposal to get the information she needed, and it was this that worried Jarod most. Had she found some other link in the weapons exchange? Had they missed something in their appraisal of the situation? His mind went back to the details of the operation. He'd been sure that he could afford Janice the perfect backup and protection by posing as her sister's photographer. It had all seemed so neatly ordered. But now Janice was missing. He sighed, and the driver seemed to sense his urgency.

"You Yanks are always in a hurry," the driver mused. "You'll find things move a bit slower here on our side of the ocean."

"I also find things cost twice as much. It doesn't mean I have to like it or agree with it," Jarod snapped.

This silenced the driver, who was quick to pull to the curb near the main entrance. Jarod paid him without another word and hurried into the gallery. *Seashells*, a painting by Albert Moore, was on display in the eighteenth- and nineteenth-century British, Pre-Raphaelites, and Victorian room. This was the agreed-upon meeting place for Liverpool, with several backup locations assigned in case this area became off limits for one reason or another.

Jarod stood looking at the portrait of a female standing on the seashore, the wind playing at a gossamer cloth that enveloped her body. The subtle shading and look of dissatisfaction on the face of the woman left Jarod little appeal for the work. He glanced around the room, then sighed again and returned his gaze to the portrait.

God, keep her safe, he prayed silently. He tried to go over all the events of the trip that had led up to Janice's disappearance. He knew Butler was getting bolder in his threats, but he hadn't expected this turn of events. Perhaps Janice was on to something that required her leaving the hotel. But even if this were the case, why hadn't she left him a message or gotten word to him through Gabby? *Please God, don't let her be in trouble.*

"I suppose one might prefer gathering seashells out of doors," a strictly business-like voice sounded from behind Jarod.

"Yes, but I heard it might rain," Jarod countered.

"So the Albert Moore will have to do."

Jarod turned around to face an older man whose weather-worn face and gray hair gave him cause to wonder just how helpful the man might actually be. "Janice Fleming is missing."

"Your partner, I presume?"

Jarod nodded. "I thought you folks were fully apprised of the operation."

"Oh, we are," the man replied with the hint of a grin. "Come along, we'll talk."

∾

Gabby wasn't surprised when Breman separated himself from the group after their tour of the maritime museum. What *had* surprised her was the strange absence of their bus driver, Roper. Breman himself had

200

taken the wheel, as well as handled the city and museum tour. No one offered any explanation for Roper's absence, and no one seemed overly concerned about it, so Gabby, too, kept silent.

They were to have a free afternoon, and Breman was already halfway down the block when Gabby made the decision to follow him. Gabby kept a noncommittal pace in order to remain unseen. *He must know where she is,* she reasoned. He'd been too smug, too unconcerned about Janice's disappearance. It just didn't figure. Her mind displayed a million images, all of them hideous and frightening. Maybe Janice had stood up to him and in a rage he had hit her and . . . She couldn't even bring herself to imagine the possibility that Janice might be seriously hurt or even dead.

Glancing around, Gabby found no other familiar face in the crowd. She felt terribly alone and overwhelmingly foolish. Jarod would no doubt be angry with her and with good reason. Here she was in a foreign country following someone she was convinced had brought harm to her sister. She was so lost in thought that she nearly missed seeing Breman stop in front of a small shop. He glanced up the street and then down and finally checked his watch.

Gabby felt her nerves tingle with anticipation. Breman was obviously up to something, she thought and watched as the two brothers from southern France appeared from the opposite direction. They were an odd pair. Always silent, never joining in with the others. They certainly didn't fit the normal appearance of tourists.

The dark-headed men hailed Breman with a silent salute, and Gabby found herself seeking some haven of shelter to avoid being recognized. Remembering her camera, she pulled it from her bag and zoomed the lens in to snap several pictures of Breman and the men. Still, she couldn't hear what was being said, and it was enough to drive her insane. What if these men had something to do with Janice's disappearance? What if they were conspirators of Breman's? She had to move in closer.

Mingling in with a crowd of people, Gabby let herself be caught up in the street traffic. She maneuvered slowly, always keeping her eyes on the three men at the corner. None of them seemed to notice that she was among the people passing by. When most of the crowd went forward to cross the intersection of Whitechapel and Church Streets, Gabby ducked around the corner not five feet from where Breman engaged his companions on the other side of the wall.

"You have your proof," one of the brothers was speaking in his heavily accented voice. "Now, when can we expect the exchange?"

"Soon enough," Breman replied in a hushed tone. Gabby had to lean forward to catch the rest of his sentence. "I can have the goods delivered to Istanbul on the Friday after the tour ends."

"Here is the address."

There was only the sound of fluttering paper, and Gabby found herself longing to know exactly what "goods" Breman was dealing. Was it drugs? Did it have anything to do with Janice?

"You won't be sorry you chose to accept our offer" came the heavy accent again.

"Nor will you," Breman replied. "Let's make our way back to the hotel. Remember, keep quiet about the details of this and forget everything you know about me. In two weeks, you'll be heroes to your people."

The men laughed and the sounds of their voices faded from Gabby's ears as they moved down the street. The noisy Liverpool traffic was picking up in such a way that for several moments Gabby stood rather mesmerized by the sounds she'd tried so hard to tune out while listening to Breman. The sound of screeching brakes and cursing brought her back to rational thought. In the street, a pedestrian shook his fist at a small blue car before crossing to the other side.

Gabby looked around her as if seeing everything for the first time. Nothing seemed familiar or overly friendly. A group of leather-clad young people were making their way toward her. The women wore a variety of jewelry, including nose rings and chains that extended from nose to ear. The men had their heads shaved in bizarre fashions, and all of them, men and women alike, wore mascara and eye liner. She'd seen groups like this in America, as well, but right now it troubled her to the very core of her existence.

They passed her in a chatter of English accents and vulgar expressions. Behind them came a group of businessmen and through them sailed a boy on in-line skates, headphones blocking out any sound of life around him. Gone were the expectations of quaint English villages and castles. Gone was the feeling of warmth and joy Gabby had known earlier. England now seemed an oppressive place, and she longed to return to America.

But she couldn't.

She couldn't leave without Janice. Breman Butler was obviously involved in more than mere blackmail. But what was it that he planned to deliver to these men in Istanbul? And exactly how was Janice involved?

She began to walk, not paying any attention to the direction or time. Her mind was a jumble of confused thoughts. It was as though someone had plunked down a jigsaw puzzle in her head, spilling millions of seemingly unrelated pieces together — expecting her to form them into a coherent picture.

She tried to relate Janice and Breman and the dark-skinned French brothers together but found it impossible. Breman wanted five million dollars from Janice for something. But what? And did the French brothers, who would soon pick up "the goods" in Istanbul, have anything to do with Janice's disappearance?

It was dark by the time Gabby realized she was hopelessly lost in the huge industrial city. Feeling a sense of trepidation at the sight of run-down tenements, she hailed a cab and gave him the name of the hotel before easing back into the seat. There had to be an answer. Somehow all of these strange, unrelated things must add up together.

Making her way into the hotel, Gabby

stopped at the front desk and inquired about Janice one more time.

"I was wondering if my sister, Janice Fleming, has . . ." She paused. *Has what?* It wasn't like she needed to check in. She had a key to their hotel room, and there'd be no real reason for her to inform the front desk of her whereabouts.

"You must be Gabrielle Fleming," a matronly woman said.

"Yes. Yes, I am," Gabby answered hopefully.

"Well, here you are, love." The woman handed her an envelope. "Your sister left this for you this morning."

"She did!" Gabby snatched up the envelope, feeling a flood of relief. "Is she upstairs now?"

"I can't rightly say," the woman replied.

Gabby nodded and made her way to the elevator. Tearing into the envelope, Gabby heard the floors click by, and when the doors opened at the second floor, she was already focusing on the words Janice had hastily written.

"Sis, I ran into some old friends from the university. I'm going to stay with them a few days and will join you in Edinburgh. Don't blow your top over this, Mittens. You know how I hate it when you fuss. I promise I'll be just fine. Be sure to mail my postcards and take good care of my things. Queenie."

Gabby stood in the hallway outside her hotel room, rereading the note over and over. The handwriting was Janice's — Gabby would recognize it anywhere. And it was highly possible that Janice had run into friends whom she'd want to spend time with. It was even like Janice to take off without warning and do something irrational. What *wasn't* like Janice was to use their ancient childhood nicknames. They'd had code names when they played their spy games as kids. Gabby was Mittens and Janice was Queenie. What troubled Gabby was not so much the use of the nicknames, but what they represented.

Unlocking her door, Gabby went in, switched on the light, and nearly screamed at the sight of Jarod Walls sitting quite angrily in the chair he'd left her in hours earlier.

Sixteen

Crumbling the note in her hands, Gabby tried to compose herself. "Did you find her?" she asked weakly. She felt like a child who was about to be taken to the woodshed.

Jarod's eyes narrowed and seemed to reflect fire from the light of the table lamp. "No. Did *you?*"

Gabby shook her head. She could feel her heart pounding at such a rapid pace that she wondered quite seriously if she might pass out. Jarod kept watching her with the same unforgiving look, making it quite impossible for her to calm her nerves.

She jutted her chin out, hoping to strike a defiant pose. "Look, I had to go. I had to see if I could find her myself. You just have to understand that. I'm a grown woman and —"

Jarod jumped up so fast that Gabby could scarcely blink before he'd taken hold of her shoulders. Shaking her so hard that her teeth rattled, she barely heard his words.

"You just scared me out of ten years of life I didn't have to give. I told you to stay here for a reason — one I didn't have time to explain. Don't ever go against me again. Do you understand? Do you?"

Gabby nodded, mostly because the way Jarod was shaking her made it a reasonable response, and also because she was fearful to indicate anything else.

Then without warning, he pulled her into his arms, and for a long moment Gabby thought he might squeeze her to death in the bearlike hug he gave her. "I was afraid something terrible had happened to you," he whispered against her ear. The bristly whiskers of his chin scratched her cheek, but instead of irritating her, it sent a current of electricity throughout her body. Shaken by this, Gabby knew she had to put distance between them in order to think.

Finding the strength to pull away, she stared at him for a moment. "Why? Why are you so upset, and why are you so worried about this?"

Jarod shrugged noncommittally. "You were frantic this morning. I wanted to help."

"No," Gabby said, feeling strongly that he was hiding something. "You know something, don't you? Something about Janice. What is it?" Her voice took on an edge of desperation as she remembered the note in her hand. Grasping it tightly, she felt her resolve to be calm give way.

Jarod shook his head. "I can't tell you anything you don't already know. I didn't find Janice or anybody else who knew where she might have gotten off to. Look, Gabby, I care about what happens to you. I knew you were upset about Janice, and I was afraid you'd do something irrational."

"Like go look for her?" she retorted sarcastically.

"Look, there's no need to take that attitude."

Suddenly their roles seemed reversed and Gabby felt increasingly angry. Jarod had ordered her to stay put while he went in search of a woman he barely knew. Jarod had broken into her room to await her return, and *now* he was telling her that she had no right to take up an attitude of indignation. Sitting down on the edge of the bed, Gabby folded her arms across her chest. "I think you know more about this than you're letting on to me. Why don't you tell me what's going on?"

Jarod looked blankly at her for a moment. She thought his face looked paler than before, and in his eyes she couldn't deny the look of concern. No, it wasn't just concern, it was fear. He looked genuinely afraid of something. What was it? It certainly couldn't be that he was afraid of her, and if not, then what was he afraid of?

"You're keeping something from me," she muttered, trying to force the pieces of the puzzle into place.

"I don't have the answers you want." He spoke forcefully but sounded very unconvincing.

Gabby jumped up and shook her closed fist in Jarod's face. "I'm not going to play these games. If you know something, then tell me. I'll go crazy if I can't put it all together. Running off to meet friends might be Janice's style, but I don't believe her note for one minute."

"What do you mean, running off to meet friends might be Janice's style? What note? Have you had some word from her?" It seemed to be Jarod's turn to grow angry.

"It's none of your business!" she declared and turned away to distance herself from his explosive expression.

Jarod's hand gripped her arm tightly and whirled her back to face him. Gabby's breath caught, but she held her ground. "Leave me alone." There was something in his eyes that warned her she'd overstepped the bounds of his patience. Fear welled up inside her, and the only way she knew to fight it was to remain angry.

Jerking away, she backed up a step. "Get out of my room. I have work to do, and you shouldn't even be in here."

"I'm not going anywhere until you level with me," he said in a deadly calm that further unnerved her.

She shook her head. "I'm not a child, Mr. Walls. We're co-workers, remember? You have no authority over me, and I'd appreciate it if you would respect my request and leave." The words were delivered through clenched teeth because Gabby knew that if she didn't hold her jaw tight, fear would have her teeth chattering like castanets.

"You may not be a child, but you're acting like one!" he declared, stepping forward in an intimidating manner.

Gabby held fast to her facade of courage. Looking up, she tried to match his fierce expression. "Whether I am or not, I don't need you to baby-sit me."

Jarod's expression seemed to soften a bit at this. Memories from their first meeting flooded Gabby's mind, but she pushed them aside. "If you know something more about Janice, then tell me. Otherwise . . . I . . . I want you to go."

"You don't know what you want, that's the problem."

"How dare you —" There was no way to finish her words because Jarod suddenly pulled her into his arms and kissed her quite passionately. Gabby didn't resist the action. It was wonderful to be suddenly enveloped in strong arms. Slumping against him in defeat, Gabby felt all the fight go out from her. Tears formed in her eyes and began to stream down her face just as Jarod released her.

"That wasn't the effect I was hoping for," he said with a sheepishness to his tone that rather endeared him to Gabby.

"I'm sorry," she whispered and wiped at the tears with her hand. "I just can't take any more. I can't stay angry at you when I'm worried about Janice. I know you aren't the enemy." She paused. Did she really know that?

As if sensing her sudden concerns, Jarod dug out a handkerchief and handed it to her. "You're right. I'm not the enemy."

"But I don't know who is the enemy or even if there is an enemy. Not really. I guess I have my suspicions. Especially now."

"Why especially now?" Jarod led her to the edge of the bed and waited for her to sit down before joining her. "Why, Gabby?"

She opened her hand and revealed the tightly crumbled note. "This is from Janice."

Jarod's face tensed. He grabbed at the note quickly and began to straighten it back out. "Why didn't you say so in the first place?"

Gabby shrugged and stared at the wall. "I don't know. I guess because this note might fully explain things for most folks, but it doesn't do a thing for me."

Jarod said nothing for a moment and Gabby knew he must be reading the note. "You're sure it's from her?"

"Yes. I'd know her handwriting anywhere. And," Gabby paused, reluctant to go on.

"And what?"

"And she's the only one who ever knew to call me Mittens. It was a game we played."

"What kind of a game?" Jarod questioned.

Gabby looked back at him. "It was my code name when we played spy games with Daddy."

"And Queenie was hers," he deduced.

"Yeah."

"So you can be confident that this note is definitely from Janice." He sounded almost relieved. "When did you get this?"

"Just a few minutes ago. The lady at the front desk said that Janice had dropped it off this morning. She would have had to leave it sometime after the bus tour departed, though, because I checked again before I left with the group."

214

"This woman actually saw Janice?"

"I don't know. She just said that my sister had dropped it off."

Jarod grew thoughtful for a moment, studying the note in more detail. "Someone must have seen her, otherwise how would they have known it was from your sister? Your name is the only one on the outside of the envelope."

"I know, and it's not Janice's writing." Gabby dabbed at the fresh tears that formed.

"Someone else addressed the envelope? But why?"

"I don't know. All I do know is that Janice is not with friends. Of that I'm certain. She's in trouble or she'd have never used our old nicknames. Those were names we only used when we wanted to make absolutely sure we could confide things to each other without anyone else knowing where the message had come from. It was all part of a very intricate code we invented as children. Janice is trying to tell me something. I just don't know what it is."

Jarod looked at the note one final time before handing it back to Gabby. His heart nearly broke at the resolve in her voice. Resolve that suggested defeat, maybe even hopelessness. He almost wished the anger would return. He knew it hadn't really been intended for him anyway. Gabby seemed to deal with vulnerability by getting mad. It was her trademark in every meaningful confrontation he'd been a part of.

He watched her wipe her tears, and it was almost his undoing. A part of him longed to tell her everything he knew. Tell her that Janice was a part of a CIA investigation and that they were trying to pin down the group responsible for trading arms to the IRA. Tell her that they'd used her position with the magazine to make it reasonable for Jarod to accompany Janice to England. It would blow the lid off his cover and expose the entire operation, but he hated seeing the anguish in her eyes. Why not be honest? Surely she'd keep her mouth shut if she knew Janice's life depended on it.

If Janice was still alive, he reminded himself.

"I'm sorry for all of this," Gabby said, suddenly getting up from the bed. "I'm not good at things like this. I fell apart when Daddy was lost at sea. Janice was always the strong one. Janice always had that carefree kind of spirit that made the bad times seem not quite so bad, you know, like maybe there really was hope that it would all work together for good. Funny thing about that," Gabby said with a forced laugh, "Janice never really wanted anything to do with God or spiritual matters, yet in many ways she was better about facing the future and life's ups and downs than I was."

Gabby paced the short distance to the window and drew back the drapes on the blackened night outside. "I always wanted to be more like Janice," she said softly. "I never had her flair for living, and now . . ."

"Don't," Jarod said firmly. He crossed the room to stand beside her. City lights pierced the darkness with strangely angled reflections that left haunting shadows on the street below. "Don't imagine what might or might not be. Your imagination can be a very defeating thing." He put his hands on her shoulders, but she remained with her back to him. Rigid. Defensive.

It was in that moment that he realized how very deeply his concern for her ran. He hated the fact that she was hurting. Hated even more that he couldn't help her. He wanted to protect her, comfort her, love her. He tightened his grip on her shoulders. Yes, he had fallen in love with her from the first moment they'd met. Jarod Walls, the impenetrable fortress, had actually given up his heart to a woman. And she didn't even know it.

Well, she had to know he had feelings for her. After all, they had kissed and spoken about it in brief. But love? That was different. Love was commitment and promises of a future, and frankly Jarod didn't know if he had a future to promise.

The perfume she wore was very floral, yet muted, almost faded from the long day's wear. He wanted to bury his face in her hair and inhale the scent, but instead, he wrapped his arms around her and pulled her back against him. She didn't resist, but neither did she respond.

"We'll find her," he whispered.

"I know she's out there — somewhere. I'm so afraid for her." Gabby shivered in his arms.

Jarod drew her away from the window and turned her to face him. "God does have this under control." She nodded but looked unconvinced. "Tomorrow we'll get on that bus as though nothing has happened and —"

She jerked away. "I'm not getting on the bus. I'm not leaving Liverpool until I know what happened to Janice."

Jarod sighed. "You have to get on the bus. We both do. If someone on the tour is responsible for Janice's disappearance, then we have to pretend that the note satisfied our concerns."

"But I said nothing about thinking that someone on the tour was responsible for Janice's disappearance." Her eyes narrowed as she considered him for a moment. Jarod knew he'd just made a big mistake. Gabby hadn't uttered so much as a single word about her suspicions, except to know instinctively, or by way of the coded nicknames, that her sister was in trouble. Jarod licked his lower lip and tried to think of a way out.

"It stands to reason that the only people who would know to leave you a note from Janice would be people on the tour."

"But we don't know that Janice didn't put the note there herself," Gabby replied flatly. "You have some other reason for suspecting someone on the tour, don't you?"

Jarod shoved his hands deep into his blue jeans. "Just a hunch, really." He hated lying, but for now it was his only recourse.

"What kind of hunch?" She sounded more hostile. The anger was obviously returning.

"Janice told you herself that Breman Butler was putting the moves on her. Trying to persuade her to get a whole lot more serious about their relationship, right?"

Gabby nodded, but her brows knit together, leaving her expression almost doubtful.

"I figure maybe something went wrong between them. Maybe Janice had to leave because of something that happened with Breman. Or maybe Breman got out of hand altogether and Janice couldn't leave."

Gabby swallowed hard and looked away. In that moment, Jarod knew that she, too, suspected Breman but wasn't letting on. What did she already know?

"You suspect him, too, don't you?" he finally questioned.

Gabby had moved back to the window and was toying with the curtain. "I suspect everyone. I don't believe that note for one minute. Janice may be spontaneous, but she isn't stupid. There was something driving her with regard to this tour, and I know she would never have left on her own accord." Then as if realizing she'd said too much, Gabby turned on her heel and headed for the door. "I think you'd better go. I want to go through Janice's things and see if I notice anything is missing."

"Let me help."

Gabby picked up her sister's two bags and tossed them on the bed. "No. I can do this alone."

Jarod knew that he had to find out what Gabby knew. His people had known nothing of Janice's disappearance, and any clue, no matter how seemingly unimportant, might help him to locate her before it was too late.

"Why do you suspect Breman Butler?" he asked softly.

Gabby was already unzipping the larger of the two bags. She'd tensed up after making her comment about Janice being so fixed on the tour. And after her reaction to his mentioning Breman, Jarod knew she suspected a great deal more than she was letting on. He could only hope that in her suspicions, there might be an answer or two to Janice's dilemma. Taking the small bag in hand, Jarod began to go through the contents.

"What do you think you're doing? I told you I could handle this alone." Gabby stopped long enough to stare at him in disbelief. Jarod held up one of Janice's T-shirts and inspected it a moment before Gabby snatched it away from him. "Stop it!"

"Answer me. Why do you suspect Breman?" Jarod continued going through the bag, even though Gabby had reached out to take it away from him.

"Don't touch her things. I don't want anyone else touching her things. She might be dead for all I know, and you're messing everything up." Hysteria seemed to edge her tone, and Jarod could see that she was on the verge of tears again. He tried to reach out but she flinched, and he couldn't force himself on her.

"Okay, I'll go. But we're not finished with this. If we're going to find her, we have to work together. You're going to have to deal straight with me and tell me what you think or better yet, what you know. Whatever you do, keep Janice's things away from Breman."

Jarod went hesitantly to the door and turned. "I'll come back in the morning and take you to breakfast. Stay here until I come for you, okay?" He saw the look of confusion and knew there was a war going on inside of her. "You can trust me, Gabby. I care about her, too."

"Why?" Gabby asked, searching his face for the answer.

"Because I care about you."

Seventeen

Sleep was impossible. Gabby tossed and turned all night, until finally when the palest glow of light touched the sky, she threw back the covers and gave up on the night. Dressing in jeans, she layered a lightweight knit top under a zippered sweat shirt in case it warmed up later. With exception to the very most southwestern cities, her trip to England had been chilly and wet, and she wasn't about to spend the day shivering in case the temperature refused to rise. They would go north today. North to Glasgow, Scotland. Away from England. Away from Janice.

She looked at the packed bags and felt tears come to her eyes. Not knowing what had happened to her sister was the worst kind of torture. She pulled out the note Janice had written and read it again to make certain she hadn't missed anything.

"I promise I'll be just fine. Be sure to mail my

postcards and take good care of my things. Queenie. "

"You promise to be just fine, but how can you and how can I ever know what's really going on?" Gabby whispered to the room.

Crossing to the window, she caught sight of movement in the street below. It was Breman! She was certain of it! He was wearing his tour guide uniform. Watching him a moment longer, Gabby saw him make his way into a small park across the street where a lone figure stepped from behind a tree. Forgetting about Jarod's warning to stay put, Gabby suddenly realized that maybe she could go have a look around Breman's room. The night before, she'd finally managed to get the room number from a less-conscientious clerk by calling down and stating that she was to meet Mr. Butler in his room but had forgotten which room it was. Seeing that Breman was still talking, Gabby hurried to grab her own room key before racing to the elevator.

Room 410 was at the end of the east corridor. Gabby glanced up and down the hall before reaching out for the doorknob. Just as she touched the cold metal, noises from inside the room could be heard. Holding her breath, Gabby panicked. She glanced to the right and saw the door of the maid's storage closet ajar. Darting in there, she barely had time to pull the door closed when Jarod stepped out of Breman's room.

Putting her hand to her mouth, Gabby suppressed her gasp of surprise. Jarod! What was he doing in there? He walked out of the place like he owned it, and a strange feeling formed in the pit of Gabby's stomach. What if Jarod was *with* Breman? What if his part in this trip was rigged in order to help Breman?

But help him do *what?*

Now she was truly troubled. It had seemed strange to her all along that Sandy suddenly wanted her to take a photographer. What if the whole thing was a big conspiracy? Breman and Jarod were both from New York and both of them could have known Janice from some previous encounter. Maybe Janice had gotten herself into some kind of trouble with them. But five million dollars' worth of trouble? It just didn't make sense. Besides that, how could they have managed to bring Sandy in on the whole thing?

She waited at least ten minutes after Jarod had moved down the hall to open the door. Chiding herself for such foolish attempts at espionage, Gabby almost laughed at herself cowering there in the tiny closet. How had she expected to get into Breman's room in the first place? As a child, she would have pretended to pick the lock, but as an adult she knew nothing of such things. Gathering up her courage, Gabby peered out the door and down the corridor. She found no one, not even another guest, stirring.

As quickly as she could, Gabby made her way this time to the stairway exit. It would be just her luck to step on to the elevator and find Breman stepping off. What would she say if she did run into him? But the hall remained empty and the elevator never opened.

She went back to her room only long enough to pick up her things, along with Janice's. They were to meet with luggage in hand before breakfast, and there was no way she wanted to give Breman or Jarod a chance to go through her things. Jarod had already proved himself capable of getting in and out of her room at will, and suddenly the thought terrified her. Trembling, she waited for the elevator and wondered how much danger she might be in. She forced herself to calm as the doors opened and revealed the elevator to be empty. She was overloaded with the bags but managed with only minor difficulty to get everything on before the doors attempted to close.

With a deep sigh, Gabby pressed the button and waited for the elevator to descend. She thought about Jarod, and somewhere deep in her heart she couldn't bring herself to totally suspect him of evildoing. Maybe he was just trying to be nice because he'd come to care for her. It was possible, she reasoned. She liked him, too. At least she had liked him before Janice's disappearance. Now she wasn't sure what she felt.

The doors opened to the lobby floor, and Gabby wrestled the bags to the place where they were supposed to be gathered for loading onto the minibus. Fred and Ginger were just depositing their bags, and Roper was already gathering them up to load. Gabby set the bags on the floor and contemplated their safety. If Roper loaded them immediately, surely that would keep them out of harm's way.

"We missed you on the tour yesterday," Ginger was saying to Roper.

"Had me a bit of stomach trouble," Roper answered and hoisted up a bag. "Nothing to write about."

Ginger spotted Gabby and instantly struck up a conversation. "Oh, we've hardly had any time to talk with you."

"I know. This trip has been a real whirlwind," Gabby replied with a forced smile.

"Jarod tells us you write for a travel magazine and that you're covering England and Scotland for a big article."

"Yes. Jarod is taking the pictures."

"Yes, he told us. It must be *very* exciting to travel to *new* locations and try *new* things all the time. I keep telling Fred *we* should get out more, but this is the first time in *ten years* I could drag him away from his beloved university."

Gabby smiled at the man. "The travel can be both exciting and exhausting. The first few years weren't so bad, but now I think I might enjoy settling down."

"Marriage and a family is just the thing!" exclaimed Ginger.

"Well, I don't know about settling down *that* much." Gabby glanced around the lobby and saw Ronny Davis approaching them. Typical of Ronny, she tripped over her own bag and nearly stumbled headlong into Gabby.

"Sorry, I have two left feet today, or maybe I should say two right feet," Ronny said with a laugh. "Either way, I'm as clumsy as an ox."

"Don't worry about it," Gabby remarked.

Just then Roper returned for Gabby's bags. "Are you loading them right onto the bus?"

Roper looked at her as if confused. "Wouldn't do to load them anywhere else."

Ronny and Ginger laughed, but Gabby pressed the issue. "It's just that it looks like rain outside and I hated to think of them sitting out in the open."

"Now, don't you worry a bit," Roper said, his British accent more pronounced. "I've not lost a bag or passenger yet."

Gabby frowned and bit her lower lip. *You've lost one now,* she thought as a vision of Janice came to mind.

As if reading her mind, Roper looked around. "Say, where's that pretty sister of yours?"

To her horror, Gabby's eyes filled with tears. "She's, ah . . . she took a side trip," Gabby finally managed to say. Roper nodded but offered no further comment.

"What kind of side trip is she on?" Ronny asked pleasantly. She moved her things aside to make room for Jim and Jason Evans, who were just now approaching.

Gabby shrugged. "Something with friends. That's all I know. Janice has never been one to give out too many details. Now, if you'll all excuse me, I'm going to grab a bite to eat." She wasn't really hungry, but it seemed imperative that she get away from the growing crowd.

"Why don't you eat with us?" Ginger suggested. "We can talk a bit and get to know each other a little better."

"I'm afraid I need to discuss business with Mr. Walls." Gabby knew the excuse was a weak one, but in all reality she also knew that Jarod would hunt her down and insist they spend time talking about Janice.

"All work and no play . . ." Ginger began, but Fred hushed her up.

"I'm sure the young woman works on deadlines, Ginger."

"Yes," Gabby replied and moved away. She could still hear Ronny's animated conversation as she crossed the lobby and slipped away to the dining room where breakfast was already being served. Helping herself to the buffet-style meal, Gabby chose eggs, toast, tomatoes, and bacon, then moved down the line to take up a cup of very black coffee. She moved around several empty tables before choosing a rather secluded one in the back of the room. Sitting down, she wondered how long it would be until Jarod arrived in his angry fashion to chew her out for not waiting upstairs.

She didn't have long to wait.

Entering the room with a strained look of concern, Jarod quickly spotted her and made his way to the table. "I thought I told you —"

She raised her hand. "I couldn't remember everything you said, so just calm down." His features relaxed a bit at this lie. She kept her emotions under control by taking long sips of coffee between deep, relaxing breaths.

Jarod took a seat and leaned across. "Did you sleep at all?"

"No," she said honestly. Looking into his eyes, she had to doubt her concerns about him being in on some evil scheme. He seemed so sincere and so open. He'd shared conversation with her about God and never once did it seem to be a put-on act. Either he was one very accomplished actor, or he was unequivocally what he claimed to be.

"I'm afraid I couldn't sleep, either." He yawned as if to give validity to his statement. He got to his feet. "I guess I'd better get some chow. It looks good. I have to admit, they've had some pretty decent breakfasts here."

Gabby nodded and watched him go. *Who is he, and why was he in Breman's room this morning?* Then the thought suddenly came to her that she was going to try to get into Breman's room herself. What if the roles were reversed and Jarod had found her coming out instead of the other way around? She didn't want to doubt that his actions were innocent, but in all honesty, she didn't know who she could trust.

A dozen Bible verses raced through her head, along with old sermons from her church back home. *Put your trust in God,* she reminded herself. That was the theme of the remembered messages. Trust God, not man, not circumstances or emotions. Trust God.

"So where are the bags?" Jarod asked, sitting down to a plate heaped with food.

"Roper took them and put them on the bus. I asked him if they were going to be loaded right away, and he assured me they were."

Jarod bowed his head, and Gabby suddenly remembered that she'd not even thought to pray. *Oh, God,* she prayed silently, *I need you now more than ever, and I didn't even think to tell you. I've been so upset that praying hasn't seemed like an important thing. I don't feel like I'm doing anything and yet I know that talking to you is the first thing I should have done. Forgive me and please help me. I don't know where Janice is, and I'm so afraid for her. Father, show me who I can trust and send someone to help me find Janice.*

"Hey, this is good," Jarod commented.

Gabby looked up from her prayers and from the plate of food she'd been toying with. "Is it?" she questioned without really caring for a response.

"You have to eat, Gabby." His voice was soft, full of concern and gentleness.

"I don't have much appetite."

"I understand, but you have to make it appear that you believe that note. At least for now. Someone was responsible for seeing to it that you received it, and in order to play the game you'll have to make it appear that the note was a logical excuse for Janice's absence. I don't know what's going on yet, but I'm working hard to find you some answers. I went to Breman's room this morning."

"You did!" Gabby exclaimed in surprise. Here she had doubted his purposes, and he was going to tell her all about it. "Did you find anything?"

"No, he'd taken his suitcase with him, and except for some trash in the waste can and the messed-up bed, there wasn't anything to suggest he'd ever been there."

"Oh." Disappointment and relief washed over her. At least he had told her about being in Breman's room. It was more than she'd have done for him if she'd been the one to succeed at spying.

"Look, you can't give up hope. Are you sure there's nothing else you can remember? Has Janice given you anything on this trip? Notes, souvenirs, anything?"

"She's been too busy with Breman. Even when I forced my company on her, Janice was closemouthed and very nearly hostile whenever I suggested she put Breman aside and do something with me."

They ate in silence for several minutes. Jarod shoveled food in as though he might have been starving, while Gabby continued to pick at the meal until it no longer resembled anything edible.

"I've been giving this whole matter a great deal of thought," Jarod said, stopping long enough to speak in between sips of coffee. He leaned closer and looked deep into her eyes. "If we stick together, Gabrielle, we just might beat them at their own game."

"Beat who, though?" Gabby said without thought. "And what game? What game includes my sister's disappearance as part of the rules?"

"I can't tell you that."

"Can't or won't?" Gabby asked irritably. "No one has any answers, and no one is talking except in riddles. I'm not cut out for this, and I'm not convinced that handling it this way is wise. I should have called the police. I suppose I still could. But most of all, I really resent your insistence that I leave Liverpool. What if Janice shows up here? What if —"

"You can second-guess your decisions all day, but it won't change the facts, nor will it bring Janice back. She knows where you're headed. After all, it was Janice who instigated your coming on this trip, right?"

"Right."

Jarod surprised her by putting his hand on top of hers. "Don't worry. We'll work at this together, and we will find Janice." Looking at his watch, Jarod threw his napkin on the table. "Come on, the bus leaves in two minutes."

"Two minutes?" Gabby looked at her own watch in disbelief. While she'd agreed in words to leave Liverpool behind, her heart wasn't yet ready to walk away from the last place she'd had contact with Janice.

Jarod waited for her to get to her feet. "Remember, act like the note convinced you. At least for now."

"Okay, I'll play it your way," Gabby said, resigning herself to the inevitable. "But if I don't hear something soon, I'm going to the police."

They'd no sooner climbed on board the bus and taken a seat at the back than Breman appeared to make an announcement. "Due to some unforeseen local problems, I'm afraid our tour of Liverpool is to be cut short. We will, however, be adding a delightful side tour in order to make it up to you. The Moffat Woolen Mill will provide you with a unique shopping experience. You'll be able to see for yourselves how wool is transformed from its raw state into those wonderful handcrafted sweaters everyone seems to so covet."

There were murmurs amidst the group, but no one made any protest. Breman motioned Roper to move out, and Gabby felt her hands begin to tremble. For a moment, she even wondered if she might faint. A part of her wanted to scream to be let off the bus, and as if sensing this despair, Jarod reached out and took hold of her hand. Rhythmically, he stroked his thumb over the top of her hand, and all the while he looked at her with those intense green eyes. Gabby shook her head and tried to draw a decent breath.

"I can't *do* this," she whispered.

"Yes, you can." Jarod's voice was tender and reassuring. "Trust God, Gabby. He has everything under control."

She tried to focus on that point, but at the same time images of Janice in torturous misery kept coming to mind. Without even realizing what she had done, Gabby had reached her free hand across to tightly grip Jarod's arm.

"What if she's hurt? What if she's . . ."

Jarod leaned close to whisper against her ear as though they were far more intimate than co-workers. "Don't borrow trouble. You'll go crazy if you let your imagination run wild. We'll find her. Be strong."

Gabby sought his eyes, desperately seeking reassurance. He had to be right. She had to believe they would find her sister. Jarod reached up and slanted her head to meet his lips. The kiss only lasted a moment, but in it was a kind of promise that Gabby clung to as a drowning person might take hold of a life raft. She wanted to trust him. She needed to trust him. Glancing up she caught sight of Breman staring at her strangely, and in that moment her mind was made up for her. She would trust Jarod Walls and seek his help. Her mind might still hold questions regarding him, but of Breman she was certain. The man was evil, and somehow he had caused the disappearance of her sister.

Eighteen

The minibus traveled across M58 to where it joined up with M6. This would take them north through Blackburn and Preston on their way to the Lake District National Park. Jarod knew this was a wonderful photo-op for the article, but his heart wasn't in the research any more than Gabby's was. He'd been unable to learn anything from his contacts, and his own frustration, along with Gabby's private anguish, was enough to make him want to leave the tour. Mile after mile of scenic countryside clicked by, but with every town they passed, Jarod's own sense of urgency grew. How could he convince Gabby that they were doing the right thing when he couldn't even convince himself?

He looked over to say something encouraging and found Gabby sleeping. She had rested her head against the window of the coach and allowed exhaustion to claim her. *It's better this way*, Jarod thought. *If she sleeps, she won't worry so much.* At least he hoped she wouldn't. He watched her for several moments, remembering the fear in her eyes. She looked at him as though she expected him to reveal all the mysteries of the world. She looked to him for answers he couldn't give her. At least a hundred times that morning he'd wanted to confide in her, but each time he held back, knowing it would do little good. She trusted him now, at least in part. Even so, he could sense a tremendous battle raging within her. Her fear was stronger than her anger, but her love for Janice was strongest of all. She'd not take kindly to the truth of his and Janice's working relationship, of this he was very certain.

A frown marred her otherwise angelic features, then faded as though the images in her mind had changed. The furrows in her forehead relaxed, then tensed again as her brows knit together over eyes squeezed tightly shut. She was far from at rest, and Jarod longed to hold her safely in his arms and assure her that it would be all right. But would it be? He trusted God, but what if God's plan was different from his own this time? What if Janice, in her devil-may-care attitude and intolerance of spiritual matters, had endured this episode in her life in order

239

to learn the value of God in her life?

I didn't plan on falling in love with you, Gabby, he thought and clenched his teeth together so tightly that his jaw began to ache. In his business, friends and loved ones could become instant liabilities. Janice had assured him that by bringing Gabby along, she would have built-in excuses for keeping Breman at bay. Gabby would become her excuse to back off when Breman got too personal, and Gabby's job at the magazine provided the perfect excuse for Jarod to join up with the tour. Jarod hadn't liked it from the start. His suggestion had been that they travel as an engaged couple, but Janice felt she could get more information out of Breman by cuddling up to him than by interrogating him. Had she been right? He had no way of knowing. What little he and Janice had discussed wasn't very helpful now.

He prayed for what seemed like hours, hearing very little of the interpretive narrative Breman offered on the countryside. In Glasgow, another contact would await him, and hopefully this one would have news of Janice's whereabouts. Until then, he had little information and positively no other leads. For an amateur like Butler, he'd certainly managed to cover his tracks. If, indeed, Breman Butler was responsible for Janice's disappearance.

Gabby was stirring now, and Jarod was drawn again to her pale face. Already there were dark circles beneath her eyes. She wasn't eating or sleeping properly, and in time, it would really begin to take its toll. Somehow he had to convince her that she had to take care of herself, for Janice's sake if for no other reason.

She rolled her head toward him and, as she did, opened her eyes. Jarod smiled and for the briefest moment she smiled in return. Then memories of her surroundings and Janice seemed to flood her mind at once and the smile faded into a tight-lipped expression.

"Where are we?"

"Just entering the Lake District National Park. You know, William Wordsworth and Beatrix Potter country?"

Gabby nodded. "I fell asleep."

"Yes, I know. You didn't use my shoulder this time, although I wouldn't have minded if you had." He tried to sound lighthearted.

Breman began telling them about the glorious scenery that surrounded them. Mountains like Fairfield, Hart Crag, and Loughrigg Fell were pointed out as they neared Grasmere and Rydal, former home villages of poet William Wordsworth.

"Wordsworth was born in the Lake District and lived his life here with his wife and children. He's remembered as one of the romantic poets, probably one of the best," Breman announced and then began to recite one of Wordsworth's poems.

"She dwelt among the untrodden ways
Beside the springs of Dove,
A maid whom there were none to praise
And very few to love:

A violet by a mossy stone
Half hidden from the eye!
— Fair as a star, when only one
Is shining in the sky.

She lived unknown, and few could know
When Lucy ceased to be;
But she is in her grave, and, oh,
The difference to me!"

Jarod felt Gabby tense at the final stanza and knew she was losing it. He looked at her, tears welling in her eyes, worries for her sister clearly written in the anguished expression on her face.

"Dove Cottage is where the poet spent his most creative years. We'll be stopping here for a very short time," Breman remarked, but Jarod barely heard those words, nor the ones that followed.

"Don't do this to yourself," he said softly to Gabby. She was dabbing her eyes with a tissue and trying hard to remain under control.

"This is too hard." Her lips barely murmured the words.

"I know." He wanted to be comforting, but it had exactly the opposite effect.

"You can't possibly know," she nearly spat the words at him. "Janice is nothing to you, but she's everything to me." She jerked away from him, turning to the window, shutting him out.

Jarod stared at her back for a moment, then straightened in his seat with a sigh. *Janice is nothing but my partner,* he thought. *Nothing but the one person I was responsible for backing up and keeping alive.*

They covered miles of inspiring scenery without a word between them. Gabby knew it was her fault. She'd put up the angry wall of defense in order to keep from feeling too vulnerable. This time, however, it wasn't working. Not only did she find herself extremely vulnerable, but she longed for Jarod's comforting touch and the reassurance of his words. Although, she'd put an end to that by being so callous and indifferent to his attentions. He'd not spoken to her since the Wordsworth house and now, nearly to Glasgow, Gabby felt the burden of the wall she'd created.

He didn't even comment on my not eating lunch, she remembered painfully. Normally, she would find it irritating if anyone kept close tabs on her, but Jarod's words always seemed to come because of his genuine concern. At least that was how it had been.

"We're just now coming into Glasgow," Breman announced. "Our accommodations here are very nice, and I believe you'll find the people quite eager to please and make your stay a pleasurable one. Glasgow gets its name from the Celtic words *glas cu,* which means 'dear green place.' Although with the storm that seems to be blowing in from the west, you'll probably think it's an awfully *gray* place." A few chuckles rose up and gazes moved to the westward horizon. He continued. "It is the largest city in Scotland and boasts many fine examples of Victorian architecture. In the past, Glasgow has been voted The European City of Culture and now rivals Edinburgh in the area of the arts. There are wonderful art galleries, museums, and cathedrals here, but unfortunately our tour will only allow for a brief drive through the city tomorrow morning. Tonight, dinner is on your own, and I can suggest several wonderful restaurants or public houses that provide delicious Scottish cooking."

Gabby stared at Breman the whole time he made the announcement. Her mind conjured images of him fighting with her sister. She tried to imagine Breman bringing up the matter of the five million dollars, and Janice laughing at him in her devil-may-care way.

It started to sprinkle rain as Roper maneuvered the minibus through the busy city streets. Breman continued speaking about supper choices, but Gabby ignored him and would gladly have gone on in silence, but Jarod turned to her with a stern expression.

"I'd like to take you to dinner," he said without so much as a hint of emotion in his voice.

"No, thank you," she managed, even though her heart shouted acceptance.

"You have to eat. You haven't eaten all day."

So he had noticed! Gabby shrugged indifferently. "I had breakfast."

"No, you *mutilated* breakfast, but I saw very little of it pass through your lips."

"I'm not hungry," she insisted and it wasn't a lie. In fact, her stomach felt quite sour and the mere thought of food caused it to do a flip that left her feeling rather green.

"It would do you good to get away from the tour group." The bus had pulled up and stopped in front of their hotel.

"I just want a hot bath, and then I'm going to call Sandy," she insisted.

"Sandy? Why?"

"Because I'm canceling the articles. I can't work under these conditions," she said with more hostility in her voice than she'd intended. Seeing his expression wavering between what looked like hurt and insult, she sighed. "Look, I know you're probably counting on this job for income, but this doesn't have to put an end to your own productivity. I'll tell Sandy that you're still hard at work and encourage her to buy the photographs for future use. Besides, maybe you could create another tabletop book."

Jarod's jaw tensed, and Gabby saw his eyes narrow slightly. "I'm not hard pressed for money. Money has nothing to do with my concern. I know you better than you think, and without the task of compiling information for your articles, you're going to sit in your room and stew over Janice. I can see it even now."

The others were already getting off the bus, and Breman was pattering about something insignificant. "You can't make me do the articles," she said firmly. "Now, please get up so I can go to my room."

"Not until you listen to me. If you all of a sudden give up the articles, Breman will be on to you in a flash."

"Still sure that it's Breman, eh? Well, it's just as well that you are, because I am, too." She glared at him hard. "I don't care what Mr. Butler thinks. I hope he worries every time I cross his path. I hope he reads the hostility in my eyes — that I feel in my heart. He's not getting away with this, but in order to devote myself to seeing to that fact, I need to be free of my other obligations. I can't very well have Sandy sitting at home with plans for the December issue on England and produce nothing to fill that magazine."

"You've already covered England," he paused, "well, at least in part. Look, I know this is difficult, but just try to stick it out."

"No, Jarod. I'm *not* writing the article. I'm *not* eating and I *don't* plan to be very sporting about any of this. I'm sorry, but on the way up here I've had a great deal of time to think...."

"To get mad, you mean." His expression dared her to defy his statement.

"All right, have it your way." She crossed her arms and snapped her chin up defiantly.

Jarod's own anger seemed to get the best of him. He grabbed up his photography equipment bag and got to his feet without another word. Making his way down the narrow aisle, he paused only briefly at the door as if to say something else, then thought better of it and departed from the bus.

Instead of feeling relief, Gabby suddenly felt deserted. She'd brought it all on herself, but nevertheless, she was afraid of Breman Butler and of what he might be capable of doing to her. Glancing out the window, Gabby noted that Breman was nowhere in sight. Roper was opening the cargo bin, but other than that, Gabby saw no one she recognized. Slowly getting to her feet, Gabby thought of Jarod's demand that she keep Breman away from Janice's bags. The thought of Janice having something planted inside her bags had haunted Gabby all the way from Liverpool. What if there was something she was missing?

She stepped from the bus into the sprinkling rain, just as Roper deposited Janice's two bags on the sidewalk. Hurrying to where they lay, Gabby grabbed them up.

"I need these," she explained.

"They'll be delivered shortly," Roper replied, lugging still other pieces from the compartment. "And I promise they won't be waterlogged."

"That's okay . . . my bags," she hesitated and changed her mind. "I'll just take these."

She hurried away into the hotel before Roper could offer further protest. Getting her check-in information and key, Gabby hurried to her room and locked the door behind her. She shed her zippered sweat shirt and stretched in the chilly room. A day of being cooped up on the bus with only two rather hurried stops had made her stiff and sore. Deciding the bags couldn't wait, she gave up on the idea of a hot bath for the moment and sat down on the bed beside her sister's things.

First, she opened both carry-ons and sorted the contents into neat, orderly piles on the bed beside her. Outside the rain came down in earnest and pelted her window as the wind picked up. It looked to be an intense storm.

Rummaging through her sister's clothes, Gabby unfolded each piece, inspected it, and refolded it before moving on. There had to be some clue as to how she could help Janice. The sudden knock at her door caused Gabby to jump.

"Who is it?" she asked, pressing against the door to look through the peephole. There was no one, and just as she started to get edgy, Gabby remembered that this had been the routine for baggage delivery since starting the trip. Opening the door a crack, she found her own luggage deposited to one side. She took them in quickly and locked the door behind her once again.

Driven to know what secrets Janice might share via the stacks of clothes and paraphernalia on her bed, Gabby dropped her own things rather unceremoniously and returned to her quest. She started to move the bags from her bed, then noticed Janice's small purse was tucked at the bottom of one case. Bringing it out, Gabby was surprised at the weight of it. Opening it and spilling the contents onto the bed, she quickly found the reason for the weight. The small revolver glinted up at her from the rather drab navy spread on the bed.

Gabby stared at the piece for a moment. What in the world was her sister doing with a gun? All manner of nightmarish thoughts began to run through her mind. Suddenly the urge to dig through the remaining things overpowered her ability to reason. Putting the gun carefully aside, Gabby turned to the task at hand.

An hour later, after diligently inspecting every single item, including the bags themselves, Gabby had only a stack of postcards to consider. Postcards. Janice had mentioned postcards in her note. Gabby quickly went to her purse and pulled out the letter.

" 'Be sure to mail my postcards and take good care of my things. Queenie,' " she read aloud. Flipping the postcards over, Gabby could see they were all written on and addressed to their aunt Margaret Getty. The only problem was, Aunt Margaret had been dead for twenty years and Janice had never known the old woman!

Now Gabby felt she had an actual clue. Turning on every light in the room, Gabby went to the small table and sat down. The cards were addressed to a post office box number that Gabby didn't recognize. The city was New York, but Aunt Margaret had lived in Rochester. Gabby read the first card, but it made little sense about anything, much less did it give any reason as to why Janice had disappeared.

"Having interesting summer. S. Holmes in Mom's book says sweet dreams.

"Can't say how very innvigorating" — she'd spelled invigorating wrong, Gabby noted — "Bath Trust turned out to be." What in the world was Bath Trust? "Paper is actually only my 5th. Jan." Gabby read it through twice. It made no sense.

She read the others and they, too, were nothing more than garbled nonsense. Thinking on the message of the first card, Gabby studied the words. "Having interesting summer" made sense. The reference to Sherlock Holmes, although confusing, was still related to England and the trip. Maybe there was a book that the recipient of this card would understand to check. The Bath Trust was completely baffling, as was the comment about the paper.

Gabby toyed with the card. Seven lines of words and very little of it made even marginal clarity. Walking to the window, Gabby tapped the postcard against her chin. There had to be something missing. Janice had specifically noted the postcards in her message, so they had to be important. Aunt Margaret was dead, so it was certain that the cards were never intended for her, but if a total stranger saw them, he'd never know that. The messages, though garbled in meaning, might well hold all of the clues to her puzzle.

She called me Mittens, Gabby thought with a smile. Mittens had become her code name because she abhorred gloves as a child and always insisted on wearing mittens in the wintertime. And Janice was Queenie because someday she planned to enter a pageant and be a beauty queen.

It was pouring outside when the revelation suddenly came to Gabby. Aunt Margaret had been the code for their secret hideout. Aunt Margaret's house! If you found yourself in the midst of other kids and said, "I'm going to Aunt Margaret's after school," the two sisters immediately understood to meet at the hideout. Looking back at the card, Gabby smiled. Seven lines. When they were children they'd developed a writing code that involved counting the letters in a sentence. Punctuation didn't count and however many lines were in a message, it was that number by which you counted. Looking at the message this way, Gabby hurried to the table and wrote out every seventh letter. ITEMMATCHIRATOPAY5. ITEM MATCH IRA TO PAY 5.

Gabby looked at the words, which hardly made more sense than the garbled message. Was it about a bank account? Some Individual Retirement Account paying five percent? Nothing made sense. Quickly she pulled out the other cards and began to decode them using the childhood method.

Two hours later, Gabby held the final card in her trembling hands. The messages were much clearer now. One card explained a Swiss bank account transfer. Another mentioned side deals being cut with Croatians. There were fifteen cards in total, and each one indicated details that could only connect Janice with the Irish Republican Army.

Dumbfounded, she dropped the card on the table as though it had started to burn her hand. Janice was working for the IRA? It didn't seem possible. Her baby sister was involved in an international weapons exchange with terrorists? No wonder she needed someone to provide her cover, but even now that small detail wasn't completely clear to Gabby.

She picked up the last card that after decoding simply read, "Am proceeding with my nuptials at 5."

The earlier reference to five had turned out to bring closure to the conversation Gabby had overheard Janice having with Breman in the Hampton Court gardens. Five million dollars would be the price of purchase for the IRA weapons. But what did the five in this message represent? And was Janice really planning to marry someone, maybe Breman, in order to get her weapons?

It was all too much. Gabby gathered the cards together and shoved them back into the bag. She hesitated. Janice had said to mail the postcards, but what if by doing so Gabby helped the terrorists obtain their guns? She couldn't do that. Janice may have lost her senses, but Gabby's mind was clearly in place and spinning a mile a minute.

Catching sight of the spiral notebook on the table, Gabby quickly gathered it up and tore off her message work and several blank pages beneath it. If she was going to play spy, she would have to immerse her actions in the part. Pressing onto tablets of paper left indentations of the message on the pages beneath it. Taking the evidence with her to the bathroom, Gabby shredded the contents piece by piece and flushed them down the toilet.

She sat on the edge of the bathtub and stared down at the swirling water as it washed away the last bits of the message. Janice worked for the IRA. It was almost too much to comprehend. When and where had she become involved in such a thing? Didn't she realize how deadly it could be to play *real* spy games?

Then a nauseating wave washed over her. Maybe Janice knew only too well how deadly it could be. Maybe Janice was already dead and her last message to Gabby held the only clues as to what had happened.

Nineteen

Breman sat alone in his Glasgow hotel room. He was impatient for Roper Davenport to appear and give him the details of Janice's demise. For reasons that still troubled Breman, Roper had made himself unavailable for discussion ever since taking Janice from the hotel in Liverpool.

Toying with the edge of his briefcase, Breman could still imagine the expression of shock on Janice's face when he'd caught her going through his things. It was a good thing he'd forgotten the banquet tickets for the group. His plan that night had been to simply set up the tour group with the medieval banquet and then meet Janice for a cozier evening elsewhere. But Janice's snooping had changed all of that.

He cursed under his breath at the sound of the knock on his door. "Come in," he commanded, and Roper entered the room with a newspaper in hand. Slapping the paper down on the table, Roper gave Breman a questioning look.

Breman picked up the paper and read the headlines from Liverpool. "I thought you said you'd keep it from becoming public for a while."

Roper shrugged. "I got spooked. A group of locals showed up nearby and I had to do some fast footwork. Don't worry, they'll never trace her back to us."

"Unless her sister gets a good look at this," Breman replied snidely.

"No chance. The hotel doesn't sell Liverpool papers, and what with the rain and all, I doubt Ms. Fleming will venture outside her room. She seemed pretty upset this afternoon. Grabbed up her sister's bags like the end of the world had come and she needed to make the last train."

Breman looked at Roper oddly. "She didn't worry about her own bags, just Janice's?"

"Yeah — strange, don't you think?"

Breman thought for a moment. "Janice said there were other operatives in this group. I believe she called them her 'back-ups.' "

Roper nodded.

"Perhaps Gabby is Janice's partner, after all. I've pondered this since last night, but nothing seems to fit. No one has bothered to contact me, and the only thing Gabby has bothered to do is stare at me with those marvelous blue eyes of hers."

"Well, someone's going to have to contact you soon," Roper replied.

"Why? What's wrong?" Breman suddenly felt panicked.

"I've been trying to figure out how to tell you," Roper said, looking rather sheepishly at the floor.

"Tell me what?"

"Janice, well, you see —" Roper paused and looked up. "She didn't make the call. The money was never transferred to the Swiss account."

"What!" Breman was on his feet instantly. "What do you mean she didn't make the call? I told you not to kill her before she called her contacts and insured that the money was being transferred."

"I know, but like I said, there was this group of locals, and, well, they surprised us. Janice started to cry out, and I hit her over the head. I didn't mean to kill her then, but —"

"But you did and then you dumped her body in the river and left me holding an empty bag." He cursed again, and Roper's features darkened.

"It wasn't *my* idea, either, but the way I

figure it, you're the one who felt it necessary to do her in. We'll just have to trust that when she doesn't call her contacts, they'll contact her partner, and they, in turn, will contact us."

"But *who* is Janice's partner?"

"You said yourself it might be her sister. I didn't see her getting friendly with anyone else."

Breman nodded. "Okay, if that's the case, then perhaps I should make the first move." He glanced around the room, then went to his briefcase and took out a pen and paper. "Have this delivered to Gabby's room. I'm going to ask her to join me here for a private meeting."

"She may not agree. She's kind of straightlaced, if you know what I mean."

Breman continued to write. "I'll mention having word of her sister's disappearance."

"Are you going to show her the paper?"

"If it gets me my five million dollars, you'd better believe it. I'll promise the same demise for her if she fights against getting me the money."

"What if she isn't the operative? How are you going to figure out what she knows and doesn't know?" Roper questioned.

"I don't know, not for sure." Breman folded the piece of paper. "Hand deliver

259

this, then I have a particularly important job for you."

"What?" Roper took the note and eyed Breman cautiously.

"I want you to take up company with Mr. Walls. Get him completely out of the hotel. He and Gabby seemed at odds when we arrived here, but that doesn't mean they haven't kissed and made up. I want him out of the hotel so there's no chance he'll barge in while I'm discussing matters with Ms. Fleming."

Roper nodded. "That's a whole lot easier than the last assignment." He grinned broadly and added, "I know this great place where —"

"I don't want the details, just get him out of here."

Roper stuffed the note in his pocket. "On my way."

Just then the telephone rang. Breman reached for it but waited until Roper had exited the room. "Breman Butler," he said in a stern, businesslike tone.

"We're sorry, Mr. Butler, but my associate and I will be leaving your tour. A matter of grave importance has come up, and we will not be going through with our arrangement."

Breman felt his head grow light and sat on

the edge of the bed in order to steady himself. He instantly recognized the heavy accent of his Croatian dealer. "I don't understand."

"You don't have to. My people are taking back their money."

"You can't believe I'll give the money back at this late date," Breman replied with a rueful laugh.

"It's already been taken care of, Mr. Butler. It seems a terrible computer error was made. The accounts represented in our transaction were, shall I say, invalid? It only took a short matter of time for the error to be suspected and checked out, but it gave us the time we needed. A better deal has come our way."

The click on the other end of the line let Breman know that the man had hung up. He'd just lost a million dollars! Outraged, he started to throw the telephone across the room, then thought better of it and replaced the receiver. Gabby Fleming had to be the answer. She must have been Janice's partner, Breman reasoned. He'd simply tell her that the price had gone up. If he couldn't get his money from the Croats, he'd get it from the Irish!

Gabby was stunned when Roper delivered her the handwritten note from Breman. She was even more surprised to read the content of the note. Breman wanted to meet her in his room in fifteen minutes to discuss news of Janice.

She looked at the clock and then again at the note. Her mind immediately conjured pictures of the possibilities. Janice was safe and would soon be joining them. Janice was injured and lay near death in some English hospital. Janice was dead and Gabby was needed to identify the body. All these things went through her mind at the speed of light.

Jarod came to mind as an afterthought. She really should tell him what was going on. After all, he, too, suspected that Breman had played some part in Janice's disappearance. But he didn't know about Janice's postcard messages, Gabby reasoned. Jarod knew nothing about her sister's involvement with the Irish Republican Army, and she'd just as soon keep it that way.

Grabbing up her things, Gabby considered the situation for a moment, then added Janice's gun to her purse. She opened the door just in time to hear Roper's voice in the hall. Cautiously, she maintained a crack only wide enough to catch a glimpse of two men. One was Roper, the other was Jarod.

"You'll like this place. The food is great,

the women are beautiful, and the drinks are cheap," Roper told Jarod.

Jarod, whose hair was still wet from either a walk outside or a shower, laughed. "Then lead the way, by all means. I've nothing to keep me entertained here."

Gabby bit her lower lip and waited until the men were long gone in order to open the door. Nothing to entertain him, eh?

She muttered under her breath, "That man can be so . . . so . . ." and slammed her door shut without finishing the sentence.

Breman's room was on the same floor, only located at the far end of the corridor from hers. The red carpet and gold-trimmed fixtures did little to capture her attention. Overhead a half dozen replicas of crystal chandeliers lighted the hallway, but Gabby only gave them a brief appraisal as she lifted her eyes heavenward and prayed for strength.

With a shaking hand, she knocked three times on the door and waited for Breman to answer. What would he tell her? She trembled in earnest and suddenly wished very much that Jarod had not gone off with Roper.

Breman opened the door with a serious expression in his eyes but a hint of a smile on his lips. "I must say, you're very punctual."

Gabby felt a wave of anger wash over her at his rather sarcastic tone. *Good,* she thought. *If I'm angry, I won't appear as nervous or weak as I feel.*

"You wanted to talk to me about news of my sister. So talk."

He waved her into the room with a glass of liquor in his hand. "Not out here. Come in here where we might have a bit more privacy." Gabby glanced nervously over her shoulder and Breman laughed. "Don't worry, you aren't my type."

Gabby turned back to face him with what she hoped was a look of scathing dislike. "Neither are you my type, Mr. Butler. I simply find the arrangements abhorring."

"Well, you have no choice." He waited for her to make the first move.

"Very well." She came into the room and looked around.

"We're alone, if that's what has you worried."

"Actually, being alone with you *is* what has me worried," Gabby snapped.

Breman leered suggestively. "Like I said, you aren't exactly my style, but I suppose an exception could be made."

"Just get to the point. What do you know about my sister?" Gabby gripped her purse tightly to her waist. She could feel the gun against her arm through the soft cloth exterior.

"Please, sit down." He motioned to the table where two wooden chairs awaited.

Gabby took a seat, never letting her eyes leave Breman's severe expression. She said nothing, fearful that if she spoke again it would be her undoing.

"Would you care for something to drink?" Breman asked, motioning to his own in-room supply. A half-empty whiskey bottle stood on the nightstand beside his bed.

Gabby shook her head.

"Very well." Breman took a seat opposite her. "I suppose this might seem a bit strange to you, but a rather delicate matter has arisen and I thought it best to discuss the situation with you."

"I thought you said you wanted to discuss Janice."

"Oh, I do," he assured her. "The fact is, Janice and I were conducting a bit of business before she went away."

Gabby swallowed hard. "A bit of business?"

"Yes, I thought perhaps, since you were sisters and traveling together, that . . . well . . . perhaps Janice's business might be your own."

Gabby knew this was it. Breman was

feeling her out in regard to Janice's terrorist activities. She knew just enough to be dangerous.

Licking her dry lips, Gabby replied, "Janice and I had no secrets, if that answers your question." She tried to play it cool and forced herself to ease back into the chair. Striking what she hoped was a relaxed pose, Gabby waited for Breman to continue.

"Janice left unfinished business. I was hoping maybe you could help me in this matter."

"It isn't my place. Janice promised to rejoin the group in Edinburgh. I suggest you wait until then."

"It can't wait!" Breman declared, slamming his drink on the table. Amber liquid sloshed over the sides and trickled down onto the folded newspaper on which he'd placed the glass. "What I mean," he said, only marginally calmer, "is that the situation is such that I can't put off the transactions any longer."

"And what do you expect me to do about it?" Gabby tried hard to sound authoritative, but inside she was falling apart piece by piece.

"If you know your sister's business, you'll understand what I want you to do about it."

"I know my sister's business. What I don't

know about is you," she replied flatly.

"I want my money."

"The five million?" she dared to question.

Breman's eyes flashed recognition. "The price had been upped to eight million."

"Eight million for a bunch of guns?" She said the word guns without really meaning to.

Breman smiled. "So you *are* Janice's backup."

Gabby knew she had to play along. She'd come this far and there was no sense in backing out now. "Yes, I'm her backup."

"What a relief. You know, I had my dealings with the IRA before, but this was my first time dealing with women in the negotiations. Now, I need that money transferred by noon tomorrow or the repercussions are going to be astronomical."

"I didn't deal with the money end of things," Gabby answered sharply. Her mouth felt like dry cotton. She had no idea, with the exception of the Aunt Margaret post office box, as to how in the world to contact Janice's Irish counterparts, much less how to get them to part with eight million dollars.

"Then you'd better start. I want my money *tomorrow* or your people can forget about the weapons."

267

Gabby began to panic. "Look, just wait for Janice and I'm sure she can take care of everything. When Janice gets back —"

"Janice isn't coming back!" Breman declared and with a sweeping motion that sent the glass of whiskey across the room, he yanked up the newspaper and threw it at Gabby. "Your sister double-crossed me. *This* is what I do to double-crossing women who have no business in my world."

Gabby picked up the paper and read the headline. Fighting the urge to throw up and faint at the same time, she dropped the paper in stunned silence. For several moments neither one said a word, but finally Gabby had to know the truth. "My sister is dead?"

"Yes. I came back to my room last night and found her going through my things. I questioned her about it, but you know Janice." Breman got to his feet and began to pace. "I gave her every chance, just as I'm giving you. I don't deal well with people who double-cross me." He stopped only a foot away and leaned down on the arms of Gabby's chair to put his face in hers. "Now, you will do *exactly* as I tell you, or you can join your sister for a swim."

Gabby didn't dare even blink. Breman's whiskey-laden breath was enough to further

her nausea, but somehow she managed to contain her fear. When Breman finally pulled away, Gabby jumped to her feet and headed for the door.

"Where do you think you're going?"

Gabby whirled on her heel. "You kill my sister and expect me to sit here and calmly discuss weapons and eight million dollars?" She felt dangerously close to giving in to the urge to pull out Janice's gun and put a bullet through Breman's head. "I can't discuss this anymore, and if you can't understand that, then go ahead and kill me, too." To her horror, tears started to stream down her face.

Breman, seeming to sense that he'd pushed her as far as he could, backed off. "We'll talk again tomorrow. We'll reach Inverness early, and there'll be time for us to continue this matter then. I suppose the transfer can wait long enough for you to have a short period of mourning."

Gabby's rage nearly got the best of her. "Thank you," she spat the words, not meaning them at all. "You are *very* generous."

She hurried away from Breman and ran as fast as she could back to the haven of her own room. Closing the door, she slid to the floor and buried her face in the cloth cover of her purse and cried. "Oh, Janice," she sobbed. How could this nightmare be true?

Twenty

The next morning, Gabby joined the bus tour with eyes still swollen from crying all night. Everyone was concerned and made comments just as she'd known they would, but Gabby said nothing and moved to the back of the bus for privacy. Seeing that she was unresponsive, most everyone left her alone. Everyone but Jarod.

Sliding into the seat beside her, he tucked his camera equipment beneath the seat. "You look awful."

Gabby looked at him for a moment and shrugged. "Bad night. Thanks for noticing."

Jarod reached out to touch her hand, but she jerked it away as though he might hurt her. "What?" he questioned in a tone that couldn't hide his surprise. "If you're still mad at me from yesterday . . ."

"Just leave me alone," she said, and to her horror, her voice broke and sounded more like a sob.

Breman was explaining that the French brothers had to leave the tour for some unforeseen reason. He joked about losing people, and Gabby couldn't help but throw him an ugly look.

"Hey," Jarod said, taking hold of her, "what gives?"

"Nothing," she replied between clenched teeth.

Jarod sighed deeply and let go. "I'm sorry about yesterday. Really I am. I know I should have come to talk to you about it last night, but I went out and —"

"You don't owe me an explanation about anything," said Gabby. She turned to look out the window but totally ignored Breman's discussion on Glasgow.

"Did you call Sandy?"

"What?"

Jarod patiently asked the question again. "Did you call Sandy? You know, to cancel the articles?"

"I forgot."

"So you want to try to keep up with it after all?"

"No," Gabby snapped. "I do not want to concern myself with the countryside and quaint villages of Scotland. I don't want to do one single touristy thing."

"Gabby, where is all this anger coming

from? I'll admit I got mad yesterday, but I thought after we both had the evening to cool off, you'd at least be civil to me."

Gabby felt badly for the way she'd treated him. She also knew that if she softened and let him see her pain, there would be no stopping the tears from coming anew. She searched his face for understanding and found compassion in his eyes.

"It isn't you, okay?" She bit her lip to keep from saying more.

"Then what is it?"

"I can't talk about it here. Please."

"Okay, then when?" Jarod insisted on asking.

"When we get to Inverness," she replied, thinking that a great many things were going to come to a head in that ancient city.

Jarod fell silent, which almost made matters worse because now Gabby had to listen to Breman's speech about Scotland and the passing countryside.

"I'm sure that when you think of Scotland, a variety of things probably come to mind. The Highlands, sheep herding, plaids, the famous Loch Lomond, and Mary, Queen of Scots, to name a few. Scotland is all of those things, but so much more. We'll see a variety of countryside on this tour, including both the lowlands, which are around you now, as well as the highlands. We'll explore battlefields and cathedrals. And we will enjoy some traditional Scottish entertainment, including the piping in of the haggis. I'll explain more about that later."

Gabby grimaced at the animated way Breman delivered his speech. He was a cold and calculating man without a hint of emotion for the ruthlessness he'd displayed in killing her sister. Janice was dead. It was impossible to comprehend. Then for the first time since hearing the news, Gabby thought of her mother. *Dear God, how will I ever tell her? How can I explain to Mother that Janice was caught up in international terrorism and managed to get herself killed?*

"The Scottish plaids are one of the more special and intriguing points of interest. Tourists always want to know more about the Scottish tartans, and I can offer you a little bit of information," Breman continued. "The clan system dates back to the twelfth century and divided the Highland people into tribes or clans. Each was led by a chieftain, and each clan had its own plaid. All members of the clan bore the name of their chief, often Mac-something, meaning *son-of.* They bore this name whether they were related by blood or not, and their tartan plaids were used as a means of identifying the various people on sight. After the Battle of Culloden in 1746, all of the clan lands were forfeited to England and the people were forbidden by law to ever wear their tartan plaids. In fact, the tartans were banned for nearly one hundred years."

Gabby glanced over to find Jarod making notes. He was doing her job, or so it appeared. She was there to do a travel story, and Sandy was counting on a wonderful spread for her magazine. For the first time in her career, Gabby was going to let down an editor. She hated herself for it, but there was nothing else to be done. She couldn't and wouldn't give her time over to something as insignificant as an article when her sister lay dead in an English morgue and her mother had no idea what had happened to her child.

Breman continued to discuss the various battles between the Scots and the British, but Gabby stopped listening altogether. Somehow, she promised herself, somehow, someway, she was going to make Breman Butler pay for what he'd done. In order to do that, however, she was going to have to approach the matter rationally and unemotionally. She looked up to watch him, but it was as though the volume had been turned off. All she heard was the pounding of her own heart and the racing of blood through her veins. Breman had spoken of clans and wars to avenge their own. Well, she would take a similar line and avenge her sister. If it meant playing Breman's game for a time, then she would. But sooner or later, Breman would slip up, and when he did, Gabby would be ready.

～

Roper pulled into the off-loading zone and brought the bus to a stop. Breman jumped up with a smile. "We have an early day of it. Inverness is a wonderful town with many historical places that you'll be sure to want to see. You will also remember that when we arranged the tour, you filled out paper work on whether to pick up the Loch Ness Monster tour or the Urquhart Castle Tour. Meet here at three o'clock for both. Those of you going on the Loch Ness tour will be deposited in Drumnadrochit with your tour guide, and the rest will go farther south to the castle. Any questions?"

There was chatter about the choices among the people on the bus, but no formal question was offered up to Breman, and so the group dispersed to be assigned to their rooms.

Jarod gathered up his things, as did

Gabby. She was the last one off the bus, and most of the others were on their way upstairs to their rooms by the time she entered the lobby. She felt so isolated and alone. Fear penetrated the wall she'd put up around her heart, and the very idea of spending another night alone made her tense. What if Breman decided to sneak into her room at night? What if he came demanding what she couldn't give him?

Father, she prayed silently, *I need a miracle. I need to be kept safe, and I want very much for this man to pay for what he did to my sister.* She lingered in the lobby a moment before going forward to receive her room packet. Other guests moved past her, oblivious to her needs, and even Jarod was nowhere in sight. Finally knowing the truth about her sister had done little to ease her anxiety, and Gabby felt a helplessness wash over her that left her weak. There was nothing she could do to bring Janice back to life.

In complete turmoil, Gabby made her way to the front desk and took up her information and room key. She looked at the room number and made her way to the stairs. This was a smaller establishment. In fact, it was the smallest they'd yet stayed in. Gabby knew from reading the tour information that this accommodation only held thirty-five rooms and had been reserved, nearly in total, for the tour group. It was a charming bed-and-breakfast with stone walls that spoke of centuries long past and black iron railing at the windows that added a quaint charm.

Her room was to be number 14. The owner had advised her that it was at the far end of the west wing and was one of the finer rooms in the house. Gabby smiled, tried politely to make the necessary conversation, and then all but ran up the stairs to escape the prying eyes of her host and hostess.

Gabby nearly ran over Roper, who was just returning from depositing baggage outside the room doors.

"Hey, now," he said, taking hold of her shoulders.

Gabby wrenched away as though Roper's very touch had burned her. She looked at him, feeling an odd sensation that she couldn't possibly begin to describe.

"Ya nearly ran me over," he said, his blue eyes twinkling.

Gabby ignored him. "Sorry." She moved on down the hall and nearly jumped out of her skin when Jarod stepped out of the room next to hers.

"Hey, you okay?" he asked, seeing her condition.

"No. Well, yes." She sighed and shook her head. "Never mind."

Spying her bags along with Janice's, Gabby brushed past. "I'd better get these inside." She opened her room door and reached back for a bag.

"I'll help," Jarod said, his hand closing over hers accidentally.

The contact was electrical for Gabby. She felt the strength in his touch, the calm and peace that always seemed to follow him. She drew a ragged breath and felt her body tremble. Without thinking, she allowed her slender fingers to slide apart, giving Jarod's fingers room to press down between her own. She held his hand this way for a moment, needing desperately to find some kind of reassurance.

"Hey, if you want to hold hands, just ask," Jarod teased and laughed. But when Gabby raised her fearful eyes to his, he stopped laughing and pulled up, drawing Gabby with him. "What is it, Gabby? What's wrong?"

"Oh, Jarod." She breathed his name as if the very word said everything that was in her heart.

"You're shaking like a leaf. Here, let me carry these bags in for you and we'll talk."

Gabby reluctantly dropped her hold on

Jarod and let him carry the bags into her room. The double bed was covered with a lavender comforter and looked so inviting that Gabby very nearly threw herself across it. Jarod put the bags near the small oak dresser and glanced around the room.

"It looks snug," he said with a grin.

Gabby hugged her arms to her body and nodded. "Yes. I suppose it is."

Jarod's expression turned serious. "You want to tell me what this is all about?"

"I can't."

"Can't or won't?"

Gabby shrugged. "I guess it doesn't matter. The thing is, I wouldn't know where to begin, and you shouldn't have to be burdened with it. I'm sorry to have been such a poor traveling companion, and I'm equally sorry for falling down on the job. I saw you taking notes on the trip, and I know that you're trying to cover for me, but honestly, Jarod, I've lost my heart for this job."

"But why? Surely it can't hurt anything to tell me why."

He looked almost hurt that she'd refused to confide in him, and Gabby wanted nothing more than to spill out the whole story.

"When I can tell you about it, I will."

Jarod moved forward and put his hands

on Gabby's shoulders. "I really do care about you, Gabby."

Gabby swallowed hard and forced herself to hold his gaze. "I know."

"So long as you do."

He walked to the door and then was gone without another word. Gabby had never felt more deserted. She looked around the room and started to take off her sweater when a knock sounded. She went to the door but found no one there. The knocking sounded again, only this time it came from behind her. Closing the main door, she turned to find another door, which she presumed was the bath. Turning the latch she was surprised to find Jarod.

"What in the world?" she gasped and looked past him into another bedroom.

"We have adjoining rooms," he said with a wink. "Pretty convenient, huh?"

Gabby felt her face grow hot. "Maybe *too* convenient."

"Well, there's a lock on both sides. I plan to keep my side unlocked so that you know I'm there if you need me. I know Janice's disappearance has been hard on you, but I promise I will be the perfect gentleman and give you all the space you need. I just want you to feel safe and I don't want you to be so afraid."

"Afraid? I didn't say anything —"

"I know," he interrupted, his voice low and husky. "You didn't have to. Your eyes said it all."

Twenty-one

Gabby had barely finished with a much-desired bath when a knock sounded at her main door. She was stunned to find Breman Butler on the other side.

"What do you want?" she asked hesitantly. She quickly pulled the towel from her hair and tried to act nonchalant about his appearance. "If you don't mind, I'm trying to unwind."

"I do mind," Breman said, coming in only far enough to close the door behind him. Gabby leaned nervously against the door that adjoined her room to Jarod's.

Remembering his promise to leave it unlocked made her feel safer, even though she had no way of knowing whether or not Jarod was still inside the room. "I'm going to ask one more time, what do you want?"

"I want to know about the money. I want to know how soon I can count on your people to deliver what I've asked for." His green eyes narrowed threateningly. "I can't wait forever, you know."

"Yes, I realize the limit of your patience."

"Well, your sister certainly didn't," he said rather sarcastically. "We're running out of time on this trip, and I want all matters resolved well in advance of the final day here. I'm giving you forty-eight hours, no more. That will put us in Edinburgh. If your people can't meet my demands, I may well have to send them another message. Two dead operatives will surely make them sit up and take notice."

"Look, Janice always handled the money end of things. I've not even been in contact with the financial people in the organization. Surely you've been educated in the way organizations such as this one work." Gabby was grasping at straws and pulling information from her memories of television documentaries on terrorism. "No one person is ever privy to the entire organization. Janice and I were responsible for very different things."

"Oh, really?" Breman said in an air of disbelief. "And just what were your responsibilities?"

Gabby felt her hands grow clammy. "That's none of your business."

"I beg to differ," Breman said, stepping

closer. "I think your very *existence* is my business. Now, enlighten me on how your precious IRA works."

"Well," Gabby said, folding her arms defensively, "they use cell structures just like other organizations. One person at the top sets up several cells, and in turn, the person they've placed in charge of those cells take on their own operatives, and so on. That way, if one person is caught or if you have a leak, they can't betray the entire organization."

Breman's expression changed. "I suppose that makes sense." He seemed to think on this matter for a moment. "Janice was in with the funding cell, I suppose."

"That's right," Gabby said, trying hard to sound authoritative.

"Again I must ask, what is your business with the IRA?"

Gabby drew a deep breath. "I . . . well . . . how should I put this?" She wondered silently what sensible thing she might tell him. It would have to be something logical. Something she knew enough about that if he wanted to discuss it, she'd be capable of doing just that. Smiling as a sudden revelation came to her, she said, "I research."

"Research?" Breman looked at her warily and shoved his hands deep into the navy blue jacket he wore. "Research what?"

Gabby tried her best to feign boredom. "Oh, come now, Mr. Butler. What do you suppose I research?"

"Tell me." He spoke as though he'd grown impatient with her game.

"I look for people, contacts, if you will, who will afford us additional support. America, as you may well know, is positively filled with folks of Irish descent. I search out potential recruits, people with safe houses for our other operatives and so forth."

Breman seemed satisfied and, to both Gabby's relief and dismay, moved back to the topic of money. "It is hardly my fault Janice got greedy and stupid. I can't abide a double-crosser. Still, if Janice is the one who knew the wherewithal of the funding, I suppose I can extend you a little more time. I'll give you seventy-two hours, no more. That will put us in York and back on English soil, but that's it. That's my final deadline. Do you understand?"

Gabby nodded. "You're coming through loud and clear. I'll do what I can, but remember, I'm only one very small cog in a rather large mechanism."

"Don't give me excuses, just do it. Eight million is my last offer. If your people want the weapons, they'll cooperate. If not . . .

well . . . I'm sure you don't want to disap-
point me," he said, reaching out to cup her
chin with his hand. He pressed close to
whisper, "Your sister didn't have much
fight left in her when the end came. I can be
a very cruel adversary. It would be a pity to
see you wind up in the river."

Gabby jerked her head away from his
touch. "I'm certain my superiors would be
very grieved to see such a thing happen, as
well. You might keep in mind that you have
a commitment holding you in Great Britain
for the next week. That's an awfully long
time to keep looking over your shoulder."
She saw Breman pale a bit and drove home
her final nail. "They won't be happy when
they realize that you gave the death order for
Janice." She played the game like a consummate actress. "You know, she was engaged
to one of the top people in the organization.
Who knows, they may well forget all about
the weapons and simply come after *you*."

Breman's jaw grew taut and his eyes
began to dart back and forth as though
trying to figure a way out.

Gabby walked to the door and opened it
wide. "Good day, Mr. Butler. I believe you
have tours to give, and I have people to contact."

Breman left with a look that seemed to

waver between worry and frustration. Closing the door behind him, Gabby wanted to laugh at her own false bravado.

"Well, I have seventy-two hours," she said aloud. "Seventy-two hours in which to figure out who Janice's contacts were and what to do about it."

Jarod pulled away from the adjoining door with a frown. He'd listened to Gabby's entire conversation with Breman. Now he understood her emotional state when she'd appeared on the bus that morning. Breman had obviously told her about Janice.

Janice. Just the thought of her death made Jarod seethe with a cold, hard hatred. He would make Breman pay for his part in all of this. He'd personally see to it that Breman Butler was never allowed to enjoy a dime of his ill-gotten gains. But that would come later. Right now he had to find a way to help Gabby. He didn't understand how she'd learned so much, but at this point in time, it really didn't matter. She'd bitten off more than she could ever hope to chew and probably knew just enough to get herself caught in a cross fire from both sides.

Rubbing his stubbly chin, Jarod paced the tiny room and tried to work out a plan. Perhaps if his people contacted Gabby as though they were Janice's IRA superiors. He might have them tell Gabby that Janice herself had made Gabby a secondary contact. They could emphasize that it was too late to put anyone else in place and encourage Gabby to continue what she'd already started. It might work.

Either way, Gabby was going to have to have some help. There was no way she could face the seventy-two-hour deadline without someone rising up to offer her assistance. He ached to think of the misery she was going through. It wasn't fair or right that she should suffer. He hadn't wanted her on this trip, he reminded himself. Now he was certain that his protest against such action had been the right approach. Too bad no one else had listened to him.

He grimaced and clenched his teeth tightly together. Gabby should never have left the States. From the first moment he'd met her, Jarod had felt a spark of something more than mere business. That was his first warning sign. The second one was Gabby's naiveté and lack of knowledge where terrorist activities were concerned. She wasn't trained for this kind of work. She wasn't equipped with the knowledge that might keep her from being killed.

Then again, Janice *had* been trained and

was even noted for her achievements with the organization. It hadn't kept her alive. Eaten with guilt, Jarod plopped down on the small double bed and stared up at the ceiling. He should have kept a better eye on her, but Janice was so insistent that she had it all under control.

"God," he whispered, "I let her down and I'm to blame that she's dead." He put his hands under his head and continued to stare into space. "I couldn't save her, and I may not be able to save Gabby, either. I need some help with this one. Please show me what to do."

After the rest of the tour group, with exception to Gabby, had departed for the Loch Ness adventures, Jarod made his way to a nearby pub and sat down to await his contact. It wasn't long before a burly red-headed man of at least two hundred seventy pounds sat down at the next table. Leaning over, he beamed a toothy smile at Jarod.

"Ya knough," he said in a thick Scottish brogue, "the loch's full of monsters."

"I've heard that, too, but then the land can be just as treacherous."

"Aye, but then the tourists dinna come for that." The man smiled and stroked his red beard.

"I suppose they come for the haggis,"

Jarod said, quite seriously referencing the Scottish concoction of spiced sheep's innards.

The man laughed and gave Jarod a nod. "So what can I do for you?" His Scottish accent was considerably less at this point.

"We've got some real headaches with the operation. My partner is dead, but of course you, no doubt, already knew that."

"Yes."

"It seems," Jarod continued, "that her sister, Gabrielle Fleming, has somehow picked up enough about the operation to get herself in over her head."

"How?"

"I don't know. Maybe Janice left her a letter or note. If she did, Gabby isn't saying and I haven't had the chance to really pursue it. She won't let me have time alone with Janice's things, so for all I know there might have been a letter that Gabby has long since destroyed."

"But surely the lass wouldn't have been stupid enough to write down the entire operation to her sister."

"She wasn't stupid," Jarod replied angrily. He studied the menu in his hand and tried to bring his temper under control. "I don't know how Gabby found out, but she knows enough and that much has put her on

Breman Butler's hit list. He threatened to kill her if she didn't get eight million dollars for him within seventy-two hours. Gabby lied well enough. She told him she wasn't involved in the financial end of the organization, and he bought it. She's very intelligent, and I'm sure, with the right help, she might yet be able to help us nail Butler once and for all."

"She's not trained."

"It doesn't matter. If you have someone contact her, just establish a link for her, then I believe she'll carry it on from there. Look, she knows the man is responsible for her sister's death. I don't believe for one minute that Gabby is going to do anything to help him out, but I worry that if we don't give her a hand, she'll make a stupid mistake in order to get revenge. If you won't help her, I'll have no other choice but to tell her exactly who I am and why I'm here. That will further blow our cover, but I can't have her out there in the cold, floundering for answers."

The man nodded. "Just tell me what you need."

Hours later, Jarod met Gabby in the lobby of the hotel. He'd finally convinced her to accompany him to a late lunch/early dinner in Inverness, but it hadn't been easy. Jarod smiled broadly and extended a hand to her as she came down the last two steps.

"You look beautiful," he said, truly meaning the compliment. Gabby wore a white silk blouse and dark navy slacks that accentuated her trim form. A matching navy jacket was on her arm along with her purse.

"Thank you." She glanced around. "Is it cold out?"

"Damp, chilly. I think you'll be glad you have that," he said, motioning to the jacket. "Let me help you with it." He reached out and took the jacket from her before she could protest, and as he did, their hands touched.

Gabby froze, and Jarod squeezed her hand. He stared into her teal-colored eyes and lost himself for a moment. He had to keep her safe. He owed it to Janice, and he owed it himself. But most of all, he owed it to Gabby. The feeling inside him was one of pure protective instinct. He wanted to keep her safe for a hundred thousand reasons, not the least of which was the fact that she held his heart.

Smiling, he took the jacket and helped her into it. Maybe this was what God had in mind all along. Maybe this was his real ticket out of the CIA. He needed stability. A family, a home, something and someone to whom he could belong. Extending his arm for her to take hold of, Jarod began to know the first real pangs of desire for those things. It was time to put the espionage world behind him and begin a new life. A life with Gabby.

Twenty-two

After dinner, Gabby bid Jarod an early evening and went to her room to think. She was deeply disturbed by the flood of emotions that had come to the surface during their meal. Jarod had been so sweet, and his lighthearted manner and stories of his youth had given Gabby a few moments of pleasure. Moments when she'd actually forgotten that her sister was dead.

She shuddered and hugged her arms close as if to ward off some external cold. In truth, however, she knew the feeling had come from somewhere deep inside. She thought of her life and the spiritual truths she'd been taught from childhood, and for the first time since her father's death, she found herself really questioning God.

Why would God allow Janice to be killed?

Why had God not given Gabby better insight to know that her sister was up to something illegal?

There were so many things she didn't understand. Her mother had always assured her that God covered all the bases, but this time it seemed as though He'd forgotten the game altogether. There had to be answers, Gabby reasoned. Taking up Janice's postcards, she spread them out on her bed as though assembling a cryptic puzzle. She first looked each one over for any strange markings or other clues that might shed further light on the topic of Janice's contacts. Nothing revealed itself, and Gabby had no choice but to go over the message on each card again. Always it was the postcard from Hampton Court with the word "nuptials" that stumped her. Gabby knew it was probably a code for something, but what? Janice wasn't stupid enough to get married to one of her contacts, was she? She was stupid enough to get involved in this IRA mess in the first place, Gabby reminded herself. Why not further the cause by marrying herself to it, as well?

The first rule of any spy game was simple. Trust no one. This, in and of itself, caused Gabby a great deal of turmoil. Jarod Walls seemed very supportive, attentive, and . . . She could hardly face the next thought that came to mind. Jarod had done something to her. He'd sparked to life a dying ember that

Gabby had thought would never blaze again. She was falling in love with him. More and more every day. With every passing moment, with every new revelation and heartache, Gabby wanted nothing more than to secure herself in Jarod's arms and forget about the world outside.

Then another thought came, even more troubling than the first. What if her feelings for Jarod were merely transferred affections for the sister she'd lost in death? She knew she'd still not fully dealt with Janice's murder, and to put her thoughts and feelings on Jarod, or even to pretend that her heart was wrapped up in him, might be her only way of coping with the loss. This created a whole new sideline of concerns. Jarod seemed to be quite serious about her, and for Gabby it appeared that he was close to making some sort of declaration. What if she countered with her own only to learn later, after the worst of her grief had passed, that she was only using Jarod as a buffer?

She sighed and fell back against the mattress. She hadn't wanted to have feelings for Jarod in the first place, but right from the start he had stirred something deep inside her she couldn't ignore. At first, she'd just chalked it up to animal magnetism — the visual influences of a handsome man to a lonely woman. But as the trip wore on and Gabby had gotten to know Jarod better, she'd actually *liked* him. At least when they weren't fighting.

She smiled to herself. Jarod had been quite attentive, almost glued to her side from the very start. His feelings seemed genuine, but then she reminded herself that *his* feelings were never the ones in question. Not really.

The knock at her door brought Gabby upright in an instant. What if Breman had returned to harass her? Glancing at her wristwatch, she knew he should still be out with the tour group. They weren't scheduled to return until six, which clearly gave her another twenty minutes. Quickly, she gathered up the postcards and shoved them into her bag.

"Who is it?" she called at the door.

"Front desk. I have a message that was to be hand delivered to Ms. Gabrielle Fleming."

Gabby opened the door and stared at the man. "I'm Gabrielle."

He handed her a sealed envelope and turned to leave. Gabby started to close the door, then realized she hadn't even offered the man a tip. She grabbed up her purse and went to call after him but saw that he hadn't gone far. In fact, he was knocking at Jarod's door. He repeated the knock, then slid an envelope under the door.

Gabby quickly retreated and waited several minutes until she was certain the man had gone before stepping out into the hall. She could see a tiny edge of the white envelope sticking out from beneath Jarod's door. Curiosity got the best of her, and putting her own missive into her pocket, Gabby cautiously retrieved Jarod's note.

Holding it for a moment, she contemplated what she should do. She chided herself silently for her nosiness, but at the same time she couldn't seem to make herself return the letter. For reasons beyond her understanding, she found the urge to open it to be far more compelling than the sensibility of returning it.

Turning the envelope over, Gabby was relieved to see that it wasn't sealed. She glanced down the hall and found no one to concern herself with. Trembling, she pulled the note from within and read the contents.

Nuptials to proceed as planned.

That was it. The entire message consisted of no more than a single line. She replaced the note inside the envelope, and then it hit her. *Nuptials.* Janice's postcard had mentioned nuptials, and now here was a second reference to the word, but this one was tied to Jarod. A strange sensation began to creep over her. Taking the note with her, Gabby returned to her room and locked the door. She pulled Janice's postcards from her bag and found the one that spoke of nuptials.

Decoding the mix-matched message, Gabby read, *Am proceeding with my nuptials at 5.* She then pulled out Jarod's message. *Nuptials to proceed as planned.* She was getting a very bad feeling about all of this. The entire game was taking on a whole new set of players and rules, and it seemed that Jarod Walls was at the head of the pack.

"What a fool I've been!" she declared to the empty room. "I *trusted* him. I thought he really felt something for me." It all seemed only too clear. Jarod had been using her to work with Janice. Now that Janice was dead, and no doubt he knew full well about that little fact, he was still using her to find out what Janice had left behind.

She wiped away tears of anger and contemplated what she should do next. There was the little matter of eight million dollars and a very threatening Breman Butler who expected to be dealt with in seventy-two hours. Her mind raced with a million images and always her conclusions focused in on Jarod. Who was he? Was he IRA or an

American connection like Janice?

Storming around the room, Gabby went to the adjoining room door and unlocked it. Throwing it open, she found Jarod's room empty. Remembering that he'd mentioned needing to buy more film, Gabby looked again at her watch and bit her lower lip. She wasn't about to let him get away with this. As soon as he returned, she was going to force him to admit his connection to Janice and the IRA weapons.

Plopping down in a chair, Gabby crossed her arms and tried to contain her anger. She wanted to appear calm and collected when she confronted him. She wanted to be able to sense if he was lying to her. At this thought she laughed bitterly. She hadn't been able to see through Janice's lies and she certainly knew Janice better than Jarod. What made her even begin to think she could read him?

Staring at the open portal connecting her room to his, Gabby felt regret mingle with her anger. Why had he done this? Why had he pretended to feel things for her, and why had he played at this game until she had feelings for him? And it was useless to deny those feelings any longer. Putting her face in her hands, she quietly cried for what might have been. She was twice unlucky in love, and if she ever had any chance of control in the future, she'd never give her heart to anyone ever again.

∽

When Jarod opened the door to his room, the first thing he noticed was the adjoining door. It stood wide open and the light from Gabby's room fell across his in a single beam. Fearing the worst had happened and anguishing that he'd again failed to protect the person he was responsible for, Jarod threw down his sack and bounded into Gabby's room without so much as a warning call.

He saw her immediately and called her name. A flood of relief washed over him, lulling him into a false sense of security. "Gabby, are you all right? I mean, I saw the open door and thought —" He stopped. The look on her face was one of pure hatred.

"How could you?" she asked quietly. "How could you?"

Jarod shook his head. "What are you talking about? How could I what?"

Gabby stunned him by jumping to her feet and crossing the room. She raised her hand to slap him, but he caught her wrist and frowned. "What's wrong, Gabby? Tell me now."

"*You're* what's wrong!" she spat the words

and pulled free from his hold.

"I don't know what you're talking about. Why don't you calm down and tell me what's on your mind?"

Gabby's eyes fairly blazed holes into his heart. "You, Mr. Walls, are what's on my mind. You, my sister, and the Irish Republican Army. Care to elaborate for me?" She put her hands on her hips and stuck her chin defiantly into the air for effect. It was a good effect because already Jarod had begun to sweat. How had she found out his connection to Janice?

"Look, Gabby," he began, walking very slowly toward her so as not to appear threatening. "I don't know what you're thinking, but I'll bet it's all wrong."

"Don't come near me, or I'll scream so loud the walls of this place will crumble."

Jarod stopped and with arms akimbo asked, "What's happened to make you ask these questions?" He glanced around the room and finally his eyes fell upon the bed. The top was covered at one end with a dozen or so postcards. Janice had mentioned postcards in her note to Gabby. That had to be it! Jarod felt a surge of exhilaration. Gabby must have learned about the operation through the postcards.

As if reading his mind, Gabby shook her

head. "No, the postcards didn't tell me about you, but this did." She held up the note she'd taken from under his door. "The delivery man left this curious little message for you. Funny thing is, it very nearly matches up with a curious little message Janice coded on the back of her postcard. I believe the word 'nuptials' put me in the mind of connecting you two together. Nuptials is a very old-fashioned word, don't you think?" Her voice was thick with sarcasm, and Jarod winced.

"Okay, look," he began, pausing to rationalize what he would say. He had to tell her everything, or very nearly, but she had to stop looking at him with those hurtful, accusing eyes. "Things aren't as they seem. I'll tell you everything, but you have to calm down, and you have to trust me."

"Ha! That'll be the day!" Gabby began to pace. "You've done nothing but lie to me from the first day we met. Isn't that so?" Her voice was growing louder by the minute.

Jarod nodded. "Yes, but —"

"And to think you made me believe —" She stopped abruptly and shook her head. "No, I won't even go into that subject."

"Gabby, you have to quiet down and listen to me."

"I don't have to do anything you say."

Jarod crossed the room and took hold of her by both shoulders. The time for gentle talk had passed. "You do if you want to stay alive," he said, holding her firmly as she struggled to get away.

"Why should I believe you?" she asked, raising her arms to push at his chest.

Jarod found no other recourse but to pull her tightly against him, pinning her arms between them. "Because you have no one else, and in seventy-two hours Breman is going to expect answers you can't give without my help."

This did the trick. Gabby instantly went quiet in his arms and Jarod sighed. "I've wanted to tell you everything from the start. In fact, I never wanted you to be involved at all. Things just kind of got out of hand and —"

A firm pounding on Gabby's hotel door caused them both to jump. She looked up at Jarod with questioning eyes. She was frightened, and he could feel her begin to tremble. "You can trust me, Gabby. I'm going to protect you."

She searched his face as though looking for proof of his worthiness. Tears were forming in her eyes, and it caused him more pain than he'd have ever admitted to anyone. The knocking sounded again.

"Answer it. I'll be just on the other side of the door in my room," Jarod said, releasing her.

Gabby straightened her blouse and pushed back her hair. Finally, she wiped her eyes and nodded. Jarod took up his place and closed the door.

"Who is it?" he heard her call.

A muffled response revealed it to be Breman Butler. Jarod had suspected as much. He'd seen the tour bus pull up to the hotel just as he'd returned from town.

"What do you want, Breman?" Gabby questioned as she let him enter her room. "As nearly as I can tell, I still have plenty of time before my deadline is up."

"Yes, but I know for a fact that you received a message today. I've kept a man watching your comings and goings, and he learned from the front desk that you were to receive a very special hand-delivered letter."

"I resent being spied on, Mr. Butler." Jarod noted the change in her voice and wondered what she was planning. "For your information," she said nonchalantly, "I forgot all about my message. I stuck it in my pocket, and as you can see, it hasn't yet been opened."

There was a faint sound of paper being

rattled and Breman's response. "Well, tell me what it says!"

Gabby replied, "Your eight million will be transferred tomorrow."

"See there, good things do come to those who wait," Breman said snidely. "Is that all the message contains?"

"No, here, read it for yourself. They want you to give me the details on the arms transfer."

"I'll do that only after the money is safely in Switzerland."

"Is that what I should tell my people?" Gabby questioned.

"Exactly that. I want to see the money in place, and then we'll talk about transferring the weapons. This way, should your people be minus the necessary funds, I won't find the guns stolen and my throat slit. I'll come to you tomorrow and we'll discuss the matter in detail."

"Very well."

Jarod listened to Gabby open and close the room door. He wondered if she'd ever believe him when he explained that her sister had actually been one of the good guys. Or if she'd ever believe that *he* was one of the good guys.

The adjoining door opened slowly, and Jarod could tell by the look on her face that

Gabby was rapidly reaching the limits of her strength. He didn't say a word but instead led her to the chair and gently nudged her shoulders to make her sit.

"We need to talk *now*," he said firmly, and Gabby, refusing to look up at him, nodded.

Twenty-three

At midnight they were still talking in hushed whispers, and the conversation showed little sign of coming to an end anytime soon.

"So you see, your sister isn't a terrorist. She's a highly regarded professional with the CIA," Jarod explained softly.

Gabby was overwhelmed with the amount of information he had given her to digest. Janice was a CIA operative. Janice was on the right side of the law, but nevertheless, she was still dead. "And you're her partner." Gabby said this aloud, not really asking for confirmation.

"I was, and now I'm yours whether you like it or not." He smiled and reached out to touch her hand. "I know this is hard for you, but please believe me, we have to work together now. Otherwise, everything Janice did will be for nothing. Even her death."

Gabby looked at him and nodded. "I'll do whatever I have to do." She felt a lump in her throat and sobbed out, "I just don't *know* what to do."

Jarod stood and drew her into his arms. "It's all right. I'll teach you what you need to do. I'll keep you safe and alive, and I won't let anyone ever hurt you again." He stroked her hair and kept whispering the words over and over until she'd stopped shaking and crying. He had no reason to lie to her now, she realized. She wanted so much to believe that he really meant the words he was saying.

"How can I trust you?" she asked, pulling away. "I want to believe you, Jarod. I really do. But as far as I can see, everything you've said and done has been a lie."

"Not everything." He lowered his lips to hers and gently pressed a tender kiss on her mouth. "Not this."

She reached a hand to his stubbly jaw. Greens eyes searched her face for some sign of acceptance. Gabby felt him tighten his arms around her.

"God will work this out, Gabby. I didn't lie about Him. I've trusted Him with my life, and there's no way I could go out and face the work I have to do without knowing He's with me."

"He wasn't with Janice," she said, abruptly stepping away.

"Of course He was. We have no way of knowing Janice's heart, but I'm telling you that God was dealing pretty firmly with your sister. We were in a situation once where we had to sit out an undercover operation in a two-man life raft. It was cramped and uncomfortable, but that was nothing compared to what we went through when a nor'easter blew in. Janice was really scared. I could tell because she looked at me then like you're looking at me now.

"Anyway, I thought for sure we'd end up swimming that night, but I prayed — out loud — right there. At first, Janice thought I was crazy, but later I noticed she was murmuring her own prayer. At least I like to believe it was a prayer. When we came out of it, no worse for the wear, Janice asked me if I really believed that God had heard us, and I told her yes. We had a good talk about God."

"Really?" Gabby took hold of his arm. "Tell me everything. I want to know what Janice asked and what she knew before . . ." She shuddered. "I need to know if she was saved."

Jarod's expression told her that he understood. "Look, I can't remember everything, but I shared Scripture with her and told her how to make it right with God. I explained to her that without accepting Jesus as her Savior, she would be forever trying to bridge a cavern between herself and God. A cavern that she humanly could never fill with enough good deeds, pleasant attitudes, or perfectionistic thoughts. She understood that the only way to get straight with the Father was to go through the Son."

"I'm glad to hear you say that." And she truly was glad, and for more than just one reason. She now felt confident that Jarod was telling her the truth. The sincerity of his expression and the truth of his words gave her a peace that left her finally capable of accepting his help.

"So what do I do now? You heard Breman. He wants proof that his money is safe and sound in Switzerland before he'll talk about the weapons. Speaking of which, where in the world did he get his hands on so many guns?"

Jarod stretched and yawned before taking a chair. "There was a weapons heist in South Carolina. One of the National Guard armories was hit, and Janice and I felt pretty confident that it might have something to do with this case. We'd been watching Breman for over a year. He uses his travel agency to allow easy access to people from all over the world. This way he avoids using telephones, letters, and even couriers. All of which could ensnare him later, when and if he's caught. He had a substantial operation, and frankly, if he were less an amateur, we'd have never caught on to his game."

Gabby shook her head and gathered up Janice's postcards. "I suppose these are intended for a centralized check-in of some sort. Some CIA post office box in New York?"

Jarod shrugged. "Probably. I think it was Janice's way of covering her back. When you work in this game long enough, you come to question everyone and everything."

"I have just one other question," Gabby said, leaning against the wall to steady her weary frame. "How in the world did you manipulate my magazine into all of this?"

"Connections. People who owed people favors, that kind of thing. I can't say that it's all that big of a deal. Things like this happen all the time. Somebody knew somebody who, in turn, knew somebody else. The pay was right, the benefits and consequences considered, and before I knew it, I was in."

"And I became Janice's cover."

"In a manner of speaking."

"Ha," Gabby murmured and yawned. "I overheard Janice make the call. I've known this entire trip that she was in some sort of trouble or danger, but I just couldn't put my finger on what the cause was. Then when we were in Hampton Court —" She paused and looked Jarod in the eye. "When you found me in the maze, did you know then that I'd overheard Breman and Janice?"

Jarod's expression remained fixed, but his neck reddened and Gabby had her answer. "You did!" she exclaimed. "You knew and deliberately kissed me to take my mind off the entire matter. Didn't you?"

A sheepish grin spread across his tired face. "That wasn't the only reason I kissed you. I told you then I'd wanted to do that since first meeting you. Then when I found you there, so frightened and upset by what I was sure you'd heard and then by having lost your way, well, it seemed the right thing to do." He slowly got to his feet and went to where she stood. On either side of her he pressed his hands against the wall and encircled her. "I *know* it was the right thing to do."

Gabby felt her heart quicken its pace, and inside her mind many unanswered questions suddenly ceased to be so important. "I don't know what to think about all of this," she said softly. "I guess I'm afraid to care too much."

"Do I get the old boyfriend story now?"

he asked with a mischievous twinkle in his eyes that absolutely endeared him to Gabby.

"Why do you want to hear about Dustin? He means nothing to me now."

"Why is that?"

"Because we were too different. I valued God and gave Him first place in my life, and Dustin valued money and having a good time."

"What happened?"

Jarod's question was logical enough, but it probed deep into her guarded subconscious and left Gabby aching to forget everything. She lowered her eyes so Jarod couldn't see how uncomfortable she'd grown.

"What happened?" he whispered again.

Gabby gathered up her courage. "He wanted more than I could give. He wanted me to move in with him. Not marry him. Not pledge my life to him forever. He just wanted us to try each other out on a trial basis. Kind of like buying a new car." Gabby knew her voice held an edge of bitterness, but she went on, suddenly realizing that this kind of confession was good for her soul. "I'm not that kind of person, Jarod. I can't go to bed with a guy just to 'try it out on a trial basis.' You might as well know up front that I take my relationships very seriously."

"Is that what we have? A relationship?"

"I don't know," she said, still refusing to look him in the eye. She knew what she felt inside and by now was completely confident that she'd fallen in love with Jarod Walls. What she wasn't so confident about was whether that love was simply a mask of emotion, a crutch so to speak, to help her through Janice's death.

"Well, I do." He slid his arms around her gently and held her close for several silent moments. "I love you, Gabrielle. I didn't want to fall in love with anyone, but I fell in love with you."

Gabby couldn't keep from smiling and buried her face against his neck to avoid letting him see her expression. It had to be real. *Please God*, she prayed, *let it be real.*

Jarod continued. "In my line of business you can't afford to share your love with too many people. Your family is a constant worry because you never know when the enemy will use them to get at you. I couldn't risk that. I couldn't risk losing someone I loved because of something I'd done or failed to do. But you might as well know, since we're making confessions, that I intend to leave the CIA. I'll still be called upon as a consultant, and I plan to write some training manuals and such, but I won't be a field agent anymore. I want to settle down and have a home and a family." He pulled away and forced her to look at him by raising her chin with his hand. "I want you," he added simply.

Gabby felt the blood rush from her head. Her mouth went completely dry. What could she say? What *should* she say? To make her own declaration of love seemed wrong at this point, but emotionally she wanted to take the plunge and tell him how much she wanted him. Needed him. Loved him.

As if guessing her turmoil and understanding, Jarod rubbed his thumb across her lower lip. "You don't have to say anything. It's enough that you know how I feel."

He lowered his lips to hers and kissed her as though desperate to make her believe his sincerity. Gabby wrapped her arms around his neck and sighed. She never wanted this kiss to end because it wasn't given in order to comfort her fears or shut her up or counter her anger. This kiss was a devoted statement of love.

Jarod finally pulled away, and when Gabby opened her eyes, he was looking at her with such intensity that she almost felt frightened. "I'd better go," he said huskily.

Gabby nodded, knowing that he was feeling all of the same pent-up emotion and confusion that was coursing through her own body. They both believed in God and His word, and to back away from each other now was the only right thing to do.

"My side of the door will stay unlocked," he said, lingering a moment in the opening. Then he smiled most suggestively and said, "But I'd lock your side if I were you." With a wink, he closed the door between them.

Gabby went to do as he'd instructed her, but as her hand touched the lock, she stopped. *I trust him,* she thought. The feeling was one that consumed her. She smiled at the door and turned to get ready for bed without bothering to put the lock in place.

Twenty-four

Edinburgh marked the first phase of her espionage career, and Gabby faced it like a stoic soldier going into battle. Their hotel, the King James Thistle, was a modern establishment with stylish furnishings and a central location in the heart of the city. Breman had informed them of the next day's schedule, reminding them that the remainder of the day and evening were theirs to do with as they chose.

After unpacking, Gabby changed her clothes and waited for Jarod. He'd suggested that they at least pretend to cover the magazine article, and Gabby had agreed, realizing the sensibility in keeping up appearances. Enjoying their first real sunny day in Scotland, Gabby jotted down notes regarding Edinburgh and followed Jarod along Princes Street in the heart of the old city.

Next they covered the Royal Mile, a section of town encompassing four ancient streets, including Castle Hill, Canongate, High Street, and Lawnmarket. At one end they began by covering Gladstone's Land, a restored seventeenth-century merchant's house on Lawnmarket Street. The house clearly depicted for tourists the lifestyle of the merchant in 1617. The tour revealed many exquisite furnishings, including an ornate chest that was believed to have been the gift of a Dutch sea captain to the Scottish man who had saved him from a shipwreck.

Across from this, Jarod snapped pictures of the Tolbooth Church, or *Kirk*, as the Scottish called it. Built in 1840, the Kirk boasted the city's highest spire, higher even than the pinnacle of the glorious St. Giles Cathedral, which was located farther down the Royal Mile on High Street.

Gabby would later remember Edinburgh for many things. The piping in of the haggis, a spicy dish of sheep's innards mixed with onions and oatmeal, made for an interesting evening. Despite the impressive bagpipe serenade, Gabby was unimpressed with the liver-flavored dish. Edinburgh Castle made a great photo-op for Jarod, who contrasted the sooty stones against a crystal blue sky. Holyrood Palace, where Bonnie Prince Charlie was said to have held court in the early days of the Jacobite rebellion in 1745, was most inspiring. But it was the tiny shops and people that Gabby loved best of all. She couldn't help but think that Janice would have liked it, as well.

As their last day in Edinburgh drew to a close, Gabby allowed herself to relax and walk hand in hand with Jarod. She no longer cared what Breman thought. He'd cornered her that morning, informing her that once they reached York, he would summon her to make preparations to transfer the arms. She'd relayed the information to Jarod, who in turn had relayed it to his people. It was all very matter-of-fact and businesslike, but Gabby couldn't help feeling a consuming desperation to be finished with it all.

She struggled in her mind to decide what she would tell her mother. It wouldn't be easy to break the news of Janice's death to the woman who'd given her life, and Gabby faced the very idea of such a task with more dread than she felt in working with Breman Butler. Jarod had already told her that the CIA would take care of getting Janice's body back to the States, but it did little to comfort Gabby. As far as she was concerned, the CIA was a nonentity. Faceless, nameless, and without emotion for the sister Gabby had loved and lost. But there was nothing, absolutely nothing, she could do about it. Breman had forced her into this game, and now, in order to see him brought down, Gabby knew that she'd give her own life in return for justice.

Walking under the now cloudy skies of late afternoon, Gabby was only vaguely aware of the man at her side. She felt safe with Jarod, and that was enough to allow her mind to wander over the events of the weeks to come. Jarod would understand, she reasoned. He would sympathize and be gentle and loving and everything she needed him to be.

"You haven't heard a word I've said," Jarod commented, pulling Gabby into a quaint shop with him.

"I suppose I haven't," Gabby replied, then smiled up at him innocently. "Did I miss much?"

"Only that I suggested we overthrow the government and install ourselves as king and queen," he replied quite seriously.

"Oh." She glanced around and seeing no one close enough to overhear, she raised up on her tiptoes. "How about I get Scotland and you overthrow Ireland? With those green eyes, you're bound to be a hit with the natives."

Jarod laughed. "Naw, too many people

are already trying to take over Ireland. Don't forget," he paused, leaning down to whisper, "you're buying weapons for one of those groups as we speak."

Gabby rolled her eyes and sighed. "Only because the Scots haven't organized themselves yet."

"But you're Irish!" he said as though shocked.

"My ancestors were Irish. I'm American and very proud of that fact." She turned to walk away and gasped at the sight of a beautiful handwoven shawl. "Oh, look at this!"

Jarod reached out to feel the material. "Soft."

Gabby rubbed it against her cheek, the ultimate test of whether she could ever tolerate it as a garment in her wardrobe. "It *is* soft."

"The colors suit you," Jarod commented.

Gabby nodded. She held up the tartan shawl and admired the red, yellow, and black of the Mackenzie Clan plaid.

"Why don't you try it on and let me see if it really suits you," Jarod said, already reaching out to wrap the cloth around her shoulders.

Gabby snuggled into the shawl and smiled. "I love it!"

"Then I'm going to get it for you." Jarod

beamed her a smile and headed for the shop clerk.

"No! Jarod, you can't. Did you —" She paused, waiting until she reached him so she could whisper, "The price is too high. It's almost one hundred twenty pounds."

Jarod shrugged. "I don't care. I haven't bought much else on this trip. Besides, it'll be an investment."

"An investment?" she asked innocently.

"Sure. It's one less thing I'll need to buy you in the future."

It wasn't until Jarod had paid for the shawl and Gabby was watching the clerk wrap the purchase into tissue paper that she dared to think about his words. She waited until Jarod had taken the package in hand and was headed to the front door before saying, "What did you mean by that statement?"

They were on the street surrounded by milling tourists and more than halfway down the block before Jarod answered simply, "It means whatever you want it to mean."

I want it to mean "forever," Gabby thought to herself. She said nothing, however, and merely kept pace beside the man she'd come to love in only a couple of weeks.

Jarod had promised to arrange a very special dinner for their last evening in Edinburgh, and because of this, Gabby was going to painstaking lengths to make herself beautiful. She'd bathed early in order to have more time to fuss with her hair, and after nearly an hour of fussing, she was finally satisfied.

She eyed herself critically in the mirror. Her blond hair, pinned in a French twist, looked very chic and sophisticated. She had donned the pearls she'd worn their first night in London and liked the effect they created in correlation with her elegant hairstyle.

Lastly, instead of choosing something from her own wardrobe, Gabby selected something of Janice's. The red dress was made of an incredibly light, wrinkle-free material, and for a moment Gabby was tempted to forget the idea of wearing it. It clung to her much tighter than she'd anticipated, and while it definitely accented the charms of her figure, Gabby wasn't all that sure she wanted to be quite *that* charming. At least it was long, she mused, making certain that the hem fell properly in place.

Still uncertain as to whether she could actually leave the room wearing such a dress, Gabby spied the shawl Jarod had purchased for her. Suddenly an idea came to her and she regained her confidence in a moment. The shawl would offer her the perfect way to accent the gown and cover the tighter outlines. Pulling it around her, Gabby reappraised herself in the mirror and liked what she saw.

She was giddy with anticipation and wondered if Jarod would like her ensemble when the telephone rang. Rushing to answer, Gabby was less than pleased when Breman's voice sounded from the other end of the line.

"Are you alone?"

"Of course. What do you want, Mr. Butler?"

"My money has been confirmed and transferred into yet another account. So as you can imagine, there is no backing out of the deal now. I want you to come to an estate just outside of the city. I am here now, and when you arrive we will discuss the arms transfer."

"But I have plans for this evening, and besides, you said we would discuss this tomorrow in York," Gabby said, frantically stalling in order to think more clearly.

"Things have changed, and I wish to end this matter as soon as possible. Are you interested or not?"

"Of course. But explain how I'm suppose

to get to wherever it is you have in mind." She glanced at the room door, hoping and praying that Jarod's knock would sound.

"Roper is waiting with a car downstairs. If you aren't there in five minutes, he will leave without you."

"Five minutes? But I have to —"

"I don't care," Breman interrupted before she could complete the thought. "I don't care what you have to do in order to make the trip, just do it and be in that car in five minutes."

The line went dead and Gabby could only stand in dumbfounded silence. She knew she needed to wait for Jarod, but Breman had issued her yet one more deadline, and she couldn't afford to be late.

She pulled out her notebook and wrote a quick note to Jarod, explaining her predicament and promising to share dinner and information as soon as she returned from the meeting with Breman. She thought of changing her clothes, then realized there simply wasn't time. Pulling her purse out of the travel bag, she hurried out of the room, even forgetting to turn off the lights.

She slipped the note under Jarod's door and made a mad dash for the elevator. One way or another, with or without anyone's help, Gabby was going to see this thing through. She stepped onto the empty elevator, clutching her purse tightly against the shawl, and only after the doors closed did she remember that Janice's gun was still in the travel bag.

Desperately, she pressed the button that would take her back up to her room floor, but when the doors opened in the lobby, Roper Davenport was already awaiting her arrival. She had no choice but to step out and join him.

"I see you decided to dress up for the occasion," he commented in his refined British accent.

"I wasn't given much of a choice," Gabby replied with a regretful glance back at the closing doors of the elevator.

"Come on, then, I have the car." Roper offered her his arm, but Gabby refused to even touch him. "Have it your way," he said and headed out across the lobby.

Gabby frantically surveyed the room for any sign of Jarod, but there was none. She kept hoping he would step through the front doors as she was forced to exit, but again she was disappointed and reached Roper's rental car without passing so much as a single familiar face.

Roper opened the door for her and waited until she adjusted the shawl and dress be-

fore securely closing it. The sound reminded Gabby of the movies where prison
doors were poignantly slammed and left to
echo in the ears of the incarcerated party.
She was trapped and weaponless, and she
realized Jarod would have no idea where she
was going — because she had no idea where
Roper was taking her.

Twenty-five

Roper said very little as he maneuvered the car out of town and headed south. At least Gabby thought it was south. She tried to memorize every detail of the road in case she found herself stranded or on the slim possibility that she got a chance to call Jarod. As they left the main road and headed down a narrower country lane, Gabby wanted desperately to ask Roper what his position was in Breman's underhanded dealings, but she held her tongue.

When Roper pulled into a long gravel lane, Gabby felt a chill run up her spine. No one in the world knew where she was. No one but Roper and Breman. *That's not true,* she told herself. *God knows. God's been with you all along, Gabrielle Fleming. You have to trust that He's with you now.* She tried to swallow the lump that had formed in her throat. She knew God was with her, but it was hard to understand how He was going

329

to get her out of the mess she'd so willingly stepped into.

A huge stone Edwardian mansion came into view, and Gabby shuddered. It looked sinister and foreboding with all the rooms darkened except for one downstairs. The glow cast from that single light did little to dispel her concern. Roper pulled into the circular drive and parked the car just outside the main entrance.

"Come on, he's waiting" was all he said as he exited the car.

Gabby tightened her hold on the shawl and prayed silently for protection and strength. Then, almost as an afterthought, she prayed that God would somehow miraculously send Jarod to rescue her.

Timidly, she opened the car door and joined Roper where he waited for her on the cobblestone walk. She refused to look at him, fearful that if she did, he'd read her instantly and know how frightened she was. *Somehow, I have to appear professionally removed,* she told herself. *Somehow, I have to act like this happens all the time and that there is nothing at all out of the ordinary.* Gabby knew it would be the performance of her life, but if she wanted that life to continue, she'd have to be convincing.

Roper opened the huge oak door and

pushed it wide. "Ladies first," he said in a tone somewhere between sarcasm and irritation.

Gabby walked into the house noting the winding staircase that dominated the entryway. The carpeted stairs seemed to ominously disappear into the darkened upper story, and beyond them Gabby had little impression as to what else might be there. Her gaze darted quickly to take in the rest of the room. She wanted to memorize every detail, just in case it was needed later. Squinting against the dark, she could barely make out the hall of closed doors that extended past the staircase.

"He's in here," Roper said, nudging her through the open door to their right.

Gabby stumbled through the door and instantly sidestepped to where the lighted lamp and wing-backed chair stood by the still-open door. She could instantly see that the room was some type of study or office. Breman Butler sat rather comfortably behind a dark walnut desk. There were papers strewn recklessly from one end of the desk to the other, and in the middle lay a snub-nosed revolver. Gabby felt her blood run cold at the sneering expression on his face.

"Well, Ms. Fleming, I see you were able to meet your final deadline."

Gabby licked her lips nervously and refused to go forward, even when Roper came to stand beside her. "What's this all about?" she asked, folding her arms and pulling the shawl tight around her.

"This is all about finishing our business."

"You said we'd do that in York."

"Yes, well, York became a little bit of a problem. It seems someone has reason to concern themselves with my whereabouts. I thought maybe you might know a little something about that."

Gabby shrugged. "I told you once before, I'm only one small part of a much bigger organization."

"Are you, now?"

"Why don't you just fill me in on how you intend to transfer the weapons to my people and put an end to this farce?"

"And what farce would *that* be?" Breman asked, lightly fingering the revolver.

The hair on the back of her neck stood taut. She glanced at Roper, who seemed indifferent to the entire affair, and then back again to Breman. "This pretense of being amicable business partners," she finally said. "I don't like you, and you obviously don't like me. You've killed my sister, and now you expect me to complete business with you as though nothing ever happened."

"I didn't kill your sister," Breman said unemotionally. "He did." His gaze went to Roper, and Gabby's did the same.

"*You* killed my sister?" she asked Roper, reaching down to take hold of the chair. Tightly squeezing the upholstery, she asked, "Is that true?"

Roper stared unblinkingly at her. "I do what I'm told." He moved across the room and took a seat, leaving Gabby to stand alone at the door.

"That's right, he does," Breman replied, and when Gabby looked back at him, he held the gun in his hands and looked at it as though considering his next move.

Gabby grew nervous and gave the room a quick appraisal. Her only recourse would be to go out the same way she'd come in, but she had no doubt Roper would be on her before she could even get to the front door. The lamp at her left was the only thing offering light to the room, and it suddenly occurred to her that if she darkened the premises it would afford her a few more minutes of escape time.

"Give me the weapons information and let's be done with this. I want to go back to Liverpool and claim my sister's remains." She said the words mechanically.

"Oh, you won't have to be worrying yourself about such things as that," Breman said, looking up from the gun. "You aren't going anywhere. You see, Gabby, you have become a liability to my future welfare."

"I don't understand. I thought we had a deal." She reasoned in her mind that they would both expect her to move closer to the door, so instead Gabby moved a fraction of an inch closer to the lamp.

"We did. I wanted money, and you got it for me. Now you have to be put out of my misery." He smiled a cold, cruel smile and nodded to Roper. "You should strike some kind of special deal for taking out sisters, don't you think? Maybe two for one?"

Roper said nothing, and Gabby never took her eyes off of Breman. He was her real source of worry at this point. Roper might only be a few feet away, but Breman was the one with the gun.

A noise from somewhere outside the house gave Gabby all the encouragement she needed. Without thinking, she pushed the lamp forcefully to the floor and closed her eyes as the sound of breaking glass filled the room. The darkness was almost comforting, and Gabby knew that all she had to do now was turn and run.

Breman was shouting her name, and Roper was shouting for light. She turned outside the door and in her confusion went right instead of left and stumbled into the staircase. Hearing Breman and Roper hot on her trail, Gabby took the stairs as quickly as her legs would carry her. She guided herself by the banister, and when the floor finally evened out, she felt her way along the wall until she reached a door. Trying the handle, she felt only moderate comfort as it turned and opened. Just as she stepped into the blackened room, a light came on behind her and illuminated the outside hall.

She noted for only a second that the room contained a fireplace. Spying a poker lying on the stone hearth, she quickly retrieved it and stood behind the door. *They know I'm up here somewhere,* she reasoned. *I'll hit one of them when they come in the room and deal with the other one however I can.*

Her breathing was coming in gulps, and fear froze her in place as she heard Breman's and Roper's voices grow louder in their search. It would only be a moment before they realized that she'd gone upstairs instead of seeking sanctuary in one of the downstairs rooms. Holding the poker high, she felt her heart skip a beat when the sound of footsteps fell outside the room.

She saw the shadow of a man take form and fall across the room in the muted light.

Gabby knew she couldn't be seen from the entrance, but it offered little comfort. Breman or Roper had only to turn on the light and check behind the door to find her.

She'd never hit a man before, and certainly she'd never tried to kill one. Was that what she was trying to do now? she wondered. *I just want out alive,* she reasoned. *No one can fault me for doing what I have to do to stay alive.* But inside, she knew she didn't have the heart to kill either man. She wanted justice, not just revenge. She wanted to see Breman Butler put away forever. What she *didn't* want was either man's blood on her hands.

The man stepped forward and the shadow pattern changed. Gabby made up her mind. She would hit him over the head and hope for the best. Biting her lip to keep from crying out in fear, she waited.

The man pushed the door back ever so slightly and took another step into the room. Gabby adjusted her grip on the poker and felt it slip in her sweaty palms. One more step and . . .

THUD!

She brought the poker down on the man's head, then watched in stunned silence as he fell to the floor. Without waiting to see if he'd move, Gabby jumped over him and ran to the door. Her hand fell on the light switch and without knowing why, Gabby turned on the light in order to see if it was Breman or Roper who lay at her feet.

The brilliant light left her momentarily blinded, but when she'd adjusted to it she noticed that the man on the floor had started to move. Moaning and reaching back to take hold of his head, Gabby suddenly realized it wasn't Breman or Roper who lay on the floor.

"Jarod!"

"Gabby?" he croaked out the word and fell back on the floor.

"Jarod! Oh, Jarod, I'm so sorry!" She reached down to help him to his feet. "Are you all right?"

"Gabby, are you okay?" He managed to struggle to his knees.

"We have to get out of here, Jarod. Roper and Breman are trying to kill me."

Jarod looked up at her with a lopsided smile. "I know all of that. Why do you think I'm here?" His eyes struggled to focus on her.

Gabby reached down and tried to pull Jarod to his feet. "Come on, we'll talk later."

"Oh, do talk now," Breman said from behind her. "Later, I'm afraid you won't be able to say much of anything."

Gabby nearly buckled under Jarod's weight. He leaned heavily against her, and to her horror, brought down his bloody hand to better grip her arm.

"You two make *quite* a pair, I must say." Breman waved his gun at them and laughed. "Once we take care of your girlfriend," he told Jarod, "we'll be sure to see to *you*."

Jarod let out a noise that was a cross between a growl and a moan. Gabby fought to keep her shoulder under his arm. "You have no reason to kill him," she protested.

"I have all the reason in the world, Ms. Fleming. In case you haven't figured it out yet, your boyfriend is working against us. He's with the FBI or CIA or some such thing and has only been cozying up to you in order to get the goods on the weapons operation. I'd already planned to take care of him, and you've just made my work a whole lot simpler."

Gabby fought the tears of anger and regret that came to her eyes. She had caused all of this by sticking her nose into Janice's business. If only she would have just stayed home in the first place, none of this would have ever happened.

Roper entered the room, gun in hand and a look on his face that seemed genuinely alarmed. "What happened to him?" he asked, seeing the blood on Jarod's hand and face.

"I believe she clubbed him over the head. Now, if you don't mind, I've had enough of this idle chitchat. Roper, take care of them and join me back at the hotel." He started to leave and then paused at the door. "Ms. Fleming, it has been a pleasure. I hope you enjoyed the tour."

Gabby wanted to jump him and pound her fists against his smug face, but she couldn't move. Not if she wanted to keep her hold on Jarod. What she did was turn her body just enough to put Jarod more behind her. "Since you plan to kill me anyway," she said suddenly, "why don't you explain to me what really happened between you and my sister?"

This caught Breman's attention. "What makes you think I haven't been honest with you about that?"

"Because I know my sister, and I believe you probably killed her because she knew too much." She felt Jarod ease his weight off of her but realized he wasn't making it apparent to Roper or Breman. She hoped this was a sign that he was recovering from the blow.

"Your sister double-crossed me, just as I told you. The irony of it is," Breman said with a laugh, "I double-crossed her first. She found out about it and was going to blow my cover."

"You double-crossed her how?" Gabby was stalling for time. With every passing moment she could only pray that Jarod would grow more clearheaded.

"The same way I'm double-crossing you. The weapons, my dear Gabby, are not going to benefit your precious IRA. The weapons were long ago given over to a paramilitary group in the United States."

"I see. Do you really believe the IRA will let you get away with this?"

"What are they going to do about it, Ms. Fleming? They raise American dollars and ignorantly trust people they don't bother to check out, all in order to fund a stupid war they can never win. The Brits will never give them their freedom, because in doing so they will open a civil war in Ireland. So in answer to your question, I don't at all fear the IRA. They have their hands more than full right there in their own backyard."

Gabby didn't know what to say. Her sister had died because this man had double-crossed not only her but the CIA. It was most ironic that Breman had still not managed to put all the pieces of the puzzle together. He still didn't realize that Janice had been a CIA operative and not an IRA terrorist.

Breman looked to Roper and took hold of the door. "Don't forget to clean up the mess." With that, he was gone.

Gabby looked up to find Roper eyeing her sternly. She tried to keep Jarod behind her, but he staggered forward and leaned against her.

"Jarod, no!" she said, again positioning herself between Jarod and Roper's gun. Her shawl fell to the floor, but it wasn't the cold that made her shudder. It was the look in Roper's eyes. Jarod tightened his grip on her waist and started to say something, but Gabby would have no part of it. Turning, she spoke what was on her heart. "Jarod, I know this is all my fault, but I can't let him kill us without telling you something."

"Tell me what?" Jarod asked in a weak voice.

"That I love you," she said, moving her arm under his shoulder again. "It may never matter past this point, but it's something you should know."

"You have great timing, Gabby."

Roper's laughter caused Gabby's head to snap up angrily. "Do you mind?"

Roper looked at the door and relaxed his gun arm. "I have to say this, old boy, you've certainly gotten yourself more than you bargained for this time."

"What's going on?" Gabby asked in confusion. "What do you mean?"

"He means that I'm bleeding all over the woman I love, and the bad guy is getting away," Jarod offered. "Roper's one of us . . . well, kind of, anyway."

Gabby eyed him suspiciously and raised a questioning brow. "I still don't know what you mean. Roper is CIA?"

"I'm with the SAS — Special Air Service — Great Britain," Roper said softly. "I've been helping Jarod and Janice." He paused and stepped forward to help with Jarod. "And now I'm helping you, too."

Twenty-six

Breman was feeling powerful and smug as he started down the stairs. He had managed to secure a fortune for himself, and now it was only a matter of tying up the loose ends of the tour and then he could retire.

Voices coming from somewhere outside drew his attention and caused him to stop in place. He strained to hear but couldn't make out words, just noises. His imagination was running wild, and with a nervous laugh, he took another step just as the entryway door started to open.

Someone was there! He turned and took the steps two at a time and managed to reach the second-floor landing before the hall filled with people.

"Search everywhere," he heard a man command.

Panicking, Breman ran to the room where he'd left Roper to deal with Gabby and Jarod. With any luck, they'd still be alive, and he'd be able to use them as hostages. Bursting into the room, he found everyone much the same as he'd left them.

"We've got company!" he told Roper and closed the door behind him.

He was surprised that Roper no longer held a gun on Gabby and Jarod but reasoned that, given the circumstance, neither one was much of a threat. Fleming was so far gone over her beloved photographer that she'd never do anything to bring harm to him.

"Get over here!" he told Gabby.

"No!" She stayed fixed at Jarod's side.

Irritated, Breman leveled his gun and commanded again. "Come here *now*."

The voices downstairs could now be heard, causing Roper to pull his gun. Breman felt a surge of confidence. Together, he and Roper could fight their way out of this, but first he'd have to have a hostage. Moving the gun from Gabby to Jarod, Breman got just the response he was looking for.

"Come with me now or I'll kill him."

He could tell she was torn between staying at Jarod's side and obeying his command. She needed incentive. "If you come willingly with me, Gabby, I'll let Walls live. Roper and I only need one hostage to nego-

tiate the crowd downstairs." He opened the
door cautiously and looked down the hall.
"Maybe we can make it to the back stairs
while they're still searching below."

"Stay here, Gabby," Jarod said in a weak-
ened but serious voice.

"I've had about enough of you," Breman
said, coming forward to take Gabby in
hand.

"Touch her, and I'll kill you where you
stand" came a voice from behind him.
Breman felt the blood drain from his face.
He knew that voice, and from the stunned
expression on Gabby's and Jarod's faces, he
knew his worst fears were confirmed.
Whirling around, he came face-to-face with
Janice Fleming.

"Your deadline is up, Breman darling,"
she drawled.

"You're supposed to be dead — the headlines said you were dead!" Breman said, still
unable to believe that he was actually seeing
her.

Janice smiled and shrugged. "Not quite.
Roper made a deal with the *Liverpool Echo*.
If they'd make up one copy with that headline to make sure you thought I was dead, he
promised them the inside scoop of the arms
deal once it went down. They'll be very
happy to know they're gonna get their story.

Now move away from my sister and partner."

"Partner?" Breman questioned, inching in the direction Janice was motioning him with her gun.

"Didn't you tell him?" she asked Jarod. "Shame on you." Then turning her attention on Breman, she smiled. "I'm CIA, Breman, and I've been working long and hard to put scum like you behind bars."

"But what about your Irish Republican Army?" he asked nervously. Then suddenly remembering the gun in his own hand, Breman glanced down.

"I wouldn't if I were you," Roper said and reached over to take the weapon from him.

"What are you doing?" Breman demanded to know.

"I'm helping the CIA. The SAS likes to do that whenever they can."

"SAS?" Breman's expression fell into complete dejection. He'd been had. The one person he thought he could count on for help was Roper. His world was falling apart by bits and pieces.

"You okay, Janice?" a burly redheaded man asked as he came into the room behind her.

"I'm fine. We're all finished here if you want to take our friend away."

Breman looked around the room for a means of escape. The huge floor-to-ceiling window behind him seemed the only possibility and could well mean severe injury if he landed wrong. But it was his only hope. The problem was how to get through it without them shooting at him.

He noted that Gabby was white as a ghost and smiled. She was going to faint; he could see it in the way her eyes were glazing over. He'd no sooner thought this than she did just as he'd predicted. Collapsing to her knees, she took Jarod down with her, causing both Roper and Janice to rush forward. It was his moment!

Without another thought, Breman hurled himself into the glass and panes of the second-floor window. His last thoughts were that even death would be better than imprisonment.

He got his wish.

Gabby was still sobbing quietly as the hospital doctor completed the last of six stitches in Jarod's head. His wound was her fault, and her guilt and grief were overwhelming. But so, too, was her relief. Breman was dead, and Janice was alive. She still couldn't believe that her sister was actually alive.

"You'll have a headache for a day or two. The nurse will give you some pills to take with you. They'll help with the worst of it," the doctor said as he tied off his last suture.

"Thanks, doc."

"There you are." The gray-haired doctor pulled away and smiled. "How in the world did you manage such a blow?"

Jarod smiled at Gabby, who could feel herself turning crimson. "I underestimated the power of a woman," he said with a laugh.

"Hey, are you two finished?" Janice questioned, popping her head through the curtains.

"We sure are, and I don't know about Gabby, but I'm starving to death," Jarod said, easing himself off the gurney. He swayed a bit and grimaced.

Gabby rushed forward to help him, and as she wrapped her arms around him, he squeezed her shoulders. "I could get to like this," he murmured, then straightened and put a hand to his head.

"Are you okay?" Gabby asked almost fearfully.

"I'm fine. It does smart a bit."

"A bit? Sure. Come on, Roper and Janice will get us back to the hotel, and you are going *straight* to bed."

"But I'm hungry," Jarod protested.

Janice laughed. "He eats like a bear, Gabby. You're going to have to get used to that if you intend to spend much time with him."

"I haven't ever really noticed," she said, musing on the idea that her sister knew her boyfriend better than she did.

"Come on, then, Bear," Janice teased, "we'll put you to bed and order room service." She went to help steady Jarod on the other side just as Gabby remembered her shawl.

"Just a minute." She retrieved the tartan plaid from the chair, and seeing Jarod's blood on it, she almost started crying again. "I was so stupid," she muttered and ran her fingers over the dried stains.

"You did what you had to do, Gabby," her sister said softly. "You did the right thing. You had no way of knowing that the man coming after you was Jarod."

"I don't hold grudges, if that's what has you worried," Jarod added in a teasing tone.

"I just can't stand the thought that I'm responsible for your head being like that," Gabby said, rejoining them. She slipped her arm automatically around Jarod's waist.

Surprising her, Jarod leaned over and kissed her head. "I'll see to it that you make it up to me, but for now stop worrying about it and feed me."

They made their way to where Roper was waiting with the car. Riding in relative silence back to the hotel, Gabby could no longer wait to question her sister.

"When did you start all of this, Jan?"

Janice, riding beside Roper in the front, let out a deep breath and turned in the seat. "You mean the CIA?" Gabby nodded and Janice continued. "I was recruited early on in college. You know me, I love adventure, and I have a heart for new causes. I guess I just got wrapped up in the fun of it all."

"Fun?" Gabby questioned in disbelief. "You were nearly killed. If Roper hadn't have been on your side, you would have been murdered."

"You underestimate my ability to stay alive. I only went willingly with Roper because I knew he was an ally. There were at least a half dozen places on the way out of that hotel that I could have escaped if I'd really wanted to."

"So she says now," Roper remarked.

Janice turned to face him. "I could have put you over the back stairs banister in a heartbeat."

Jarod and Roper both burst into laughter.

Gabby couldn't bring herself to join in. For nearly a week, she'd believed her sister dead, and now to find her suddenly alive again was more than she could hope for. Hot tears began to stream down her face again. Tears of relief and joy and praise for answered prayer. Turning to look out the window, Gabby tried to keep Jarod from noticing that she'd fallen to pieces again.

Jarod's hand reached out to take hold of hers, and Gabby knew he understood. He didn't say a word but merely held her hand as if to convey his promise of support and comfort.

"Did you know Janice was alive?" Gabby suddenly asked Jarod.

"Jarod knew nothing," Janice replied before Jarod could answer. "Roper and I decided it would be better that way."

"Thanks a lot," Jarod interjected. "I spend a week eaten by guilt because I'd failed to keep my partner safe, and you say you just thought it would be better that way?"

Janice shrugged. "So we were wrong. Poor judgment. Next time we'll tell you."

"There isn't going to be a next time."

Janice turned to look at Jarod. "You *can't* be serious about leaving."

"Oh, but I am. I have plans for the future, and they don't include throwing myself in the line of danger, unless you consider romantic relationships dangerous."

"They're the worst kind," Janice said with a laugh. Then relaxing back in her seat, she asked, "Anyone I know?"

"Apparently not well enough to confide in," Gabby threw out. "Do you plan to spend *your* future with the CIA?"

"I plan to go full-time into field-agent work after graduation."

"Mom will have a fit," Gabby said without thinking.

"Mom can never know about this, Gabby," Janice said quite seriously.

"And how will you keep it from her?"

Janice turned to face her sister. "The same way Daddy did."

Gabby startled at this.

"I know it's hard to believe, but I only learned about it myself after Daddy died. He was deeply involved as an operative doing much the same as I've been doing."

"No wonder he taught us to play spy games," Gabby muttered. The very thought of her father being a CIA agent was almost more than she could fathom. He'd owned a shipping company, and the ocean and ships had been his passionate love, second only to their mother. "And Mama never knew?" Gabby met Janice's expression and knew it was all true.

"She never knew because Daddy never

wanted her to know. Now you have to keep *his* secret, and *mine,* too."

Gabby shook her head and fell back against the seat. The burden of what she'd just learned was too much. "I'm surrounded by spies and family secrets. I never would have even bothered with this tour if it hadn't been for your insistence."

"I know," Janice admitted, "and I'm sorry. I never thought you'd be in any real danger because I never thought you'd suspect anything was going on."

"It was just supposed to be a quaint little adventure in which I would write a wonderful series of articles on touring England and Scotland." Gabby stared out the window, trying once again to piece all the details into an acceptable order.

"Speaking of the tour," Janice commented, "what are we going to do about all those people? There're still a few days left."

"Already accounted for," Roper said, bringing them to a stop in front of the King James Thistle. "SAS has already provided a professional tour guide and driver. The tour will go on, and no one need be the wiser for it."

"Well, I, for one, am finished with it," Gabby said, surprising them all. "I'll wing it on writing about York and Hadrian's Wall, but I'm taking the next train for London and booking an early flight home." Up until then, she hadn't really thought about going back early, and now that the words were out of her mouth, Gabby knew it was exactly what she wanted to do. Needed to do.

"Are you sure you want to do that?" Janice asked in disbelief.

"Very, and don't try to talk me out of it by telling me what a good time the four of us will have." She grew very serious and looked from Janice to Jarod. "You can all laugh about what you do. After all, it's your choice of occupation, and you apparently have a flair for it and maybe even a love of the excitement. But I can't quite deal with all of this just now." She took one look at Janice's expression and knew without words that she was blaming herself.

"Don't even think it, Janice," Gabby said before her sister could remark. "This isn't just about you. Although I do have to admit it has a lot to do with you, but it also has to do with —"

"Me?" Jarod interjected.

Gabby turned to meet his saddened expression. "Yes. It has a lot to do with you."

"I guess I don't understand," Janice remarked. "I know you care about both of us, but —"

"Don't, Janice." Gabby's voice broke and she found herself crying anew. "I can't deal with all of this now. Please don't ask me to. I just need some time to sort it all through. I will keep your secrets. All of you are safe in that regard. Just try to understand," she said, looking at Jarod. "I nearly lost you both, and now you want me to treat it as though it was just one of those occupational hazards. You laugh and make your jokes, but in the back of my mind I was planning funerals and wondering how I'd ever be able to go on without you."

They all fell silent as Gabby opened the car door. "I *do* love you," she told Jarod, unashamed that Janice and Roper were privy to this declaration. "I didn't want to, but now I do, and I'm not sure what to do about it."

With that, she hurried from the car and left Roper and Janice to help Jarod. The pain she felt at walking away was almost worse than the fear of losing them in death. Somehow she had to sort through the madness inside her head, but the very first thing she wanted to do was go to the privacy of her room and fall down on her knees in thanks to God. They had lived through the nightmare and now could go home. At least, *she* could go home.

Twenty-seven

"Gabby, this is some of your finest work!" Sandy declared as she thumbed through the article layout. "These photographs are incredible. I can see from the looks of them and the contrasting stories that you and Mr. Walls worked very well together."

Gabby forced a smile. It had been three weeks since she'd returned to the States, and the only word she'd had from Jarod had come in the form of an overnight package of photos. Even Janice had been unable to give her any insight into his whereabouts.

"He's tying up the loose ends of this operation," she had told Gabby. "He probably won't surface again until everything is said and done."

That had offered Gabby no comfort whatsoever. What if he was dead? What if the operation's conclusion had turned sour? There was still the matter of reclaiming the weapons arsenal. What if the paramilitary group Breman had sold the guns to put up a fight?

"So you never told me how you kept from killing each other," Sandy said, forcing Gabby's attention. "Did you have any real problems on the trip?"

Gabby wanted to laugh out loud, but instead she shook her head. "Not once we got past our pride. Jarod is a very capable photographer, and I have to say I enjoyed working with him a lot more than I thought I would."

"I'd like to see you two working together on future projects," Sandy replied and picked up one of the photographs from Hampton Court. "It makes me want to take the trip myself."

"I'm glad you're pleased, Sandy."

Gabby felt a bittersweet tug on her heart. She had Jarod's photographs but not Jarod. Despite Janice's assurance that Jarod was one of the best in the business, Gabby couldn't still the worries of her heart. She wondered whether he'd managed to end his career with the CIA, or if he was already assigned elsewhere and knee-deep into another covert operation. She couldn't help but worry about him and wonder if his feelings for her had changed. Three weeks and no word. It was a long time to hash through her fears.

"So what do you think?" Sandy asked.

Gabby realized she'd not heard the question. "Think about what?"

Sandy laughed. "If I didn't know better, I'd think you were bored with your work. I asked if you would mind taking on another big assignment with Jarod Walls. I'm going to see about bringing him on board as a full-time photographer."

A tolerant smile formed on her lips. "I doubt seriously you can get Jarod for another assignment. He's busy with other things."

"I wouldn't bet on that," the familiar voice came from behind her.

Gabby felt her chest tighten and turned very slowly in the seat. She met his face and saw the love and desire that had been there for her in Great Britain. "Jarod." She mouthed the word but no sound came out.

He was really here.

Crossing the room in his faded jeans and opened-collar oxford shirt, Jarod reached out to shake hands with Sandy. "I'd love to come on board for another job, but only if I'm working with Gabby. I've kind of become accustomed to her way of doing things, and since I don't need to baby-sit her or be baby-sat," he said with a wink, "she shouldn't protest too much."

Sandy laughed, and Gabby waited for him to take the seat beside hers. He was even better looking than she'd remembered, and her mind remembered a great deal. Sometimes more than she wanted it to remember. He reached out and automatically took her trembling hand and held it as though it was the most natural thing in the world.

"Well, what do you say about that, Gabby?"

Gabby shook her head. "I don't know what to say." She turned to Jarod and lost herself in the brilliant green of his eyes. "What about your day job?"

He grinned. "I've recently become unemployed. I thought full-time photography would be more to my liking anyway."

"I know if I had any say in the matter, it would be more to my liking. But if you only did it because of what I said in Scotland, then . . ."

"I'd already made up my mind before I got the job working with you. So," he paused with a determined look on his face, "if you think you had something to do with my choice, forget it."

"I see," Gabby replied, earnestly trying to take in this new information. Jarod had really gone through with his plan to quit the CIA! But hadn't he told her himself that no one ever really quits? "And you're serious about photography?"

"Serious enough that I bought a huge camper . . . you know, an RV. I can drive all over the country looking for that perfect picture now. Just think of the books I could create." He grew very sober. "But I was kind of hoping for a partner."

Gabby held her breath and bit down on her lip. Sandy leaned forward with an expression of absolute curiosity. "What kind of partner?" Sandy asked before Gabby could say a word.

"The kind who will be responsible for helping me out, working at my side, keeping me out of trouble — things like that. Of course, it should be someone who enjoys my company and can hold their own against me. Know anybody like that?" he asked Gabby directly.

"I might. I suppose it would depend on the contract between parties."

Sandy was thoroughly stumped by now, and it was to her consternation that her secretary appeared in the door. "Sandy, there's a problem with the November issue, and they need you right away."

Sandy got up from her desk, eyeing both Jarod and Gabby suspiciously. "I'll be back in a few minutes."

"I promise we won't hurt each other while you're gone," Jarod replied, his gaze never leaving Gabby's face.

When Sandy had left the room, Gabby couldn't help asking, "Did you get your weapons back?"

"Did you doubt I would?"

She shook her head and smiled. "No, you seem to get whatever you want."

Jarod drew Gabby's fingers to his lips and kissed each one slowly, lingeringly. "I've missed you," he said between kisses.

Gabby was trembling from head to toe and found it impossible to hide it from Jarod. "I've missed you, too." She didn't trust herself to say more.

"Did you manage to get your worries all sorted into neat little organized piles?"

She smiled. "Yeah, but then I had no idea what to do with them afterward."

"Might I make a suggestion?"

"That depends."

"Oh? On what?" he asked, tugging her arm gently and pulling her into his lap.

"Jarod!"

"Do you want to hear my suggestion or not?" he asked, nuzzling her neck with a kiss.

Gabby sighed and nodded. "Yes. Tell me your suggestion."

"I suggest you throw out all the past concerns and start a new pile."

"A new pile of concerns?" she asked with a hesitant laugh. "And just what kind of new concerns should I occupy myself with?"

"For starters, how about deciding how long we need to date before you'll agree to marry me."

Gabby's mouth dropped open. He was asking her to marry him. After weeks of no word and wondering if he was dead or alive, he just walked into Sandy's office and had the audacity to ask her to marry him.

"You've left me wondering about you for three long weeks and now you have the nerve to bring up marriage? I didn't know if you were dead or being tortured someplace. I asked Janice, but she couldn't give me any information. Three weeks, Jarod! Do you know how miserable I was waiting to hear if you'd survived wrapping up your . . ." She looked around the room, wondering if there was any chance they were being recorded. "Never mind." She crossed her arms defiantly, knowing she'd already said more than she should.

"I left you alone for three weeks because I was afraid if I pushed you, you'd run out on me like you did in Edinburgh."

"I didn't run out on you," she protested,

then added softly, "I ran out on me. I couldn't cope. I'd just come through the ordeal of a lifetime and all I could think about was that you and Janice chose to experience things like that every day."

"Not quite *every* day," he said with a smile.

"I do love you, Jarod, but I don't think we know each other well enough to consider marriage." She smiled coyly and added, "At least not today."

"Then maybe tomorrow?"

Rolling her eyes, Gabby shook her head. "You are a terribly pushy man, Mr. Walls."

He smiled. "Yes, I am." Jarod had just directed her lips to his when Sandy returned.

"Well, you *did* promise not to hurt each other," she said with a stunned expression.

Gabby jumped up from Jarod's lap, looking for all the world as though she'd just been caught stealing the good silver. "I . . . well, you see . . ."

"I'm trying to get her to marry me," Jarod said, getting up in a slow, lazy manner. He smiled confidently and put his arm around Gabby's shoulder. "But she's only looking for a photographer at this time."

"I didn't say I was looking for anything," Gabby said with a stern expression that quickly faded into a grin. "But maybe, just maybe, in a few weeks or months I might have a different answer."

"What's with this weeks and months stuff? I had in mind days, hours, *maybe* even minutes."

"You drive a hard bargain, Mr. Walls," Sandy said with a laugh.

Gabby nodded. "You're telling me."

Sandy took her seat and eyed them for a moment. "I've just had an idea you two might be interested in."

"What is it?" Gabby asked, glancing up to find Jarod just as curious.

"Yeah, what did you have in mind?"

"I had in mind to run a series next June on honeymoon resorts."

"Hmmm." Gabby rubbed her chin as though trying to consider the possibilities. "Sounds intriguing."

"Sounds like an undercover operation," Jarod said with a mischievous wink at Gabby.

"Jarod Walls! You are incorrigible."

"I was just thinking how detailed we could get if we were, say, on our own honeymoon."

"June, eh?" Gabby said, looking directly at Sandy.

"Well, actually, I'd need your articles and photos by the end of March."

"I'm liking this better all the time," remarked Jarod.

Gabby could see that he was quite pleased with himself. "A March deadline seems possible," she admitted. "But it will all depend on a great many details."

Jarod pulled her close and, in spite of Sandy's presence, leaned down to whisper in Gabby's ear, "I'm positive we can work it out."

Gabby smiled. "Yes, I'm fairly certain we can."

The employees of Thorndike Press hope you have enjoyed this Large Print book. All our Large Print titles are designed for easy reading, and all our books are made to last. Other Thorndike Press Large Print books are available at your library, through selected bookstores, or directly from us.

For information about titles, please call:

(800) 223-1244
(800) 223-6121

To share your comments, please write:

Publisher
Thorndike Press
P.O. Box 159
Thorndike, Maine 04986